CHANGELING

COPYRIGHT

CHANGELING

MOLLY HARPER

CHANGELING

LIGHTBOURNE, NORTHERN ENGLAND

*O*ne wrong step and my ankle would snap like greenwood kindling.

I bolted down the cobblestone walkway connecting Rabbit's Warren to the maze of side streets that cushioned the elegant neighborhoods of Lightbourne from our neighborhoods. Heaven forbid our Guardians smell the "humors" drifting out of the more modest Snipe houses.

I ran through the early morning fog as fast as I dared on my unsteady legs, lungs burning, clutching the canvas bag to my chest. Mum had been so tired the night before, she'd taken a shirt of Owen Winter's home for mending, rather than staying late. Mum rarely took anything from Raven's Rest, for fear it would get soiled in our grimy little house or worse, that she'd be accused of stealing.

Unfortunately, Mum was also tired enough to forget the shirt when we left our house before dawn. She sent me to fetch it because she needed Mary's help getting the day started. Since starting as a maid-of-all-work at Raven's Rest two years before, I'd been trusted with small tasks like hanging sheets and drying dishes, but Mum *needed* Mary's help with jobs I was simply too sickly to do.

The house ran on a precise schedule. The Winters woke up at exactly six, followed by breakfast at seven. Washing day chores were immediately followed by dusting, sweeping, and scrubbing the water closets before any of the Winters woke. Owen left for classes at the Palmer School for Young Men at nine, while Mr. Winter retired to his study to work. Mum met with Mrs. Winter to discuss menus and upcoming social engagements before luncheon. We spent the afternoon helping Mum prepare an elaborate formal dinner, which we served and cleaned up before retreating home just before midnight to collapse into our beds and start all over the next morning.

I supposed that I should have been grateful that unlike my friends' families, we were allowed to live off-site in the Snipe district known as Rabbit's Warren. My friend, Elizabeth's, family was required to live with their Guardians full-time as a term of their employment, meaning they were available to serve around the clock. But given the uneven pavement and my weak ankles, living on-site sounded pretty good just about now.

I ran, careful to look for any cray-fire carriages that might have wandered into our neighborhood. The richer magical families could afford the new horseless carriages; quiet, smooth-running vehicles powered by the cray-fire engine and steered by coachmen. The magically super-charged crystals provided the speed and safety of a horse-driven carriage without the earthy drawbacks. The problem was that when these magical marvels inadvertently found their way into the Warren, the coachmen tended to drive at breakneck speed to get their esteemed passengers back out.

I rounded the last corner to Armitage Lane, rallying the last reserves of energy it would take to get to Raven's Rest. And I bounced face-first off of a warm mass that smelled of sandalwood and ozone. I yelped, sprawling back on the stone walkway, losing my grip on the shirt. Barely feeling the pain radiating through my backside, I scrambled to my knees, searching for the canvas bag. The rough fabric would protect Owen's fine shirt from street dirt, but not a puddle. If I damaged that shirt, Mum would make me regret it, and then Mrs. Winter would get a hold of me.

Large hands wrapped around my thin arms and pulled me to my feet. I winced as the lift stretched my abused leg muscles. A smooth tenor said, "I'm so sorry."

My head snapped up, finally registering that there was a finely dressed Guardian man holding me up by my elbows. I squinted up at him. No, not a man, though he was the tallest boy I'd ever seen. He was sixteen or so, on that awkward edge between gangly adolescence and growing up. He had the high cheekbones and long, refined features of the upper class, with large blue eyes and thick dark hair so long it brushed his high collar. An expression of bemused mortification made his features almost approachable. He was wearing the black suit and blue-and-grey striped tie that marked him as a Palmer's student. His pristine white shirt was marked with soot from my face.

I cringed in his grip, expecting at least a good telling off.

"Am I hurting you?" he asked, letting go of my arms. The sudden release of bloodflow to my hands made me suddenly aware of how badly I'd skinned my hands on the stone.

I raised an eyebrow. He was slouching down over me, turning my scraped palms over in his hands, inspecting the damage to my pale skin.

"I just wasn't watching where I was going. It's a terrible habit of mine when I'm in the middle of a good think. Alicia says I wouldn't notice if dragons fell out of the sky and did a dance on my head," he said in that soothing voice. He didn't seem at all worried about the sandy grit on my hands or the dirt embedded under my ragged nails. He just cupped them in his own hands, sending a pleasant warmth blooming through my stinging fingers.

Was this a trick? It felt like a trick.

I groaned at the sight of even more smudges on his cuffs. "Your shirt."

He scoffed at his cuffs, which were accented with silver cuff-links shaped like lanterns.

"Never mind the shirt. I can fix it. Are you all right? You bounced off that sidewalk like an India rubber ball." He was inspecting my face, craning his neck down to make up for the considerable difference in our heights. Not for the first time, I wished I was built like Mary. While my sixteen-year-old sister bloomed with health, I was under-sized and had a permanent sickly look to me that made me look several years younger than fourteen.

Oh, no. That was probably why he was being so nice to me. He probably thought he'd knocked down a little girl. Heat flooded my cheeks and I felt tears gathering at the corners of my eyes. He was only being nice because he felt sorry for me.

I looked down at the ground, careful not to let him see the tears.

"I'm fine, thank you. I just need to get to work before my mother-" I gasped. "The shirt!"

I pulled my hands from his and stooped to pick the battered canvas bag. It was dry, thank goodness, but rubbing the rough material against my hands had me hissing in pain. A tear slipped down my cheek and I wiped at it quickly.

"Here," he said. "I can help with that."

The boy patted his pockets, pulling out a tangled red silk cord, a broken pocket watch, a small blue-green egg that glowed from the inside. He handed me these items while he searched the inside of his vest. The egg felt warm to the touch and pulsed pleasantly against my injured skin. Finally, he pulled a smooth black rock out of his breast pocket.

"Aha!" he said, smiling at me. He took the canvas bag and tucked it under his arm. "Cup your hands."

He placed the black rock in my raised palms. I stared into its glassy surface, mesmerized by the rings of white, grey and purple.

"Hold… still," he whispered, carefully drawing an intricate magical symbol against the surface of the rock with his fingertip. The twisting line glowed red and I felt the pain fade from my hands. "There you are."

I sighed in relief, watching as the scrapes closed into shiny pink scars. I'd never experienced magic *directly*. I'd seen it performed plenty of times, but I never felt its touch on my skin. It was more comfortable than I expected, familiar, like being wrapped in a favorite old blanket. It only added to the collection of scars and other marks of my service on my hands. They were rough and dry and nothing like the soft, pampered skin of his fingers. "Thank you very much."

"Well, I did bowl into you, very inconsiderate of me. I didn't expect it to work that well though. You must be a quick healer," he said, smiling again. In five minutes, this boy had spoken more to me than any boy – never mind a *Guardian* boy - had in years. Boys were usually too busy tripping over themselves to get to my pretty golden sister to even realize I was there.

But again, he probably thought I was a child. No stranger believed I'd graduated from the Warren school two years before when they saw my short, scrawny frame. He was simply being kind to a child, which was a mark of good character, but crushed the tiny thrill of excitement fluttering in my chest.

Behind me, I could hear the bells of the Capitol clanging, announcing six o'clock. The boy's mouth dropped open in a dismayed expression. "Is that the time?"

"For at least the next hour," I told him wearily.

"You'll be all right, yes? You'll be able to get to your Guardian's home?" he asked, backing away from me. I nodded. "Good, just watch out for distracted boys who don't look where they're going. We're a menace."

"I will," I promised, watching him run into the swirling mist. Then I realized, he still had my bag. "Wait!"

Frazzled, the boy jogged back and placed the bag in my hands.

"Thank you."

He smiled one last time. "My pleasure, miss."

And he was off again, pumping those long legs to run down Armitage Lane. I watched him run, sure I would never see this boy, or anyone like him, again. I ran my thumb over the smooth bit of stone in my hand.

"Wait!" I called. "Your rock!"

"It's obsidian! Good for healing!" He turned, still moving as he waved his arm. "Keep it, just in case!"

I shook my head, watching until he disappeared from sight. Mum would tell me I was being silly mooning over some Guardian boy who was only trying to prevent a problem between his family and the Winters – mistreating a servant was considered the height of bad manners.

Wait.

"Mum!" I moaned, trying to dash towards Raven's Rest, but finding my legs too bruised and sore to run. I glanced at the obsidian in my hand. Maybe there was some residual magic left in it? Feeling more than a little silly, I bent at the waist and rubbed the rock in circles on my knees, trying to recall the comforting warmth that had seeped into my hands when he'd healed my scrapes.

To my surprise, the pain in my legs slowly faded, just enough to let me walk at a quick clip up the hill to Raven's Rest. I stuck the obsidian in my apron pocket and prayed my mother wouldn't question where I'd gotten it. She would *not* have been pleased with her daughter causing public scenes with a Guardian boy in view of our employer's home.

By the time I reached the servants' entrance to the sprawling Georgian manor, I was doing well to stay on my feet. The kitchen was dim, but warm, thanks to the heat of the cookstove. Mum was stoking the fire, preparing to slide slices of bread on a toasting fork.

My sister, Mary, was chattering, as usual. She was always chattering about something, lately, it was the new play at the Rabbit's Warren theatre, the dress she was piecing together from Mrs. Winter's sewing room scraps, and Owen Winter. Oh, how she could go on about Owen Winter.

Mum's worn face bathed in warm light. How much sleep had she gotten the night before, after spending an extra hour mending Owen's shirt?

"Ah, you're back," Mum sighed, her tone relieved. Her eyes narrowed suddenly. "And you've got dirt on the bag!"

"I'm sorry, Mum," I said. "Someone bumped me and knocked me to the ground, and I dropped it. But the shirt should be clean."

"Knocked you to the ground?" She spied the dirt stains on my heavy grey skirts. "Are you all right?"

"I'm fine," I said.

"You didn't overtax yourself, did you?"

I shook my head. "I told you, I'm fine."

"Well, sit down and rest yourself. We've some time yet."

Mary frowned as I slid into one of the battered kitchen chairs, feeling very tired suddenly. Perhaps I had pushed myself too hard, running home and back. I wasn't used to that sort of exercise. Mary's good mood seemed to be restored after going into the cold larder for eggs and raw bacon. Her beet-dyed pink skirts swished back and forth as she bounced between the counter and the old, black wood stove.

"I should make extra. Owen loves his bacon," Mary cooed, stretching fat, thick strips across the cast iron pan.

"*Mister* Owen," Mum corrected firmly, without looking up from the fire.

"Mister Owen," Mary repeated cheekily, winking at me. I dropped my head on the table. I didn't have the energy for her nonsense this morning.

I'd only been still a moment when I felt a nudge against the top of my head. "Sarah, you forgot your pill."

"Mum," I groaned into the table.

"You have to take them every day as soon as you wake up, Sarah, no skipping, no forgetting. We don't spend our hard-earned money on these things for you to scorn them."

I winced. Mum knew just which strings to pull, and when she wanted to save time, she simply yanked on the big one labeled, "Guilt."

"Yes, ma'am," I mumbled as Mum dropped the pressed brown tablet into my hand.

My parents paid dearly for the special medication from Mr. Fallow, a disgraced former Guild member who worked as an apothecary, in the heart of Rabbit's Warren. A mix of vitamins, herbs, and components that weren't quite legal, the pills treated an array of symptoms leftover from a prolonged battle with Japanese measles when I was three.

I'd been doing all I could to avoid the pills for weeks. They left me feeling sick to my stomach and twitchy, like I was coming out of my own skin. I'd palmed two so far that week, after being so jittery than I darn near dropped Mrs. Winter's prized orchid pot. But Mum was watching me now, and so I dutifully popped the rusty-tasting lump between my thin lips.

I accepted the cup of bone-chilling water from the sink pump and showed her my empty mouth, careful not to arch my tongue and give away the pill's hiding place. She patted my head. As soon as she turned, I spat the tablet into my hand and tossed it into the fire. The flames crackled with dirty green smoke, but Mum was too busy to notice.

It took all of my concentration to keep the triumphant smirk from my lips. Nice Snipe girls did not smirk.

"I'll mind the bacon, Mary," Mum said, shooing her from the stove. "It's washing day, so you two go gather the hampers. Be ready to snatch up the sheets after the wake-up bell, then get to the dusting. Mrs. Winter is expecting a guest in the parlor this afternoon."

Mary pouted. "I was going to help serve breakfast."

I snorted, covering it with a false cough. By "serving breakfast," Mary meant standing by the breakfast table and simpering at Owen behind his parents' backs. Fortunately for Mary, Owen ignored her flirtations in favor of the bacon. I didn't want to think about what could happen to my family if he noticed and complications arose.

"I can handle breakfast," Mum told her sternly. Mary's pout deepened and her brows drew together in a stubborn line. Mum responded with a hard stare over the top of her wire-rim spectacles. Mary's mouth bent into a mutinous frown. Mum glowered back. Sensing that the facial expression warfare was at its end, Mary rolled her eyes and snatched a laundry basket off the worktable.

Pinching my lips together to prevent a snicker, I followed Mary out of the servants' hallway. My skirt slapped dully against the kitchen door.

Like their parents before them, my parents had been working for the Winters since they were children. Mum was perpetually worn and snappish. We practically had to carry Papa home after he spent all day working on the Winters' gardens and grounds. Mary said she could remember a time when Mum smiled and hummed while she worked. She could remember Papa drinking water with supper and telling stories in front of the fire, instead of dropping off to sleep as soon as he flopped into his worn-out leather chair, a bottle dangling from his fingers. She never said that this stopped when I came along. She really didn't have to.

The worst part was that there was no end in sight, no holiday, no retirement, just years of work stretching out before me like an endless hallway – where every door was marked "Back-Breaking Labor." I already knew what my life would be like in a few years after Mr. Winter arranged my marriage to some Snipe boy and I moved away to take care of some other Guardian family. Mary, as the stronger of the two of us, would remain behind to replace Mum as head housekeeper. My future would be even more work, only without a mother to take the brunt of the kitchen chores and remind me to take my pills.

As our Guild Guardians, the Winters were responsible for "guiding" my family in all major decisions. During the death-rattle days of the Old Kingdom, organized sorcerers - disturbed by the creativity shown by non-magicals during the Industrial Revolution - melted the gates of Buckingham Palace and informed the non-magical monarch that her reign was over, Parliament was a thing of the past, and the Guild was now responsible for standing as Guardians for us helpless regular people.

The group that would eventually be called the Coven Guild took on the task of "protecting us" from the escalating dangers of our own inventions. While the Guild agreed that developments like machinery and steam-power made life easier, they feared that industrialized non-magicals would eventually create weapons beyond the capabilities of the Guardians' magic and we would leave them in our common, but lethal, dust. And there was the small problem with non-magicals being unable to go more than a few years without a war.

Having organized in secret for years, merging all forms of magic, the Guild forces rose up worldwide in any country where there was a government to take over, for what they called The Restoration of Balance. It was an awfully nice way of saying, "Why don't we just run things for you, whether you like it or not." Guild forces shredded the Declaration of Independence, the Magna Carta, any document that told non-magical people that they deserved to run their own lives, nations, or technological destinies.

The governments objected, of course, but it's hard to fight off an army that can knock buildings to the ground with the wave of their hands. Over time, the world evolved into a more feudal society, where non-magical families were assigned to magical families for employment and supervision. The magical populations created a united government, calling themselves a "Coven Guild of Magical Nations." The new Capitol city of Lightbourne was located halfway between the former textile district of Lancashire and the now-defunct iron works of Shropshire. The base of political power was moved to the heart of the once-burgeoning manufacturing industries, reducing London to a lovely second-rate town with some pretty buildings and reclaiming the northern land from what the Guild saw as misuse.

Buckingham Palace was now a museum used to display famous works of Guardian art. From what Mum said, the royal family retreated to somewhere in Wales.

Non-magical families like us, sometimes called "Snipes" (short for "guttersnipes") by the members of the upper crust, were assigned supervision from Guild families as our new "Guardians." We were paid a fair, living wage for our services. The Guardian government wrote laws to protect our health and safety, but the unwritten laws were very clear. We were the servant class and that's the way it would stay. There was no hope of becoming more.

The Smiths were fortunate enough to be assigned to the Winters, who had been Guardians to our family almost one hundred years, from generation to generation since the Restoration. Mrs. Winter never paid much attention to us personally, treating us as particularly useful household articles.

Of course, Mrs. Winter provided the kindnesses expected of

our Guardians, new clothes on the day after Yule, food baskets each Sunday. But knowing the special Sunday sugar cookies were given out of obligation made them heavy on my tongue. Mary tended not to worry about these things, so she often ate my share of the sweets.

"C'mon, mopey," Mary teased cheerfully, snapping me out of my gloomy thoughts. She gave the parlor mantel a long swipe with her cloth. "Less thinking, more dusting. I don't want to have to do *all* of your work today."

I frowned. Mary did more work. There was no denying it. I wanted to do more, but my body wouldn't let me. I couldn't lift the heavy *objet d'art* pieces for cleaning or move the bulky chairs to sweep around them. I was just grateful that she didn't seem to resent me for it. She just smiled, made some silly joke and went about the cleaning. She used the same silly jokes to make me feel better after she'd had to defend me from Deborah Green, a horrible, pock-faced girl from the next block over, who liked to throw mud at me while I read on our stoop. After dragging Deborah away by her braids and tossing her into the gutter, Mary told me that Deborah only called me "horse-face" and "mush-brain" because those were the only names people used for her. And then she'd tell me some joke and we'd go inside for some of Mum's scotch tablet candy.

I tried to thank her the only way I knew how, a pretty hair ribbon here, a cough there when she was staring into Owen's portrait with a particularly moony expression on her face. But I would never be able to make it up to her.

That morning, I moved about the Winters' formal parlor in our usual sequence – floorboards, shelves, knickknacks, then tables. The Winter family crest, featured prominently in a marble carving on the mantle, centered on a large raven, frozen mid-lunge against a field of white. It was an homage to the crest of House Mountfort – the larger "mother house" that included the Winter family – which showed a set of golden scales with a raven on one side and an apple on the other.

Death and health constantly swinging back and forth, out of balance.

Winter House Sigil

It seemed that the theme had inspired Mr. Winter's father and his father before him to be fascinated by birds, so avian skeletons, eggs, and other specimens were used as part of the décor of the house; the white bone contrasting starkly against expensive black and grey furnishings. The parlor's icy grey walls with their blinding white trim and dark furniture were just as inviting as the words "formal parlor' implied in a place called Raven's Rest. The best black enamel and ivory pieces were kept in this room, where Mrs. Winter greeted important guests and "ladies who lunch." It was to be kept spotless at all times.

Mum appeared at the entrance, wordlessly presenting Mary with the fresh arrangements of white freesia and anemones Papa harvested every day from the grounds. Their delicate scent mixed with beeswax and furniture polish, created the familiar perfume of Raven's Rest. On a normal day, I would find those aromas comforting, but today I was agitated, my thoughts restless and spinning off in a dozen directions.

More than ever, I resented doing chores that our Guardians' magic could easily finish. Magical folk wouldn't dare waste their power on stasis charms that could keep rooms dust-free or floors shiny. Oh, no, they reserved that magic for such vital tasks as wrinkle-cloaking glamours or potions that kept their bodies slim. And it was good for us, Snipes were told, to have work to keep our hands busy. Otherwise, we were prone to dangerous ideas.

I moved to the antique writing desk, carefully wiping the ink pots free of dust as I heard the double doors slide open to reveal the woman herself. Aneira Winter moved with the sort of serenity that only forty years spent in the top tier of the capitol's social circles could afford. The pale blue-grey morning gown with its rigidly corseted bodice set off a figure ruthlessly tended with diet and medicinal herbs. (A Winter would never do anything so vulgar as exercise, or even worse, *sweat*.) Her cornflower blue eyes were as chilly as her smile. Though striking white, her teeth were her only real imperfection. She had a slightly crooked left incisor, something that could have easily been corrected by any Guild healer, but she chose to leave it as is, as if to prove she didn't need correction.

I'd once suggested to my mother that Mrs. Winter selected the stark decor to off-set her cool blond beauty, only to receive a smack.

"Girls," she sniffed, without bothering to look at either of us. "Running a bit behind schedule today, yes?"

"Yes, ma'am," Mary replied, her tone appropriately reverent. "It's washing day, so we started a bit late."

"Please learn to manage your time more wisely," Mrs. Winter said, moving to her writing desk, her stiff blue silk skirts rustling.

I moved quickly, eager to finish and move on to the next room. Mrs. Winter's discerning eye could mean another hour spent re-cleaning spaces we'd already covered, and I didn't have the patience to do that with a smile on my face.

The lady of the house set out her special writing set and stationery, charmed with her signature sword lily scent. This meant Mrs. Winter was about to send a last-minute luncheon invitation to the social chair of some-such charity. I had no doubt this would result in a big benefit party that Mum, Mary and I would have to clean for and cater. I sighed. When the noise attracted Mrs. Winter's attention, I whipped a dust rag from my apron and took my frustrations out on the baseboards.

"How are you feeling, Sarah?"

I turned, looking sharply toward Mrs. Winter. I couldn't remember the last time she had spoken to me directly. Usually, instructions were filtered through Mum or I was addressed with Mary as a unit, the "girls." What had I done to catch her notice this morning? I hoped it wasn't so bad that it was putting a wrinkle in that indomitable brow? Mrs. Winter did not look with favor upon people who put wrinkles in her brow.

Perhaps I hadn't managed conceal the burn mark I'd ironed into Mr. Winter's favorite suit vest as well as I thought.

Batting down the feelings of panic climbing my spine, I cleared my throat. I slipped my hand into my pocket and found the obsidian. I wrapped my fingers around it, savoring the warmth radiating from its surface. "I'm feeling just fine, thank you, ma'am."

"She's been a little run down, not sleeping well. Real skittish," Mary reported.

I shot my sister a warning glare, which she ignored.

Mrs. Winter gave Mary a flat, disinterested look before turning her attention to me again. She quirked her lips. "Actually, I was going to say that you look rather nice this morning. There's a bit of color in your cheeks, a sparkle in your eyes."

My dark eyebrows swung up to my hairline. Speaking to me was one thing, but Mrs. Winter never paid us compliments, particularly about our appearance. What was happening this morning? Had she seen the incident with the Guardian boy out of a window? Was this some sort of torture to get me to admit I'd damaged a precious Palmer school shirt?

"Thank you, ma'am," I mumbled.

"Well, let's not let a striking reflection keep us from our chores," Mrs. Winter sniffed, her head bent over her papers. "Move along."

Mary and I nodded and immediately began scrubbing the day's ashes from the fireplace. Mrs. Winter abhorred the task and the residual soot that might make its way onto her clothes, so she finished her letter quickly and swept from the parlor. My sister and I breathed a sigh of relief, though Mary's bottom lip poked out ever so slightly.

"What was all that about *you* being pretty?" Mary asked, pouting a bit.

"I don't know," I whispered, glancing at the beveled glass over the mantle. I looked the same as I always did, a thin girl with a long nose and too-large eyes of an indiscriminate blue-grey-green. My dull brown hair was pulled into its usual sensible knot at the base of my neck. The only difference was a rosy blush on my cheeks, probably from the agitation of being trampled by an attractive Guardian boy.

I moved to the mantle, carefully removing a large antique Chinese vase from the ledge. Rare true-black porcelain painted with white chrysanthemums, it was a wedding gift from Mrs. Winter's favorite aunt. Leaving it on the mantle while the ashes floated around was asking for trouble. Of all of the objects in this room, this was the one we had to handle the most carefully. Of all the precious items in the house, this was the only item Mary insisted that I handle, because I was less likely to be punished if something happened to it.

I tried to think of something to give Mary that would sweeten her blackening mood. She wouldn't want my books. She had no use for my dresses, since they were her remade hand-me-downs. Maybe she'd want my blue scarf? It was a Yule gift, and the one nice thing I used to make my Sunday dresses special. It would also bring out the almost-violet color of Mary's eyes.

Hang it all, I would miss that scarf.

"In all the years we've been here, she's never once told *me* that *I* was pretty. But she's full of compliments for you? The apothecary must have mixed her tonics wrong," Mary mumbled as I placed the vase on the desk.

I shushed her, knowing that I would have to give Mary my scarf *and* my share of Sunday sweets to balm her wounded pride. Mum had tried to explain Mary's ever-shifting moods as a consequence of my sister growing up, becoming a woman. All I knew was that growing up seemed to mean outgrowing me. She didn't have time for my "little girl games" anymore. She wanted to be out with her friends, finding new ways to braid their hair or tricks to catch the attention of the boys they liked. I told Mary this seemed like a pointless hobby, since their marriages were to be arranged, but Mary sniffed that I would never understand.

These outings with her friends seemed to have spurred Mary on to her less-than-subtle attentions toward Owen. A secret part of me that I would never discuss, not even with Mum, was embarrassed by this new side to Mary. I didn't want to grow up if it meant making a fool of myself over a boy, pinching my face to put color in my cheeks and stuffing cotton wadding in the front of my dress. My "little girl games" might have been baby-ish, but they didn't hurt anybody. If Mrs. Winter got too annoyed by Mary's ploys, we could be dismissed. We could end up working for another Guardian family far less distantly tolerant than the Winters. Mary was putting us all at risk.

I sighed, tightening the strings of the hand-me-down apron around my waist. I would have to visit the ribbon shop on the way home to pull her out of this mood. There went my contra-band book budget.

Shaking my head, I forced myself to focus on my task. Mary

whisked the ashes from the room before they could settle on any of the furniture. I carefully wiped my hands on my apron before wrapping my fingers around the neck of the vase and placing it on the mantle. *Slowly*, I told myself. *Slowly draw your hands away from the porcelain so you don't bump it, like playing pick-up sticks. Steady hands.*

And suddenly Mrs. Winter appeared at my left, tapping my shoulder. "Sarah, I meant to ask you-"

I shrieked, jumping back. My fingertips slipped against the cool, slick surface of the vase as it teetered on the mantle. I watched in horror as it wobbled on the whitewashed wood, then toppled over. I grabbed for the falling porcelain, but it slipped through my fingers, bouncing off of my hands in its descent to the floor. I dropped to my knees, hands grasping at thin air, hoping to reach under the falling heirloom before it hit the floor.

I closed my eyes, imagining the vase reversing mid-air and floating back up into place on the mantle. I prayed, *Oh, please, no. Not her favorite. Not that vase. Please don't let it fall. Please. Please. Please don't let it fall!*

I could feel my will, every cell inside my body, reach outward in a rippling wave.

I waited, but the vase never hit my hands. There was no telltale crash, no angry cry from Mrs. Winter.

Where was the crash?

I opened my eyes to see the vase hovering there, a good six inches above my hands, spinning in mid-air like a top. My whole body seemed to flex and contract at once, as if I'd never used my muscles properly and this was their first opportunity to stretch. My fingertips warmed and tingled pleasantly as I stared at the circling object.

Mrs. Winter was kneeling on the floor in front of me, rumpling her dress terribly as she watched the vase orbit. She must have wanted to save it badly if she was willing to abuse her clothes like that. The vase bobbed, rising slightly as it spun. Somehow, I could feel the change in my head, as if there were some invisible tether from the porcelain to my brain. I knew exactly how much force and pressure it took to keep the vase afloat. I knew exactly how many times it was rotating per minute and how far it could drop before it hit the floor.

The very idea made me panic and the vase rotated higher, turning at Mrs. Winter's eye level.

"Are you doing this?" I whispered.

"No, dear, you are doing this." She studied me, her expression calculating as we watched the vase turn. There was a strange gleam to her eyes that I'd never seen before. Excitement. I'd seen Mrs. Winter pleased with her latest anniversary bauble. I'd seen her triumphant over eliminating a social rival from her ladies' club. However, my Guardian didn't feel undignified emotions like *excitement* or *happiness.*

My breath quickened and the vase dropped, right into Mrs. Winter's waiting hands. My head dipped to my chest. The string of tension keeping my body upright snapped and I sagged toward the floor.

"Yes, all right." Mrs. Winter clucked her tongue, setting the vase aside. She pulled me to my feet by my elbows and led me to the couch. I almost protested that I wasn't allowed to sit on the parlor furniture, but I was just too tired. I collapsed against the silk upholstery, leaning my head against the arm. It felt wonderfully cool against my clammy skin.

"It is always like that the first time," she assured me.

"First time doing what?" I asked weakly.

"No, no, my dear, no false modesty. I think you know that you were making the vase float," she said, arranging her skirts around both of us as she sat next to me.

My eyes went wide. What she was saying was impossible. Snipes did not have magic. We were missing the blood properties that made our Guardians so superior. And Snipes did not suddenly just *become* magical. So how could I make that heavy vase float like a misbehaving bubble?

Through the fatigue settling into my limbs, I could feel cold piercing dread. This went beyond burnt shirts or broken vases. I didn't want to know what the Guild would do to me for this.

Mrs. Winter patted my numb hands and gave me a frosty smile that made my stomach turn. "Let's have a chat, you and I."

2

PARLOR TRICKS

$\mathcal{M}$um had been horrified, summoned by her mistress's call for a cup of rosehip tea, only to find me sprawled on sacred parlor furniture. I struggled through the white noise buzzing in my head to get to my feet. Mrs. Winter patted my shoulder, gently pushing me back on the silky upholstery.

"Sarah, what in the world do you think you're doing?"

Through blurred vision, I could make out the soft, rounded lines of my mother's brown dress against the stark colors of the room.

Mrs. Winter took the rattling teacup from my mother's hands and pressed the warm china against my palm. "Drink this, Sarah, you'll feel better for it. Anna, please make sure that Mary isn't listening in the hall and then close the door."

I raised the cup to my lips and took a long draw from the raspberry-colored liquid. The tangy, slightly floral brew flowed over my tongue, warming my throat and belly. In an instant, the white noise in my head faded away. I sat up straighter. I took another drink and felt the warmth spreading to my fingers and toes.

"Madame," Mum whispered, her voice fearful. "If Sarah is ill, I can take her to the kitchen. I'm sure she didn't mean to dirty the sofa."

"I believe Sarah is perfectly fine. In fact, I believe she is returning to her natural state."

"I don't understand," Mum said, watching as I drained the last of the cup's contents. I blew out a long breath, feeling in control of my body for the first time since I'd walked into the parlor.

Mrs. Winter gestured toward the sofa as if Mum was an honored guest. Somehow, this made the nervous lines around my mother's mouth stand out even more. "Please have a seat."

Mum lifted an eyebrow, glancing at the space next to me on the sofa. "I don't think –"

"Please have a seat," Mrs. Winter repeated, considerably less friendly now.

Mum dropped onto the cushion next to me without another word.

Mrs. Winter gracefully sank onto the opposite chair, arranging her crumpled skirts around her.

"Now, I'm going to ask you a series of questions. They will seem invasive and rude, but I will remind you that you are obligated to answer; even if that answer will make either of us uncomfortable."

Mum nodded slowly, clearly seeing Mrs. Winter's use of such formal Guardian language as a bad sign. "Yes, I understand."

"Now, is Sarah your daughter?"

My mouth dropped open like a gaping fish. Mum was equally startled, making an indignant squeal before clamping her mouth shut. "Of course, she is, Madame. You remember the night she was born, right there beside the stove in your kitchen. Please just tell me what is happening! My family has served yours faithfully for years. Why would you ask me these questions now?"

Mrs. Winter eyed my mother shrewdly. "It would seem that Sarah has magical gifts that have stayed hidden up until now, very powerful gifts if her display earlier was any indication."

Mum's lips curled into a shaky smile, but her unease didn't quite show in her eyes. I knew, somehow, as sure as I knew that Mary was listening at the door, that Mum had been expecting these questions. She'd been dreading them for years, if the look on her face was any indication. Mum turned toward me. "This isn't funny, Sarah, whatever you did to make Mrs. Winter think you have magic, that's not a child's prank. You could get into a lot of trouble. You owe her an apology."

"Mum, I didn't—"

Mrs. Winter silenced me with a wave of her hand. "Trust me, Anna, when I say that it was no prank. Sarah levitated a heavy vase for the better part of two minutes. She more than levitated it. She made it dance and spin like a top. That's something that a witch with two years' training at the institute might not be able to accomplish. Now, how do you think she managed to do that?"

"I wouldn't know, Madame. Are you sure that—"

"Please don't insult my intelligence by asking if I'm sure of what I saw," Mrs. Winter snapped. "I know magic when I see it. I know what it feels like to be in the same room with magic. Now, if Sarah is your child, a child of the Smith family, a family that has no magical blood whatsoever in its known history... how could she suddenly possess such power?"

Mum looked down at her fidgeting hands. "I wouldn't know, Madame."

"Anna, you know there are far less pleasant methods by which I could extract the truth from you. It is a mark of respect for your years of service to my family that I am choosing not to employ them." Mrs. Winter's tone was all politeness, but I knew a barely veiled threat when I heard one. She could be referring to any number of tactics, from a bitter hypnotic tincture that would prevent Mum from concealing the truth to spells that could pull the truth from her lips. The Guild enforcement teams were known to use these techniques and more on Snipes who caused trouble. Mrs. Winter wouldn't have mentioned them if she wasn't considering using them.

My breath quickened as I stared at my mother's strained expression.

Mrs. Winter cleared her throat, as if this next sentence marked a new beginning to the conversation. "So, Sarah has never shown any signs that she could have special gifts?" she asked, her eyes narrowed. "She's never made the plates float at home? You've never seen an object suddenly move across the room when she had a temper tantrum? Fire and water have never behaved oddly around her when she was excited or upset?"

I gasped. Mum rarely let me have birthday candles after an incident on my tenth birthday in which the flames somehow ignited the much-scrimped-for birthday treat into a butter-fueled inferno. I don't think I'd ever cried harder than when Mum whisked the flame ball of cake into the rain barrel. The same rain barrel that froze solid when Mary provoked me into an argument during my first monthly course – in the middle of August.

Mum had blamed that on a prankster, too, as if someone in our neighborhood could afford to take our rain barrel to one of the expensive public ice houses in the name of confusing us. Images whirled through my head. The hurricane lamps that shattered without warning. Papa's smoking pipe flying off of the mantle.

"Mum." Horror had reduced my voice to a squeak.

Mum's eyes glittered with unshed tears as she clutched my

hand in hers. Her chapped lower lip trembled before she bit down on it so hard I feared that the fragile skin would give way.

"May I speak to my daughter alone, please?" Mum asked. "I'll tell you whatever you want to hear, but I would like to explain it to her first."

Mrs. Winter shook her head, her mouth set in grim lines. "Better to get it all out at once."

The elegant black grandfather clock ticked the seconds away while we waited for Mum to speak. I wanted to take it back, take it all back, pull time backwards to this morning, when my biggest problem was choking down my stupid vitamin pills. Mrs. Winter turned her head and stared hard at me. I shrank back in my chair.

"Whatever you're thinking, you need to calm down this instant. Whimsical levitation of my *objet d'arts* is entertaining and acceptable - once. Making every bit of glass in this room explode because your thoughts are running away like a panicked rabbit, is quite another matter. Take a few deep breaths and focus on your mother's voice... should she ever choose to use it."

My mouth fell open. How did Mrs. Winter know I was on the edge of blind, earth-shattering panic? Could she read my mind? She said "whatever you're thinking," but what did that mean? Where could I retreat to if even my own thoughts weren't private?

On this morning of firsts, Mrs. Winter did something I'd never seen her do before. She rolled her eyes at me.

This was not good.

"Right," I muttered. "Calm thoughts."

Mum took a long, deep breath of her own and said, "I only did it to protect you, to keep you with the family. And if that's wrong, I will throw myself on the mercy of the Coven Guild."

"I don't think we would need a gesture quite that dramatic if you would simply explain what you did," Mrs. Winter sighed.

"It started with little things when you were just a baby. The flames of candles leaping whenever you cried. A teething ring turning up in your crib when we'd left it all the way across the room. Vines growing up the wall outside of your room and tangling themselves into knots trying to slip under the pane. We thought it was just coincidence until you were three. Mary took a favorite doll of yours, and when you tried to take it back, she snapped the left arm off. Your papa took it away to fix it, but you were so upset. And Mary, well, even at five years old, she didn't understand when enough was enough. She laughed and told you to stop being such a baby. All of the sudden, you stopped crying and this calm, *determined* look came over your face. The next thing I knew, Mary was on the ground with her arm bent at an awful angle."

My stomach rose in my throat, what little I'd eaten for breakfast threatening to spill out on the carpet.

Mrs. Winter shot me a knowing look. "More tea, Sarah?"

I shook my head. "No." With a severe look from Mum, I added, "No, thank you, ma'am."

"So, Sarah broke Mary's arm?" Mrs. Winter asked conversationally. "I seem to remember a story about a fall off of a swing. And I believe that Sarah's mysterious bout with the Japanese measles occurred around this time, correct?"

Mum nodded. "The apothecary, Mr. Fallow, told us the measles were the best way to explain her looking so ill and skinny after we started giving her the pills. He was a member of the Guild, you see, before his bad habits got him kicked out of the finer circles. And he knew the signs better than we did. He knew just what to give Sarah so that her 'problems' would stop. Mr. Fallow had always liked Sarah, and he didn't like the idea of her being handed off to the same people that kicked him out of his own home. So he helped us. Sometimes, if he got the dose wrong or Sarah missed a pill, some little problem would pop up, but we were always able to explain it away."

"And Mary never questioned those 'little problems' or the pills?" Mrs. Winter asked.

"Mary has never been a particularly curious child."

Mrs. Winter snorted, a delicate sound that barely registered in my ears. "Suppressors are not a long-term solution," Mrs. Winter said, her mouth turning down at the corners. "Your Mr. Fallow should have known that. We only give them to children who aren't ready to handle their talents or adults who get themselves into trouble with the law. And even then, it's for a few months, under the strict supervision of a physician."

"The pills?" I murmured. "Those *vitamins* you've been giving me every single day since I can remember? They were suppressors?"

A change swept over Mum's worn face, a sort of determination, stiffening her features. "We were so worried about keeping it hidden, that we didn't spend too much time thinking about the why's or what it would do to her in the long run."

"No wonder the poor girl has been so sickly!" Mrs. Winter scoffed. "She's been deprived of her magic, as if you could cut a magical being off from the very source of her life's energy. It would be like keeping one of your Snipe children out of the sun her whole life."

"She is one of *my* children," Mum said stiffly. It was the closest she'd ever come to talking back to any of the Winters, and Mum was sassing the head of the household herself.

"Clearly, she's not," Mrs. Winter snapped back. "Now, we could spend this precious time dithering over what was, but I believe it would be better to ask ourselves how we progress from here. It is clear that Sarah cannot stay in your custody any longer."

Mum made a distressed sound, which Mrs. Winter ignored.

"Being able to perform untutored magic, even with the suppressors in her bloodstream, is evidence of a rare and powerful gift. And frankly, I do not trust you to protect that sort of treasure. You cannot be allowed to care for her. You've nearly killed the girl with your idea of 'doing what's best for her.'"

"What does that mean?" my mother asked, her tight grip on my hand returned and made me wince.

Mrs. Winter eyed the marks Mum was leaving on my skin and waved her hand. A powerful invisible current separated our hands and forced Mum's into her lap.

"Simply put, Sarah will become a member of the Winter household," Mrs. Winter said, as if she hadn't just psychically divided mother and child. "We will claim she's a distant cousin, twice removed, or some such thing. There are so many Brandy-wine family branches, no one will have difficulty believing it. Sarah will be dressed and presented in the manner befitting a Winter relation and stay in the family wing, in the Lavender Room, I think. After a period of rest and recuperation, during which we will allow the poisons *you* have pumped into Sarah's body to fade from her system, she will be sent to the Institute to study magic properly. She will be introduced to our social circles and find a useful, productive life within the Guardian community."

Stunned, I stared at Mrs. Winter with my mouth hanging open. She was joking. She had to be. This was some sort of trick to make me compliant and hopeful before she called the Guild enforcements on me. And if it wasn't a trick, Mrs. Winter had managed to go quickly, quietly insane over the last few minutes.

"And clearly, I will need to tutor her in etiquette and proper behavior," Mrs. Winter said dryly. "Lesson One, dear, a lady does not leave her mouth hanging open as if she hopes to catch stray insects."

My jaw snapped shut with a click of teeth.

"Why would you do that?" Mum asked. "Why would put yourself at risk for my child?"

"Because it will save us from certain ruin, from losing our home, our standing, our fortune, to the Coven Guild as punishment for somehow not noticing that Snipe girl managed to develop magical powers while under our protection, without us noticing. Other families have suffered as much after *rumors* circulated about lax supervision of their Snipes. I will not have my family name besmirched in any way because of Sarah's *abnormality.*"

Mentally, I added, "harsh treatment of housekeeping staff" to Mrs. Winter's list of qualities.

"I won't allow it," Mum insisted. "You can't just steal my daughter from me."

"You would rather lose her completely?" Mrs. Winter asked. "Because that is what will happen, when she is discovered by the Guild Enforcement. Do you really think they will just let her toddle along, flinging magic from her fingertips whenever she gets the least bit upset? She is a threat to our entire way of life. Her very existence calls into question everything we have been taught about the origins of our magic. Guild Enforcement will make 'the problem' disappear. She will be taken from you in the snap of a finger. And you will never see her again. We will never know what becomes of her. Even Mr. Winter doesn't have the influence necessary to protect her from that. And you? What sort of punishment do you think you will face for trying to conceal it for all these years? My proposal is the only option available to you, if you want to continue to see your daughter. She will be here, at the house, where you and your family will be able to visit her every day."

Mum made a helpless noise that sounded suspiciously like a sob. Mrs. Winter's voice softened as she leaned forward in her seat and gently patted my mother's hand. "Sarah has potential to lead a better life," she said. "Education, comfort, and in a few years, a marriage that will elevate her situation. Isn't that what every mother wants for their daughter?"

"I need to think about this," Mum hedged.

"You don't have time to think about it," Mrs. Winter said. "I need an answer now. We must act quickly if we are to work ahead of this debacle."

"You can't expect me to just hand her over."

"I can, and I do," Mrs. Winter told her. "And my patience is wearing thin. Now, what is your answer?"

"Do I have any say in this?" I asked quietly.

"No," Mum and Mrs. Winter chorused without looking at me.

3

THE DEATH OF SARAH SMITH

$\mathcal{A}$nd that was that.

Without any troublesome opinions from me, Mum and Mrs. Winter negotiated the terms of my "death." My parents were instructed to tell our neighbors that I had become so ill that I'd been rushed to a special hospital near London. With my reputation as being "poor, sickly Sarah," this would come as a surprise to no one. This was the pattern for most of my parents' conversations. They would tell people that my condition was getting worse and worse, until I "died" in a few weeks. Mr. and Mrs. Winter would arrange for a tasteful closed-casket funeral and headstone in the Warren's boneyard. And I would no longer be considered part of my own family.

Not everyone was agreeable to this arrangement. If my mother had been upset by the sudden change in my status in the Winter household, my father had been inconsolable. And Mary... While my father had wept openly as Mum led him away from Raven's Rest, Mary hadn't even looked back. She just marched away like she couldn't get far enough, fast enough.

My father, who normally wouldn't have said "manure," if his boots were covered in it, weakly protested the scheme as Mum shushed him. This was the pattern for most my parents' conversations. By the time Papa had grasped what was happening and came up with what he wanted to say, Mum had already decided that he was wrong and found some way to keep him quiet. Mary had been smart enough to keep her mouth shut as Mrs. Winter made it clear that any discussion of my whereabouts would result in a "sharp rebuke." I had my doubts that Mary knew what the word 'rebuke' meant, but Mrs. Winter made it sound very unpleasant.

Sarah Smith was dead, or very close to it. No more pre-dawn walks to the house with Papa absent-mindedly quizzing me on proper Latin names for the plants in his garden. No more mornings in the kitchen bickering good-naturedly with Mary and Mum while we divvied up the chores. I would never walk through Rabbit's Warren, listening to other children playing stick-ball or singing their silly jump-rope songs.

And in return, I was safe, hidden away in the Lavender Room, a cozy guest room done in a dozen shades of purple. I was given Mrs. Winter's very own castoff gown to sleep in and was buried under a mountain of soft, sweet-smelling sheets when a strange tapping noise brought me out of the deepest sleep I'd had in years.

I sprang up from bed, dizzy and confused, and scrambled for the door. I'd overslept. I *never* overslept. It was my job to brew my father's morning coffee to make sure he was... alert enough to work. We would be late for work. Why didn't Mary wake me? Why didn't Mum wake me? Mrs. Winter didn't tolerate tardiness. And it was Tuesday, silver-polishing day. If we started late, we would be buffing forks all afternoon.

THWUMP.

My face bounced off of a wall and went sprawling across a delicately worked lavender floral rug.

I groaned, rubbing my nose where it had collided with the

purple silk wallpaper. I'd run smack into a wall, right where the door would be in my tiny bedroom at home.

"Ow," I muttered, thunking my head back onto the carpet.

The tapping sounded again, more insistent this time. From the hallway, I heard Mrs. Winter saying, "The usual response is to say, 'Come in.'"

I rushed to the door, combing my fingers through my hair and slipping a pink shawl embroidered with warming charm runes around my shoulders.

I opened the door. Mrs. Winter wore a wry expression and one of her favorite morning gowns, peacock blue silk with lace trim. She was carrying a silver breakfast tray. In all my years at the house, I didn't think I'd ever seen her actually *carrying* anything, except a lace fan or a fancy handbag.

Clearly irritated with my silent staring, Mrs. Winter said, "I can see our etiquette lessons will have to begin at the very beginning. As I mentioned, Lesson One, a lady does not leave her mouth hanging open as if she hopes to catch stray insects. Lesson Two, when someone arrives at your bedroom door with your breakfast, the polite response is to invite them in and say 'thank you.'"

"I'm sorry, ma'am," I murmured. "I'm so sorry."

"Why are you whispering?" she asked, setting the tray on a little mahogany side table situated in front of the double doors leading to the balcony.

I frowned and whispered, "I'm not sure."

Mrs. Winter's lips quirked as she lifted the tray dome to reveal a small pot of tea, blueberry scones, a huge rasher of crispy bacon, coddled eggs, toast and a double portion of porridge. This was more food than I normally ate for breakfast in a week. My father, even with his hollow leg and love of Mum's scones, couldn't have put away this much food.

I hopped out of bed and dropped a curtsy, because I seemed to be physically incapable of not curtsying while in Mrs. Winter's presence.

"No, no, your curtsy is all wrong, dear," Mrs. Winter sighed, mimicking my quick bob. "That is the subservient pose of a housemaid. You have to carry yourself as someone who always been assured of her high-standing, of her self-worth. A little poise, please."

I stared at her. I had no idea what it was like to move with poise. I barely, grasped how to move without tripping over my own feet.

Mrs. Winter sighed and demonstrated a much more digni-fied curtsy, dropping smoothly until it looked like she was almost kneeling and then rising without pushing her way back up. And then, to my total shock, she sang a little song that sounded like *Twinkle, Twinkle, Little Star.*

"Curtsy curtsy, ankles strong,
Your chin is up,
Your neck is long."

There was no possible way for me to respond to this little performance that would not end in my being tossed out of the house for my blatant disrespect. And giggling.

"Please, sit." Mrs. Winter gestured to the chair. "Eat it all,"

"I've never had much of an appetite, ma'am," I said, sitting as delicately as I could while Mrs. Winter snapped a white linen napkin open over my lap.

"A side effect of the suppressors, I am sure." She tutted, while slathering butter on my toast. "Your appetite will return as you indulge in a richer diet."

Suddenly, I was struck with images from a fairy tale told to Snipe children, the evil step-mother force-feeding Hansel to fatten him up for the feast before he was rescued by the good, caring Guardian witch. I shuddered, but dutifully shoved a strip of bacon into my mouth.

I moaned and stuffed more bacon between my lips. I knew that Guild Guardian families enjoyed better food. I'd helped Mum prepare a good portion of those rich dishes since I was seven years old. But we'd never been allowed more than a testing taste. Oh, we'd had occasional special treats – peppermint candies at Yule and sponge cakes on my birthdays – but meals at home were always utilitarian, meant to fuel us for the work we had to do.

"Is this what food is supposed to taste like?" I asked. "We never had anything like this at home."

Mrs. Winter smirked as she stirred honey into my porridge. "Well, I suspect that your senses have been stunted by your daily medication."

I frowned, feeling a dull stab of resentment for my mother, and then feeling immediately guilty for it.

"The suppressors put you out of balance," she said. "Your magical life source was bottled up, depriving you of a sort of essential nutrition. It's as if one of your organs was not functioning. How is your skin supposed to glow with health and vitality when your liver has failed?"

"It wouldn't?" I guessed.

"Exactly," she said, crossing to the small wardrobe, where she'd deposited a few hand-me-down gowns the night before. She removed a rose poplin gown and a sunny yellow silk and held them against my shoulders, one after the other, which made my eating bacon considerably more difficult. I changed tactics and buttered a scone.

"The yellow will work for now, I think, but it's not your color. And neither is the pink. It washes you pale, terribly. Plums, blues, a few carefully selected shades of green, they will bring out the lovely silver quality in your eyes, I think. We'll know more when Madame DuPont brings her samples to your fitting."

My eyebrows lifted and a bite of scone nearly fell out of my open mouth. Charming.

"Madame DuPont? Your personal dressmaker is going to make gowns for me?"

"My dear, I do not think you grasp my commitment to this… project of ours. I will do everything in my power to help you assimilate into the circles in which we tread. I have just as much to lose as you do. I do not want you to simply survive in the Guardian community; I want you to thrive. I think you have great potential. You will be afforded every opportunity and luxury available to any member of this household."

"Can I see my mother?" I asked. "I'm sure I'd behave better if I saw my mother."

"Not at the moment. Your mother and sister have been restricted to the kitchen. Ruth and Martha will be taking over the other rooms for now. Should you try to enter the kitchen, you will find wards in place to keep you out. You will behave yourself either way."

Wards were complicated magic, a protective barrier formed from a combination of charm-work and potions that could prevent entry to or even hide the existence of rooms. For Mrs. Winter to have constructed one around the kitchen meant she was quite serious about keeping me away.

"I have keyed this particular ward to your magical signature, dear, so you are the only one affected. Your sister and mother can move about the house freely, but they know better than to try to speak to you against my wishes."

"How did you key it to my magic, when I've only done magic once?"

"Your magic is a part of your very being, Sarah. As I've told you, it's part of your skin, your bones, your hair. All you need is the tiniest bit of that magic, and you can do all sorts of spells affecting that person. Why do you think Guardians are so careful to do their barbering at home?"

"And how did you get a lock of my hair?" I glanced back at the bed where I'd slept. "Did you snip off my hair while I was sleeping? Is that something that proper ladies do?"

"If they can get away with it, yes," Mrs. Winter said coolly as she offered me a linen napkin and gestured to my lips. I scrubbed at my mouth with it, making her frown. "Though I will admit most proper ladies' hair-pulling runs along the lines of cutting remarks and social blacklisting."

"I thought the whole purpose of your taking me in was that I would be able to spend time with my family."

"Yes, but we don't want you to become confused, now do we, my dear?"

In a rare show of defiance, I muttered, "Oh, yes, confusion would be completely out of the question."

Mrs. Winter's hand whipped out like a snake, grasping my jaw between her vice-like fingers and yanking my face to eye-level with her. "Do not mistake my efforts to make you comfortable for weakness. I will not tolerate disrespect or ingratitude. I am vital to your survival, not the other way around. And yes, your splashy debut has the potential to give me a boost of popularity in my social circles, but so would the right dress. It would be very easy for you to become more trouble than you're worth. You so much as make a less than respectful facial expression towards me again, and I will turn you over to Guild enforcement myself, and let them figure out how best to take you apart and study you. Is that understood?"

I shrunk back and ducked my head, all defiance drained out of my system. "Yes, ma'am."

"And while we're on the subject, we must change your manner of speaking."

I frowned. If anything, "my manner of speaking" was quite polished in comparison to some of my peers. Mum wouldn't allow us to drop consonants or use "ain't" when we meant "isn't." Foul language resulted in soap in our mouths. And my reading had given me an extensive vocabulary, mocked by Mary's friends as "putting on airs."

"First, when you're asking for permission, you say, 'May I?' not, 'Can I?'" she said. "And you should reduce the number of contractions you use. It may take less time to say 'I'd' or 'I'm' but their use makes you sound coarse."

"I am coarse." I held up my hands to show her my work-roughened palms.

"Yes, well, that does not mean you have to *sound* coarse."

"Curtsy rhymes. Contractions. Color schemes." I shook my head. "I'll – I will never be able to remember it all. I will never be able to pass myself off as one of you."

She brushed her hands over her skirt and took a deep breath, a neutral smile sliding into place. "Now, now I will not have any more of this self-defeating talk in my home. This is Raven's Rest. Sniveling self-doubt has no place here. We start with the outside and work our way in. We will take this lump of clay and create a great work of art. You will be a great beauty, celebrated and sought after for your charm and talent. Soon, you will begin your lessons on comportment, etiquette and basic magical theory." She smiled blithely, a shallow expression that barely crinkled her face. "For future reference, my dear, whenever you can't find a proper or polite response to something, you simply say, 'How lovely' until you can determine the best course of conversation."

Keeping my expression as bland as possible, I parroted, "How lovely."

"A little less sarcasm in your tone, if you please. And we will have you ready for Miss Castwell's in just a few weeks."

"Miss Castwell's!" I exclaimed. "Miss Castwell's Institute for the Magical Instruction of Young Ladies?"

Miss Castwell's was not some fancy finishing school where a girl learned how to embroider cushions, pair the right wines for dinner parties and conduct social terrorism. Mrs. Winter was going to send me to one of the best magical schools in the world, where the students also happened to learn about embroidery and social terrorism. Sarah Smith had missed almost half of her days at the Warren school because of illness, but she would have access to the most talented teachers and the most diverse library available to young magical English ladies.

I would finally get a full education. I'd done well in school,

for as long as we were allowed to attend. What I lacked in
formal instruction, Mr. Winter had made up for with his selec-
tions from the library. Maybe there was some bright spot to this
mess, after all.

Mrs. Winter replied dryly, "Well, we are certainly not
sending you to Miss Castwell's Institute of Carpentry. But no
one in the know would actually use its full name. In fact, girls
from proper families refer to it as 'Miss Castwell's' or simply,
'school,' as if there is only one school to refer to, because it is the
only school that matters. Remember these little details, and you
will move about our world as if you were born to it," she
assured me. "With the right tools and just a touch of audacity,
even *you* will begin to believe that you were. And the first of
those tools is a new name. From this moment, you will be
Cassandra Reed. That is the only name you will answer to."

"I like it, I think. It's certainly fancier than Sarah. But why
did you choose 'Reed?'" I asked, unable to recall any Reed
family with a connection to the Brandywines.

Mrs. Winter gave a small smile. "Reed Warblers are a
common variety of cuckoos."

I gave an indelicate snort. She'd named me for a type of
bird that shoved eggs out of other birds' nests and swapped in
their own, forcing the parents to raise substitute offspring.

"And when I develop that touch of audacity you mentioned,
will I be allowed to see my family?"

Mrs. Winter sighed, "Your condition at the moment is very
delicate, Sarah. You're fortunate that we found you when we
did. I do not think it would be beneficial for you to see your
family. It would only confuse you. For now, your family has been
instructed not to speak to you, even if you approach them."

I took a deep breath and tried to keep the annoyance from
my tone. "How lovely."

Mrs. Winter cleared her throat. "And on that note, you must
adjust to calling me something other than, 'ma'am.' I know that
an increased familiarity between the two of us could result in

some… discomfort for both. But it's more important to convince my peers not only that you belong in their class, but that you are a member of my family. I do not believe we will be able to accomplish this if you're calling me 'ma'am' in that spineless manner. You will call me 'Aunt Aneira' or if a mischievous, though self-destructive, urge should strike, 'Auntie.'"

I stared at her, my mouth hanging open. Mrs. Winter raised her eyebrow and stared at my mouth. I closed it quickly, clacking my teeth together. She added, "Now, after your breakfast, you may sit in the garden for an hour to take some fresh air."

I nodded slowly. "Yes, ma'am." I caught myself and pronounced the familial endearment as if it were a foreign word. "Yes, Aunt Aneira."

4

EAVESDROPPERS RARELY HEAR
GOOD NEWS

*A*fter the ordeal of strapping me into the yellow gown, it took a lot of help from Mrs. Winter to get me down the stairs and through the rear garden door. It would have been easier to lower me out of a window with a rope. But I now understand why little Guardian girls never seemed to scamper around at play. They couldn't *move*.

Mrs. Winter led me through the grounds my father carefully cultivated, when he was sharp enough to focus on giving the Winters little islands of color on their rolling lawns. While Mrs. Winter gave Papa a design to follow, she never troubled herself with anything less than her precious magical specimens. Rounded beds of tall elegant irises in every shade, a statue of Morgana surrounded by a pool of delicate periwinkle, mixed rosebushes arranged so that their reds, pinks, oranges and yellows resembled a summer sunrise. Every bloom was well cared for. Every blade of grass was carefully tended by my father's hands, but he was nowhere to be found.

Mrs. Winter steered me to a smooth stone bench beneath an arbor of wisteria. She'd arranged a table stacked with books, my mother's still-warm strawberry tarts and a jug of milk. It was not lost on me that she was, in effect, serving me, though I certainly didn't think the gesture came from kindness. She wanted to keep Mary and Mum away from me, just like she had no doubt directed my father away from the garden while I was here. I noticed that she lingered, on the edge of my vision, pretending to inspect her prized fairy roses until I nibbled at one of the tarts.

Mrs. Winter helped me arrange my skirts on the bench and opened what looked like a children's book in my lap. I frowned at the cartoonish rendering of a Guardian child manipulating a dancing tin soldier.

"*A Magical Primer for Children?*" I asked. "But you said that the sort of magic I performed showed an advanced talent."

She poured a tall mug of milk and pressed it into my hand. "*Untutored* and advanced. You must learn to control your power before you try anything else that requires finesse. That means that you will begin at the beginning."

I frowned at the book. It felt like an insult, but I read, as instructed. Something in the gardens caught Mrs. Winter's attention, and she crossed to the ornamental pond, leaving me to my reading.

A few moments later, a sleek songbird with jewel-bright blue-green feathers landed at the end of my bench. It twittered sweetly, hopping toward me with its little head cocked, a bright, black eye on the tarts. I thought I detected a glimmer of hope in its look. My lips twitching, I broke off a piece of tart and dipped it in the milk.

"You're in luck. I happen to be in a generous mood," I said and I dropped the soggy mass at its feet. The bird didn't shy away. In fact, it skittered across the polished stone surface, bold as you please, and pecked at the milky crumbs without so much as a thank you.

"You're a very entitled little bird."

I read through the primer, ignoring the brightly colored, childish illustrations of a young witch and her orange tabby cat skipping across a meadow. The bird stayed at the end of the bench, pacing back and forth, eyeing the tarts. I sipped the milk and picked at the buttery pastries.

I relaxed against the curve of the stone bench. I could not remember the last time I simply sat in the sun and enjoyed a book. Explanations of magical babies being the result of moon-beams shining through the windowpanes of deserving magical couples weren't particularly interesting, but it was pleasant to just *sit* and do nothing. Even on my days off, I was so busy with chores at our own home that I rarely had time for leisure until after dark. The heat and light felt good on my skin, even through the material of the dress. The relatively warm early autumn wind feathered over my cheeks and I realized that I could breathe deeply for the first time in as long as I could remember.

I knew I was feeling better because the suppressors were fading from my system, but the better I felt, the sharper my guilt. My family was only a short distance away. I missed my mother so badly, my stomach ached with it. Could I sneak away from the garden, through the herb and vegetable beds, to the kitchen window without Mrs. Winter spotting me? No. It was better to wait, to show Mrs. Winter that I could be trusted alone... so she might relax her guard long enough to let me sneak behind her back.

I would worry about my willingness to deceive and sneak at some other time.

I finished the primer, feeling no more informed about magic than when I started. Though I did learn that magical children were very gullible about their origins.

Still, I dutifully read my assignments. I tried to tackle *A Comprehensive History of the Coven Guild,* but eventually, the complex explanations of the origins of magic and the first generations of Guardians to experience the magical "spark" made my eyes cross with boredom. To my shame, I only reached page thirteen.

Mrs. Winter had drifted from the pond to one of her experimental herb beds. Though it was difficult to imagine the ever-coiffed Mrs. Winter dirtying her hands, the magical garden was her passion. When she wasn't orchestrating the social lives of the Guardian elite, Mrs. Winter ran meetings of the Demeter Society, a prominent women's research guild devoted to the advancement of magical botany. Mrs. Winter used the talents and social clout of her fellow members to further her research, "bettering magical society" while maintaining and advancing her power base. Similar guilds existed for nearly every specialty – healing, metallurgy, astronomy, divination and more.

Entrance into the Demeter Society was even more coveted than most positions within the ever-competitive guilds. To be admitted, new members had to be legacies, related to other Demeter ladies, or have shown meteoric potential at Miss Castwell's. Lesser botanists were admitted to the not-quite-as-illustrious Epona Society, or worse yet, the Lightbourne Garden Club, which was barely a guild at all. Still the Garden Club was better than being left out of a guild entirely, which was considered a great disgrace among Castwell graduates.

From what I overheard while serving tea, Mrs. Winter was cross-breeding different varieties of tansy so it wouldn't burn so quickly when dried specimens were added to spellwork. I had no idea what that meant, but Mrs. Winter seemed very focused on growing heartier, less flammable specimens.

Closing my book, I stood and took a few steps away from the bench, waiting to see if Mrs. Winter noticed. She hadn't, because she'd slipped through the iron gate to her "restricted" garden where she grew the specimens so dangerous that she didn't dare mention them in conversation over tea. My father wasn't even allowed to enter this section of the garden, nor Mrs.

Winter's restricted greenhouse, both of which were kept under keys *and* wards only accessible by their mistress.

I took a few more steps toward the kitchen herb garden, the one full of plain old cooking grade mint and thyme, smells I would always associate with my mother. She would be baking the lemon-rosemary cakes for tea by this time of the morning. Could I sneak to the kitchen entrance before Mrs. Winter noticed?

I took another step.

Nothing.

With hurried, quiet movements, I picked up my skirts and moved toward the kitchen door. Every step I took that wasn't interrupted by Mrs. Winter's yelling, had me moving faster. I saw my mother through the window, hunched over a sink full of dishes. Mary was nowhere to be seen.

Was my mother angry with me, like Mary? Was she upset over seeing me all dressed up in a dress my family could never afford? I barely resembled the daughter she knew. Was she afraid that she'd lost me permanently? Or was it too scary to see this spit-and-polished Guardian version of the little girl who clung to her skirts all those years? And if she felt that way, what would my father say? Did he remember that I was gone, or were the empty bottles simply piling up by his fireside chair without me to collect them each night?

In that moment, I didn't care about the lies and the pills and the magic. I just wanted to see my mother. Just as Mum looked up and spotted me, I grasped the door handle.

And I was thrown back as if a horse had kicked me, hind end over tea kettle with my skirt thrown over my head. I felt like I'd been struck by lightning, my skin tingling with the shock of running into a ward keyed to keep me out.

"I think I hate wards," I grumbled.

I rolled to sit up, shoving at my skirts until they were no longer over my head. I blew my hair out of my face. Mum was pressed against the window, her eyes wide with fright. I couldn't hear her, but I could see her mouth forming the words, "Are you all right?"

I nodded, and waved away her concern. I pushed to my feet with some difficulty and brushing the stray grass from my skirts. I looked back to the window to try to have some sort of conversation with Mum through the glass. However, once Mum had assured herself that Mrs. Winter's ward wasn't going to do me permanent damage, she'd disappeared.

I knew I shouldn't let that disappoint me. Mum had been putting distance between us ever since I could remember, always shooing me toward work that needed me to be done or away from the boiling pot she was watching. I used to think she was just too busy to be a mother, but now I wondered, knowing that she'd known about my magic from the start, had she been afraid of me? Ashamed of me? Had she been afraid to get attached, knowing that I could be taken from her if people found out about my magic?

Still staring at the empty glass, I heard a sharp shout from behind the brick wall that separated the kitchen garden from the plot where Mrs. Winter grew plants for magical purposes. I glanced over to the little table and saw that the tarts had been reduced to crumbs. My shadow stretched far across the yard, almost to the feet of the statue of Queen Mab. How long had I been sitting out here?

I heard the angry voice again. "Mother, I can't believe you followed through on this ridiculous idea!"

At the commanding, but somehow petulant, tone, I nearly dropped my book. Only one person in the Winter household could get away with speaking to Mrs. Winter like that – Owen Winter, the darling boy of this proud household and the object of my sister's affections.

The very thought of him set my teeth on edge. Once upon a time, I thought we were friends, but I hadn't had much use for him since he was nine. The young boy with whom I'd once played pirates in the petunias had grown up to be cold and haughty. He rarely had a kind word for anyone but Horus.

Of course, just because Owen *could* get away with using such a tone toward his mother, didn't mean that I'd actually heard him use it. Though he was her darling boy, Owen was just as scared of his mother as the rest of us. I crept quietly toward the hedge, dragging my heavy skirts over the grass.

"Owen, I appreciate your opinion on this subject, but what's done is done," Mrs. Winter responded calmly. "We cannot let Sarah's abilities become known to the authorities. You know what that would do to our reputation. Not to mention the consequences for Sarah herself. We have struck a bargain with the Smiths and if we have taught you anything, it's that a Winter stands by his or her word."

"There was no reason to contact the Institute on Sarah's behalf! There are alternatives you haven't considered. Continued suppression, re-location – just send her across the pond and let her stay with some of your American relatives."

Through the metal slats, I could see Owen towering over his mother. He was dressed in the typical uniform for his classes, an exquisitely tailored black suit with a high-creased, heavily starched, white collar and a black-and-silver striped tie. Like most young men of fashion, he showed his family allegiance through the silver raven pin securing his tie. His auburn hair, a cross between his mother's gold and… whatever darker shade Mr. Winter had before he'd elected to shave it off, was slicked back behind his ears. He was the very picture of elegance, breeding and all things valued by his class at the ripe old age of fourteen.

Mrs. Winter sat on a stone bench in a slate blue muslin morning gown, her version of gardening clothes, culling rosemary stems. Owen threw off his silk coat and vest, choosing to rant at his mother in his shirtsleeves.

He rolled those sleeves up to his elbows as he paced, exclaiming, "No one we know will believe this charade. No one in our circle will believe Sarah comes from a proper Guardian household. Send her back to her family before you ruin us all."

I felt that sting much deeper than I expected. Owen wanted me back in the scullery where I belonged. Although we'd never been what you would call close friends, I didn't think I'd done anything to earn his disdain. But now he was afraid that I would embarrass him, that all his fancy Guardian friends would know that his mother was trotting out a servant, treating her like a show dog.

"Owen, that is enough." Mrs. Winter's voice rose to a volume I'd never heard her use. "*Cassandra* has become a part of this household. She will be a credit to the Winter name. And if she is not, there are other, more final, solutions under consideration. But for now, we will simply have to make the best of this current situation."

I pressed my hands over my mouth. A more *final* solution? What exactly did that mean? What did Mrs. Winter have planned? I'd come to think of my employer as a constant in this shifting sea of tension, but could I really trust her? Could I trust anyone?

"She's a plain little mouse, afraid of her shadow, and you want to teach her magic?" Owen scoffed, his full mouth curling into a scowl. "You'd be better off trying to teach my cat to waltz."

I dropped my book to ground, yelping when it landed on my toe.

Owen turned at my sound and saw me standing at the gate. His pale face flushed with guilt as he caught sight of my wounded expression. I backed away from the gate, willing away the hot angry tears gathering at the corners of my eyes. I gathered my skirts in both hands and turned on my heel, praying that I wouldn't trip while I ran back into the house.

I ignored Owen's voice as he shouted after me. "Sarah! Come back!"

5

SECOND-RATE FIRST IMPRESSIONS

*R*iding in the smart black carriage along McGavock Street, I stared out the window, rubbing my gloved hands together.

I tried to focus on the novelty of riding *inside* the cray-fire carriage, instead of merely staring after them from the street. I would arrive at Miss Castwell's with the faint ozone of a cray-fire engine clinging to my clothes, which was considered a mark of distinction among Guardian ladies. That didn't do as much for my confidence as I'd hoped it would.

My weeks living as "Cassandra" in Raven's Rest had not left me feeling at all prepared for this morning. In this new identity, my life was in danger. My family was in danger. And the only thing keeping them safe was me being able to pretend this fairy tale girl – Cassandra Reed – to life. If I couldn't convince the girls of Miss Castwell's Institute for the Magical Instruction of Young Ladies that I was a proper, pampered little witch, I would lose everything and everyone I loved.

Through the window, I watched young servant girls carrying

their heavy wicker baskets full of bread and vegetables from the market, and children in their ragged clothes chasing hoops precariously close to the bustling cobblestone street. Somehow, I felt jealous of them. Even though my life was supposed to be easier now, I missed being Sarah Smith. I missed being one of those magic-less servant girls, knowing my place in the world.

I caught my reflection in the glass. Over the past few weeks, my face had lost its pinched, tired look and my skin evened out to something like a fair complexion. My eyes had lost their feverish glint and settled into a clear, bright pewter color. My dull, limp hair became soft and shiny, a rich mahogany that fell over my shoulders in waves. I was still relatively thin, but I finally resembled the young lady I was, after years of looking like an underfed little girl. With the exception of the scars on my hands, I was no longer recognizable as Sarah Smith.

I stared down at the smooth, silky blue material covering my hands. These days, I often stared at my rough palms, comforted by that connection to my old life. The scrapes from my run-in with the Guardian boy on Armitage Lane had long since faded to a dull white, blending in with all the other marks and burns from kitchen work. Sometimes, I thought about that boy, wondered if he'd knocked down some other Snipe girl since I saw him, or perhaps he'd learned his lesson about looking up while in a "good think." I was sure he wouldn't recognize me now as the proper Guardian lady, but somehow, I hoped I would see him someday, in this new incarnation. I didn't want his last impression of me to be that pale, wan girl.

I did not think rationally when I was under social distress.

The carriage clattered through the gates of Miss Castwell's and I found I was too frightened to look out the window for my first glimpse of the school. It was a shame. Miss Castwell's had stood on one of the country's most beautiful stretches of property for centuries. While placing the new Capitol near the existing school was a dramatic gesture against that area's industrial development, I suspected it had far more to do with allowing magical parents convenient visits to their precious daughters.

My days had become a cycle of rich, nutritious meals, mornings spent reading in the garden, and Mrs. Winter's lessons. Martha, a slim, sly-eyed redhead who lived down the street from our house, spent hours rubbing tonics into my hair and moisturizing salves into my hands to soften the work-roughened skin. She was none too pleased about taking up the slack on my chores or serving the girl to whom she used to entrust with her lady's chamber pot, but she was smart enough not to complain about it. She did, however, seem to enjoy brushing my hair as roughly as possible.

For my part, I suffered intense table etiquette lessons and answered direct questions with practiced grammar. I discovered small pleasures to be had in life when you had the time and means to appreciate them. I had everything a little Snipe girl dreamt of, a warm soft bed, a full belly, pretty clothes. And still, I was constantly anxious and lonely. Everything in my life felt so temporary. One mistake, one badly timed word, and I would end up in Coven Guild custody. Nothing tied me to Raven's Rest, not really. Beyond Mrs. Winter's constant "attentions," I didn't feel like I was part of the Winter household. Owen pointedly ignored me. As he did in most situations, Mr. Winter was civil, but kept his distance. I got the distinct impression that he was under orders from Mrs. Winter.

I felt so guilty, being pampered while my family was working so hard just a short distance away. My hands itched for something to *do*. I was used to constant motion and employment. If I'd been born a lady, I might not have minded the idleness. But as it was, I had to settle for Mr. Winter's library and Mrs. Winter's garden for entertainment. My nightstand in the Lavender Room was piled high with editions of *Grimm's Fairy Tales*, *The Swiss Family Robinson, and Around the World in 80 Days*. Not the heavily edited versions we found in the Warren's bookstore, but the originals. The differences in the fairy tales alone were shocking. Maybe if Snipes had heeded the Grimm Brothers's warnings about witches, we wouldn't have suffered through the Restoration.

I wasn't allowed to use magic. Mrs. Winter wanted me to have some grasp of magical history and theory before I "went about casting spells willy-nilly, causing chaos wherever I went." I felt that was a little harsh. But I had sent the ceremonial blade she'd lent me flying through an eight-hundred-year-old tapestry depicting the Norse goddess, Frigg. It was possible I'd earned the criticism.

On the morning she took me to Miss Castwell's, Mrs. Winter had gifted me with her first ritual knife, a long, muted silver blade with a black stone set in the twisted silver handle. Unlike the fairy stories, Guardians did not use wands for spells. The metal of blades was more useful to direct magical energy, and each of them had their own personal athames, ritual knives, that they kept hidden, on their person or in their homes, to draw runes in the air during serious spellwork. Hand-motions, knife movements, chanting, herbs and various bits of nature all made up the strange music of charms and wards. I had to master the basics of blade dancing before I could start throwing other elements into my rituals.

It had the word *"Ingenium"* – the Latin word for wit –etched on the handle, which Mrs. Winter had explained was a family joke. The Brandywine ladies always carried their sharp wit with them. I knew that it was significant, having Mrs. Winter give me her first athame, which I'd decided to call "Wit" for brevity's sake. Mrs. Winter also gave me an elaborately monogrammed leather holster to wear it under my sleeve. But for the protection of the other students, she told me to keep it stored in my trunk for the first few weeks. An athame was normally passed down mother to daughter over the magical generations. Mrs. Winter was either placing a lot of trust in me, or wanted to make a significant show of placing a lot of trust in me.

Mrs. Winter did not provide me with a familiar, a sort of

magical servant in animal form. I thought that was odd, but I didn't want to push my luck when she was already giving me her magical heirlooms. Anything the magical person needed, the familiar would try to find a way to get it, whether it was help or potion ingredients or something as simple as companionship and comfort. The bond was supposed to last for the witch's lifetime, but I certainly didn't see any of that loving support from Horus the horrible cat. He spent most of his time licking himself. If I was to ever get a familiar, I hoped it would be something along the lines of Mr. Winter's raven, Tiberius, who bothered no one and was mindful of upholstery stains.

Mrs. Winter was very thorough in her instruction, though I wasn't sure if her information would be useful to me in real life. She did indeed start at the beginning with me, with basic magical runes every Guardian school child learned in their first year of home instruction. And wasn't I the luckiest girl in the world that she decided to teach me through embroidery? I was painstakingly embroidering each of these symbols into a sampler using a rainbow of blessed silk thread. Mrs. Winter pronounced my stitches "serviceable, but unimaginative."

To complete the Guardian nursery school theme, Mrs. Winter drew a large wall chart depicting the chapter on the six ancient Mother Houses, as if every Snipe child didn't have the various Houses, their associated families, and their symbols memorized by the time they reached working age.

Mrs. Winter insisted I study the house chart for at least thirty minutes each night before bed. She claimed it would help me prepare for the "who's who" at the parties I would be expected to attend. That education included a complete history of Mrs. Winter's family, the Brandywines. The Brandywines needed the money the Mountforts provided. The Mountforts needed the Brandywine's political influence, in addition to herbs for their healing potions. Mrs. Winter was the daughter of the Longbourne branch of the Brandywine clan, raised on an herb farm in Suffolk. Her marriage to Mr. Winter, a descendent of the

Mountforts, had been arranged by their fathers to seal yet another connection between the two families. Neither of them seemed particularly *unhappy* with the arrangement, but it wasn't a blissful union, either.

All of this effort was supposed to prepare me for my interview at Miss Castwell's. But despite the changes in wardrobe and table manners, I still felt like the tired, scared Snipe girl on the inside.

"Do stop fidgeting, dear," Mrs. Winter sighed, bringing me back to the present. Her gaze never wavered from the window. My hands dropped to my lap and I made a concentrated effort not to wring them. "Proper Guardian girls from this sphere are *expected* to attend Miss Castwell's. More importantly, they *expect* to attend Miss Castwell's. And therefore, as a proper Guardian girl, Cassandra would not be nervous about this interview. Cassandra would see it as a formality before she waltzed into her proper place amongst her peers."

I nodded, pressing my lips together in a flat, grim line.

"Take a breath. *Now.*"

I nodded, inhaling deeply through my nose.

"Perhaps without the nostril whistling."

I resisted the urge to snicker. While I had grown slightly more comfortable with Mrs. Winter, she had made it quite clear during my etiquette lessons that proper young Guardian ladies did not snicker at their beloved aunties. Nor did they talk with their mouths full, accept dances from young men to whom they had not been introduced, or touch another student's athame without permission. I had these rules copied in tiny, scrupulously neat hand-writing on a series of paper cards that Mr. Winter had provided from his desk. I also made cards for the history of the school and the members of Miss Castwell's faculty. I pulled the cards from my blue silk reticule and reviewed the faculty cards.

"Reference cards?" Mrs. Winter asked. "How very industrious of you."

I paused, my hand suspending the card mid-air as I tried to determine whether she was being sarcastic. To my surprise, she offered me a quick wink and said, "I did the same thing before I arrived at Miss Castwell's, listing the girls from the most prominent families, who I might want to befriend. Just make sure you burn them before the other girls see them. Otherwise, you might come across as 'disingenuous.'"

"What? Proper young ladies don't want friendships based on reminder cards?" I feigned horror.

Mrs. Winter smirked. "Well, they certainly don't want to *know* their friendships are based on reminder cards."

Before I could respond, I looked through the glass and caught that dreaded first glimpse of Miss Castwell's Institute for the Magical Instruction of Young Ladies. We rolled down a long white-gravel drive toward a crescent-shaped building, dotted with enough towers and turrets to make any fairy princess want to toss her hair over a bannister. The great grey stone walls stood five stories, supporting a roof set with green scale-shaped tiles. The building curved around an enormous white marble fountain depicting the Maiden, the Mother and the Crone lifting a cauldron together. The building was topped by an enormous bell tower, with all four corners supported by heavily carved green marble pillars. The green scale-tiled tower roof looked a bit like a traditional witch's hat, but I wasn't about to make that observation to Mrs. Winter. The stereotypical cone hat had gone out of fashion centuries ago.

Unlike the carefully manicured grounds at Raven's Rest, the groundskeeper had allowed the woods to reign here, the tree line creeping toward the school gnarled with outstretched fingers. Ancient stone benches were arranged in clusters here and there between clumps of herbs and flowers. I'd heard that at Palmer's, the school kept a special kennel for the few boys that brought pet wolves, but here I saw no familiar more exotic than a palomino pony wandering the backlawn.

Young ladies in day dresses of pale green stood out against

the drab background, strolling across the velvety lawn, their heads turning to watch the carriage clatter by. They moved in clusters, like birds, their heads bent together as they giggled. Under Mrs. Winter's orders, Madame Dupont made me a dozen dresses in the same pale spring green muslin prescribed to all Miss Castwell's students – known as Castwell Green. But I wasn't allowed to wear the dresses, or the dozens of matching gloves meant to hide my rough hands, until I was accepted into the school.

The girls were allowed to tailor the school "uniform" to their figure and taste, but they were expected use the same color and fabric to keep things "even" for the less fortunate girls whose families had status, but not much else. Mrs. Winter called those girls "social cautionary tales," and instructed me to avoid them. The girls were watching the carriage door, waiting for the Winter footman to open it and reveal... me. This was my first public appearance as Cassandra Reed. And if I wasn't mistaken, my breakfast was going to make an encore appearance. I sucked an unsteady breath, clutching my hand to my waist. I felt a firm hand clamp over my shoulder.

"*Radicem fortes*," Mrs. Winter murmured.

"I don't know much Latin," I whispered back. "Or any at all, really."

"It's the Brandywine family motto. It means, 'Strong roots hold.'"

"But I don't have roots here."

"No, but you have something better," Mrs. Winter countered. "My support. Now, get out of the carriage before the other girls get the impression that you are afraid. Like dogs and bees, adolescent girls scent fear."

"Could you give me a little push, please?" I asked, wincing when the gentle nudge I expected was replaced by a stinging magical jolt to my backside.

"Thank you," I murmured through a wince as my expensive shoes hit the ground.

The building seemed to loom even larger from the ground and I couldn't help but marvel up at the sheer scope of the stone façade. Mrs. Winter hooked her arm through mine, hurrying me along, all the while looking perfectly at ease.

I tugged at the high blue collar that seemed to be tightening around my throat. Madame DuPont had stayed away from exotic laces and embellishments for my wardrobe, keeping to curlicue piping, high collars and the occasional pointed sleeve. Today's selection was a creamy blue with white-and-blue striped edging at the lapels and matching silk gloves. I might have felt elegant and impressive, but the gloves were damp from the sweat gathering in my palms. Impressive girls surely had dry palms.

Mrs. Winter led me through a wide foyer, set with black-and-white floor tiles and faded emerald trim. A large, dark-stained double staircase led to the second floor, where I could hear the echo of an older woman's voice as she lectured on the properties of ground moonstone. An oversized frosted glass window bathed the foyer in light, silhouetting a dark, slim figure standing on the landing with her hands folded in front of her.

Mrs. Winter curtsied, but just barely. She nodded toward the formidable-looking woman, who was around Mrs. Winter's age, but wore her iron grey hair pulled back into a severe bun. Her moss-colored dress was also severely simple, with frog enclosures that kept the crisp collar closed at her throat.

"Cassandra Reed, this is Headmistress Lockwood," Mrs. Winter said, gesturing to the woman. "Headmistress Lockwood, this is my niece, Cassandra Reed. Your latest pupil."

Headmistress Lockwood offered an enigmatic smile, the sort that involved stretching your lips over your teeth without actually revealing any of them. "We shall see."

Without another word, Headmistress Lockwood turned on her heel and walked up two more flights of stairs. Mrs. Winter and I followed, carefully negotiating the stairs in our heavy skirts, on the hope, I supposed, that Headmistress Lockwood actually wanted us to follow. Headmistress Lockwood left the door to her office open, and Mrs. Winter had the grace to take a few deep, recuperative breaths before entering that dimly lit chamber.

I, on the other hand, stopped at the door. What was waiting for me on the inside? Would I have to pass some sort of test? An initiation? Would I have to cast a spell? Drink a potion? Mrs. Winter had tutored me, but her instruction was mostly theory. What if I was turned away from the door before I took my first class? I realized, to my shock, that possibility frightened me far more than the possibility of being exposed as a Snipe upstart fraud. As much as I missed the simple life I'd had as a servant, I wanted to study at Miss Castwell's. I wanted to know how and why I was able to do magic. I wanted to live life as a magical being. And I couldn't do that unless I crossed through the door.

I was just in time to hear Headmistress Lockwood's voice, rounded and burred by a distinct Northern accent. "This is highly irregular, Aneira. Surely, you expected some questions on my part."

Headmistress Lockwood sat in a heavy, ornately carved chair behind her desk. Mrs. Winter was seated in the leather club chair. She did not look pleased. "Questions, yes. My old friend and mentor casting aspersions on a member of my own family? No. I am telling you, Dora, the girl is of my bloodline and has powerful magic. What more – beyond the substantial donation my husband and I make to this school each year – do you need to admit her?"

I pretended I hadn't heard that, focusing on the strange furnishings in Headmistress Lockwood's office with its dark green wallpaper and heavy grey curtains. Every wall was covered in portraits of students past, dating back to the 1600s, when the pre-Restoration institute was only known as Miss Castwell's School for Young Ladies. Several specimens of exotic plants stood on special stands under bell jars. I leaned close to examine the glowing gold petals of one particularly odd-looking plant. I reached up to touch the glass, the golden flower, whose lovely foliage immediately darkened to brown, reptilian scales.

"I wouldn't do that," the Headmistress said, without looking up at me. I glanced down at the golden flower, whose lovely foliage immediately darkened to brown, reptilian scales. The flower expanded and split, revealing row after row of tiny fangs amongst the stamens. The unhinged jaw snapped up, smacking against the glass in its haste to get to my fingertip. I shoved both hands behind my back, straightening and stepping away from the stand. Having missed its opportunity to eat my hand, the plant returned to its charming, shimmering state.

How lovely.

"*Drosera aureus*," Headmistress Lockwood said, again without looking at me. She flicked her wrist toward me. A black linen-bound book, *The Dark and Dangerous Garden*, materialized in my right hand. "One of the first known magical carnivorous plants. Perhaps you could study their origins and save your fingertips. I expect one thousand words, neatly printed, on the plant's camouflaging and hunting techniques."

A small stack of writing paper and a fountain pen appeared in my other hand. I bit back the question that immediately came to mind – would I still have to submit the paper if I was not admitted to the institute? Mrs. Winter did not seem upset with my misstep, so I assumed that this was normal behavior from Headmistress Lockwood. Perhaps this was how she heated her office in the winter, by burning stockpiled essays from nosy initiates.

I was not asked to sit, something I was rather accustomed to, so I stood at Mrs. Winter's shoulder, spine ram-rod straight and the book and paper cradled in my hands.

"Some proof of her pedigree would be nice," Headmistress Lockwood insisted, not missing a beat as a silver tea service seemed to appear from nowhere on a small wooden table beside Headmistress Lockwood's desk. She poured a cup for Mrs.

Winter.. "And perhaps a school record or two, something that proves that she has had *some* formal training."

"I am afraid Cassandra's mother was very… liberal." Mrs. Winter sipped her tea, making an almost imperceptibly sour *moue* with her lips and stirring in sugar. "She insisted that Cassandra be tutored privately at home in Cambridgeshire, but was so demanding that her instructors often quit without notice. As a result, Cassandra's education is riddled with holes. She will need a specialized class course, allowing for remedial instruction in some basic areas while accommodating her natural gifts."

Headmistress Lockwood frowned. "I am assuming you have some lesson plans detailing what her tutors taught her?"

"I am afraid those records were destroyed in the fire," Mrs. Winter lied smoothly. I played my part, looking appropriately distressed at the mention of my "parents" and their tragic, fiery demise; a demise that provided a perfectly legitimate reason for me to transfer schools mid-year with no proof of who I was or what I knew. I twisted my hands around the book, plucking at my gloves as I chewed my lip. Though I didn't think it was possible, Headmistress Lockwood's expression softened, just as Mrs. Winter said it would.

"Cassandra, perhaps you should visit the library," she said, her voice a bit more gentle. "Your aunt mentioned in her letter that you enjoy reading."

"Yes, ma'am, I would like that very much," I replied, carefully imitating Mrs. Winter's sophisticated inflection.

"Morton!" Headmistress Lockwood called into a black funnel shaped object on her desk. A few moments later, an older woman in a tea-leaf colored dress and a frizzed chignon of greying curls glided into the office. The blue architect's compass embroidered at her sleeves denoted her as a member of Morton family. The Mortons were minor extension of House Drummond, masters of complicated ward construction. Her aquiline features were perfectly placid, but there was a sadness to her deep brown eyes that made me want to put my arms around her. But I was sure that hugging was something severely frowned upon at Miss Castwell's.

"Headmistress?" Miss Morton asked, clearing her throat and giving Mrs. Winter a deferent nod. "You rang for me?"

"Miss Morton, our librarian," the headmistress said, waving rather dismissively at the older woman. "Morton, I believe you remember Aneira Winter. This is her niece, Cassandra Reed, who is enrolling rather late in this year's session. Please take Miss Reed to the library to keep her occupied. When she has completed her essay, let her explore the stacks. Entry-level access only. No advanced subjects."

Miss Morton gave me a quick once-over and smiled gently, a kind expression that helped wiggle that cold weight from my chest, ever so slightly. "Of course. I would be happy to. Come along, dear. "

Miss Morton led me along a long black-and-white corridor lined with more student portraits. Her long skirts swished around her ankles. She checked her pocket watch, a blue enameled circle with a Morton House compass on the lid. It was her only ornament, besides a tarnished silver brooch securing a sprig of nightglove, a dark purple hybrid of nightshade and foxglove whose scent encouraged focus and clarity, to her chest. It seemed an odd plant to wear against the murky color of her dress, but given how frazzled she seemed, maybe she needed the boost of concentration.

Thousands of questions sprang to my tongue about the paintings, the various house symbols worked into the crown molding. But I didn't ask any of them, because I suspected that hallway conversation was also verboten at Miss Castwell's.

Miss Morton opened the double doors to reveal the library. Rows and rows of bookshelves, floor to ceiling, three stories high, lit by hundreds of cray-fire lamps. We emerged on the landing of the second story, overlooking long rows of worktables on the ground floor. Younger students, some as young as nine or ten, in matching green dresses bent their heads over books, scribbling industriously in their notebooks. Older girls wandered the stacks upstairs, their books floating behind them as if carried by an invisible servant.

I felt conspicuous in my blue gown, as beautiful as it was.

Overhead, a ceiling of stained glass showed the crests of the prominent family Houses against a smoky blue backdrop, composed of little pinpricks of light like elitist constellations – the Drummonds' black tree against the white background, the Benisse peacock, slightly imbalanced golden scales for the Mountforts, the flaming silver McCray lamp, the heavy brass Cavill hammer splitting a mountain.

The Brandywine crest was a bit more subtle than I'd expected, white apple blossoms with dark leaves and roots. As I was supposed to be a distant Brandywine cousin, Mrs. Winter had asked Madame DuPont to subtly embroider white apple blossoms on some of my dresses and handkerchiefs, and each set of gloves. She'd also given me several small pieces of costume paste jewelry featuring the floral motif. All of the smartest girls did this, Mrs. Winter claimed, sneaking their house sigils in some form into their ensembles to show allegiance to their families and remind their classmates with whom they were dealing.

I wandered closer to the cray-fire lamps, an invention of House McCray, powered by a network of magically charged crystals. They were terribly expensive to create and maintain, due to the amount of magical energy required to keep them lit. Miss Morton murmured that the McCray family had generously donated the lamps more than a century before, with the understanding that the students would be responsible for charging them as part of their coursework.

"The older girls are quite diligent in this task," Miss Morton assured me. "Though I admit that with some classes where the talent pool is, shall we say, diluted, the faculty step in to supplement."

I smiled, but didn't comment, sorely afraid that I would say the wrong thing in the wrong accent and give myself away before I even started. Miss Morton led me down the sweeping marble staircase to the ground floor, where she seated me in a little window alcove at a private desk.

"One thousand words," she said kindly. "I'm sure you'll manage it in no time at all. And then I shall show you some of the more interesting botany books, since you appear to take an interest in the subject."

I glanced down at *The Dark and Dangerous Garden*. Miss Morton snapped a green velvet curtain closed around my study alcove, separating me from the rest of the library. I cleared my throat and uncapped my pen. I searched through the table of contents until I found the chapter on *Drosera* plants. One illustration showed the plant as I'd first observed it, beautiful, golden blooms glowing against a dark background. The second illustration, labeled "actual appearance," revealed a plant covered in brown reptilian scales and a split mouth-like pod with teeth like the disgusting lake lampreys Mr. Sykes sold at the fish market.

Plants of the family drosera *use a glamour of bright petals and faint iridescence to attract potential prey. The plant requires the blood of its prey to generate the glamour, so only the strong specimens survive.*

I wrinkled my nose, wondering which of her hapless underclassmen Headmistress Lockwood used to feed her plant. Still, it was an interesting plant and reminded me of the old vampire tales Mrs. Green, our teacher at the Warren school, tried to scare us with around All Hallow's Eve. I dutifully scrawled out an introductory paragraph in my neatest cursive, comparing the plant's methods to the old vampire tales and suggesting that the familiar legends could have some link to the plant world. It might not have made any sense, but at least it would entertain Headmistress Lockwood.

Soon, I had a passable first draft – one thousand and *fourteen* words, thank you very much – but as I read over it, I realized it was missing something. Mrs. Green had insisted on supporting our essays with multiple sources, something Mary had complained about bitterly. I needed something to back up my assertions about the vampire tales. Surely, a library like this had a section devoted to folklore and legends.

I stood, poking my head out of the study alcove. Miss Morton was nowhere to be found. Come to think of it, she was supposed to come back to check my progress. Had she forgotten about me completely or I was supposed to alert her when I'd reached my goal? Was working *past* my goal considered a breach of new student etiquette? I worried my lip, considering my options. If I waited for Miss Morton, I might not finish my essay, which would definitely not help my case with Headmistress Lockwood. And I had been given permission to look at the "entry level" shelves, though I'm sure Headmistress Lockwood meant for me to have an escort. As long as I didn't touch anything, I told myself, I would be fine.

Several heads rose as I parted the velvet curtains. Though several sets of eyes followed me, each girl was careful not to appear as if she was watching. I scanned the plaque on the stairwell, listing the subject areas on each floor. The folklore section was located on the third floor. I sighed, eying the steep staircase and my voluminous skirts.

What would Mrs. Winter do, I wondered.

She would hike herself up those stairs. Or she would enchant someone to carry her.

I grabbed the bannister, pulling myself up the first step. I marveled at the sheer number of bookshelves I passed, novels, history, alchemy, astronomy, divination. Seeing Headmistress Lockwood's office and this monument to the written word made me that much more eager to get up the mountain of stairs and finish my paper so I could stay at Miss Castwell's. And I wanted to stay at Miss Castwell's, not to please Mrs. Winter or to avoid Coven Guild dissection, but because I wanted to live in this library. I wanted to wallow in these bookshelves, taking my time as I worked my way through the treasures it had to offer.

Several minutes and curses against fashion later, I'd arrived on the third floor landing. The library was even more impressive from this height, the green-carpeted levels standing out sharply from the black and white floor tiles. The ceiling's jewel-like renderings of the House crests were so close I could almost touch them.

The older students I'd seen before were still milling about, adding to the burden of their floating book stacks. They largely ignored me, but I could see the occasional intentionally casual glance thrown my way. I could see now that there was a seventh crest etched into the glass, but it had been nearly obliterated. Only a dark outline remained, a rounded blobby bird-like shape with outstretched wings.

"Or possibly a bat," I acknowledged softly to myself, tilting my head to study the blurred shape. "Or a cranky dragon."

Why would the school try to cover a House crest? For that matter, whose House crest could it be? As far as I knew, there were only six great families. Had the glasscutter made a mistake in one of the designs? The strange bird-like smudge could be the Benisse peacock, a fat, hyper-extended version of the peacock. I moved along the railing to the center of the landing, closer to the blurry bird. Distracted by its malformed wings, I bumped into a glass display case on a pedestal on the near side of the landing. The case was like another bell jar, protecting the open, blank pages of a large book the size of a paving stone.

I jumped, my hands fumbling to keep the case from falling. I leaned closer to get a better look, my breath fogging the protective glass. Tiny, evenly spaced symbols appeared on the white pages in molten, glowing gold. The glow rippled from one corner of the page to the other. The text must have been Greek or Sanskrit or some magical dialect I'd never heard of, because I couldn't make out any words I recognized.

I smiled, delighted, and rubbed at the glass to wipe away the fog. As if in response, the symbols rose from the page, bouncing against the glass like confused, insistent bees. I glanced around the floor, to the older students wandering the shelves, but none of them seemed to notice glowing, golden words, tapping testily at a glass display case... which made me question the school as an educational institution all together, really.

Also, I needed to stop examining items in glass cases. No good came of it.

The floating letters gave one last mighty heave against the glass case, popping it open like a clamshell. The smell of verbena and old paper rose immediately to my nostrils. I might have closed my eyes to enjoy the fragrance, if not for the floating letters trailing up my arms, across my chest and around my head.

My fingers moved as if controlled by some unseen puppet master, dragging gently down the corners of the book and gripping its edges. I did, I would admit much later to myself, panic, when I couldn't let go of the book. My fingers felt glued to the pages. I frantically scanned the floor, wondering whether I should call for help.

None of the other girls seemed to be reacting to this bizarre occurrence. I didn't know what sort of spell I'd activated or what sort of harm it could do. And I was certain that Headmistress Lockwood would not look kindly on removing ancient books from their perfectly nice display cabinets, which were probably in place to protect students from their own stupidity as much as from the curses contained under the glass. And I wasn't even a student, so the headmistress's patience was not likely to extend to me.

I blew out of the corner of my mouth as I could chase the floating symbols away like annoying insects. I shook the book, attempting to dislodge it from my hands. Was this some sort of practical joke? Or a cruel trick meant to punish unworthy Snipes who touch books without permission? I yowled as the silk of my gloves and sleeves burned away, flaking to the floor in ashes.

Hallucinogenic punishments for Snipes who touch books without permission. How lovely.

The ink crawled the lengths of my fingertips to my hands,

the words flowing over my skin intact. Curling black lines scrolled across the skin of my palms like climbing vines, forming an almost bat-shaped crest of stylized swirls. It burned, but it wasn't painful. It was like getting into bathwater that's just a little too hot. It felt right to have the marks carving their way into my skin. They were raised, metallic, like an inflexible vein of silver had embedded its way into my skin forming a slender wing-shape across each hand. The stylized curves were shining metal that reflected all of the colors of the spectrum. My hands finally loosened from the book and I was able to touch the shape on either palm, finding it pleasantly warm to the touch.

My gloves and sleeves disintegrating as metalwork spontaneously burst from my palms *did* seem to finally get other girls' attention. I heard soft exclamations and the rustle of skirts as I cradled my hands together, pressing my pinkies together in a cupping gesture, so that when my hands touched, it looked like a silver dragonfly was perched in my hands, the head pointing toward my fingertips. It didn't hurt. I flexed my hands gently. How could I have so much metal embedded in my skin and still be able to bend my fingers, grasp my hands? My legs twisted under me, and I fell back to the carpet on my rump.

Mum was not going to pleased. She did not like magical marks, no matter how in fashion they were in Guardian circles. I didn't think my "aunt's" reaction would be all that favorable, either.

I glanced up at the circle of strange faces around, unsure of who to ask for help. The sea of green skirts surrounding me parted and a dreadfully familiar black-and-grey striped gown approached. My cheeks flushed red. I tried to push to my feet, but my legs were tangled in about a dozen layers of petticoat and silk. I couldn't move.

I'd expected Mrs. Winter's expression to be furious, but she eyed this mottled green cover of the book in my lap, and she had to school her features from the gleeful grin that threatened to smear her lip rouge.

"The book chose you," she marveled. "How… interesting."

"W-what?" I huffed out a breath, wiping at the perspiration forming on my brow and trying against to push to my feet.

"No, no, dear," Mrs. Winter said, dropping to her knees in front of me and pressing me back to rest against the mahogany display case. "You mustn't move your hands too quickly. You will want that to set properly, like a healing bone. It takes a moment."

She glanced up at Headmistress Lockwood, who was shooing the gathered students away with practiced ease. Mrs. Winter cast a triumphant look over her shoulder. "It chose her, Dora."

Headmistress Lockwood rolled her eyes. "Oh, Aneira, enough of your foolishness. That book has been stored on school property for more than two centuries. It will remain school property."

"The book chose to show her its secrets, Dora. It belongs to her now."

"I don't think it showed me anything," I told Mrs. Winter. "I couldn't read it."

Mrs. Winter smiled, but it wasn't a warm expression meant to comfort. There was greed in her eyes, bright and gleaming, and it made a shiver run down my back.

"You will, in time." She nodded toward the decorative insect now embedded in my skin. "That marks you as the owner and translator of *The Mother Book*. The original *Mother Book*, written in magical cuneiform by matriarchs of the great families before the Houses were even formed, before we could scratch out a language so harsh and guttural as English. It represents one of the largest deposits of archaic magical knowledge in the world and is imbued with a magical will all its own

The book only allows its secrets to appear to the Translator, one person it believes to trustworthy enough to read its contents. It bounced between the old world magical schools, sharing the matriarchs' secrets, before it was brought here the year the school was founded. The book will only reveal itself to witches it deems worthy of its secrets. A Translator hasn't been chosen in how long, Dora?"

"One hundred and forty-two years," Headmistress Lockwood muttered.

"And all of the previous Translators have been much older than you, dear. The youngest Translator on record was seventeen. To be chosen at fourteen... well, the book must have felt quite the connection to you."

Mrs. Winter seemed to laying on this Translator business on pretty thickly. I could only hope this wasn't some trick she'd arranged to convince Headmistress Lockwood to admit me to the school. Because the Headmistress in question looked like she wanted to pitch me and my silver dragonfly out onto the gravel drive.

"What does the Translator do?" I asked, still wiggling my fingers, as if I thought they would suddenly stop working if I didn't flutter them.

"Study the book," Headmistress Lockwood said. "Translate the spells and determine what to share with other witches, with the Guild government. Previous Translators have only worked through about a third of the pages. You are not in for an easy road, Miss Reed."

"I didn't expect any of this to be easy," I assured her.

Mrs. Winter smirked up at the headmistress as she helped me to my feet. "So I suppose this qualifies as sufficient record of her magical ability for admission, Dora?"

"No one likes a gloater, Aneira."

6

THE WHEELS TURN

*M*rs. Winter and Headmistress Lockwood led me to a wing marked "dormitories," and I felt the faint magical sizzle of protective wards pass over my skin, warming the metalwork on my hands. The two ladies seemed to be arguing in several different languages, switching from French to Italian to German as we passed little pods of students pretending *not* to stare at the girl in the tattered sleeves being led down the hall, carrying a beloved school artifact.

The room, done in greens and greys, was laid out much like my room at Raven's Rest, though obviously less grand. A desk stood in front of the window, already stacked high with textbooks. I kept Mother Book clutched to my chest, its thick parchment pages glowing with a faint gold aura of power, making it stand out from the ordinary history and astronomy texts. Thick quilts sewn from green, black and white were piled high on a sturdy four-poster bed. The windows stretched from floor to ceiling, overlooking the grounds. A little blue-green bird hopped back and forth over my windowsill, as if it was his job to provide cheerful mid-morning chirping.

"The Peridot Suite," Headmistress Lockwood told me. "You have a private bath, through there. Your orientation packet lists other meal-times and will include your class schedule by morning." She turned on Mrs. Winter. "You will send for her clothes by this evening?"

"Her trunks are waiting on the carriage downstairs," Mrs. Winter said, looking very pleased with herself.

"Always prepared," Headmistress Lockwood said, rolling her eyes a bit. She turned to me. "I hope you know, that display in the library will not entitle you to special treatment. You have a certain amount of independent study built into your schedule for the Mother Book. But otherwise, you will meet all of the expectations set forth for the other students, is that clear?"

"Yes, ma'am."

"Magic is not what you have been told. It is mathematics, physics, chemistry, *science*," she said. In my hands, the book seemed to shudder, as if it didn't appreciate Headmistress Lockwood's sentiments. "The superiority of our bloodlines allow us to manipulate the energies around us so that we can control matter, reach between molecules and change their behavior. It is not a mystical loving force bubbling up from a spring of loveliness somewhere inside you."

"And how do you explain this?" I asked, gesturing with my recently decorated palms.

"All systems have their anomalies," she said airily. "Now, as for your first essay, while it shows a degree of original and creative thought, your margins were laughable and you used the word 'interesting' far too often. By morning, I expect a list of at least twenty alternatives for the word 'interesting' on my desk."

I nodded. That didn't seem unreasonable.

"Copied five times."

That seemed less reasonable.

"Thank you, ma'am."

"If you have any complications with your new mark, please see Mrs. Wentworth in the infirmary. She will send up medication with your dinner tray, to help balance your system after its *exertions*," she said, eyeing my hands. "See that book does not leave this room."

Headmistress Lockwood inclined her head and swept out of the room, slamming the doors shut behind us in a magical flounce.

"What is this?" I asked Mrs. Winter, sagging to the bed.

"A rather lovely, and none-too-inexpensive suite," Mrs. Winter said dryly. "We paid for you to have a private room, because we were afraid that any well-bred girl who roomed with you would recognize any quirks leftover from your... less fortunate upbringing."

"I could always come home for visits, give my classmates less time to watch me," I said.

Mrs. Winter gave a light tap to my chin with her pointer finger. "There's no leaving the school grounds for now. The book has claimed you. Dora is already suspicious and attempting to leave the school grounds right away with a precious magical relic would probably send her over the edge. She's never truly trusted me, not even when we were in school together."

I opened my eyes wide, feigning disbelief. I chose not to comment on how Mrs. Winter had managed to look about thirty years younger than Headmistress Lockwood. "I can't imagine why."

"Oh, no, I gave her good reason," Mrs. Winter said. "But no matter, with your first social dance scheduled for this weekend, your sudden, rather dramatic appearance at school should give you a bit of traction on the gossip circuit."

I shuddered. I'd forgotten about the social dances, opportunities for the girls of Miss Castwell's and the young men of Palmer's to demonstrate what they'd learned in their dance lessons while preparing for the busy spring cotillion season. The social dances were less formal versions of the cotillions, an opportunity for the ladies of Miss Castwell's to practice and demonstrate the steps we'd learned. The Palmer boys would be there to serve as partners. I would not only be expected to mingle and socialize but *dance*. In public.

Since my emergency tutoring had involved only the most basic dance instruction, I would be pleading a strained ankle.

Parents were invited to observe their students' progress in behaving like miniature adults. And since both Owen and I would be participating, Mrs. Winter would attend. Rather than looking forward to the party, as Mary or any other girl in my position might have, it hung over my head like a dark cloud. No matter how nicely I was dressed or how faithfully I remembered the etiquette lessons Mrs. Winter drilled into my head, I was sure the Guardian crowd would sniff out the imposter amongst them the moment I arrived.

"Now, we must re-think your gloves," Mrs. Winter said, carefully peeling away the charred remains of my gloves. "It's a shame to waste all of Madame DuPont's work, but it would be a greater shame to cover that mark. And, if you will notice, you don't really need them anymore."

Gasping, I lifted my hands closer to my face. The fingertips were smooth and soft, like baby's skin. It was as if the roughness of my skin, the callouses left behind by years of hard work, had burned away to leave these smooth, soft hands. Even the faded burns on my wrists from handling hot cooking pans were gone. Did that mean all of my scars were gone? My skinned knees? The mark on my neck where Mary had accidentally burned me with a pair of curling tongs? Somehow that made me sad, as if the last bits of Sarah Smith had been scrubbed away, leaving this new stranger.

"I don't know if I should show it off," I said, rubbing my hands against my skirts. "Maybe it would be better to hide it, to keep the other girls from getting jealous."

"No false modesty, Cassandra. It would be unattractive and

dull. That is a mark of prestige that women in my circle would give their eye-teeth for. That is the mark of great spellwork, when casting opens a Guardian's magical core and uses iron from the caster's own body to form the image. It is the price we pay for greatness, and is considered quite the magical accomplishment to achieve such a mark."

"But I've never seen this sort of mark on any of your society friends," I protested.

"Because they don't have them. I don't have one, myself," she said, stroking an absent hand along her corseted ribs. "You must be strong, having a gift like that will set you even further apart from the students. When the magic inside of us gives us these gifts, it is not our place to ask why or whether a mistake has been made. It is our responsibility to make the most of them. I did not give you this life so that you could hide behind closed doors and library shelves. You, my dear girl, are clearly meant for more."

I didn't have the nerve to tell her that she hadn't *given* me this life. Magic had dropped it in my lap.

"How is any of this possible?" I asked, dropping my voice to a whisper. "I'm not a Guild Guardian. I only know how to do the most basic magic, and most of that is accidental. I shouldn't have been able to talk to the book, or whatever it is that I did."

For the briefest of moments, the pretense drained away from Mrs. Winter's face.

"I do not know. The uncertainty is as infuriating as it is frightening. This is not supposed to be the way the world *works*." She took a deep breath and her resentful tone became light and breezy. "All I know is that you have been given a great gift. And, should you listen to me, you will be able to parlay this gift into a lifetime of security and comfort."

I nodded and cleared my throat. "Speaking of symbols, the celestial ceiling, in the library, there's a strange sort of smudged mark in the glass. What happened there?"

Mrs. Winter sniffed, "Oh, *that*. It was during my second year here at Castwells. We woke up one morning to a terrible fuss in the library. The faculty wouldn't let us in for two days. None of the girls knew what had been done to the ceiling, only that Headmistress Chawton was *highly* displeased that one of her girls had vandalized a very expensive gift from the alumni. They spent hours questioning us, but never managed to find out who did it. They just hushed it up. I may have mentioned to Headmistress Chawton that as a descendant of House Benisse, Dora Lockwood would be more inclined to such a prideful display, attempting to add the Lockwood peacock feather quill sigil to the ceiling. While Headmistress Chawton assured me that the feather quill wasn't the image added to the glass, Dora did not appreciate my pointing a finger in her direction. She may or may not have hexed my bed curtains to come to life in the night and slap me across the face whenever I was about to drift off to sleep."

Bernisse House Sigil

"Headmistress Lockwood is related to House *Benisse?*" I

gasped, remembering the headmistress's severe, unflattering clothes and greying hair. The Benisse family was known for their ability to produce beauty glamours and love spells so convincing that the recipients swore they'd enjoyed a whirlwind romance in a single night.

"I'm afraid Dora took my comments about her pride in her appearance a little too personally," Mrs. Winter sighed.

"So, you're leaving me at a school where you have a lifelong feud with the headmistress?"

"Oh, there's no reason to worry, Dora couldn't possibly interfere with you. You're the Translator."

"Has someone told Headmistress Lockwood that?" I asked.

As if on cue, there was a knock at the door. Miss Morton entered with my trunks levitating at shoulder level behind her. The luggage floated across the room and settled at the foot of my bed.

Mrs. Winter seemed to be waiting for Miss Morton to leave, but Miss Morton smiled serenely, folded her hands at her waist and stared at Mrs. Winter. Mrs. Winter pursed her lips. "Well, I suppose I will be going, right after I have a word with the Headmistress about her faculty's inability to pick up on social subtleties."

"I could come with you to see you off," I offered, strangely reluctant to have Mrs. Winter leave me in this place. Sure, I'd been cut off from my family at Raven's Rest, but at least I'd known they were there. At Miss Castwell's, I had no one.

Mrs. Winter glanced at my singed dress and shook her head slightly. "Not in that condition, dear. I believe you have caused enough of a stir for one day." Her expression softened and she took my hands in hers. "You will do very well here, Cassandra. Now, settle in. And I will send a special treat for you on mail day." I was shocked when Mrs. Winter pressed a kiss to my cheeks. "Good luck. Bring honor to your family."

I dropped a curtsy. "Yes, Auntie Aneira."

Mrs. Winter gave Miss Morton one last stern look and swept

from the room. I rubbed my hands up my arms, peering out the window as the Winter carriage pulled in front of the school entrance, waiting for its mistress.

Miss Morton clucked her tongue, placing a hesitant hand on my shoulder. "Do not fret, Miss Reed. This can be a wonderful place. Excellence can be a lonely lot in life. It doesn't necessarily lead to the things we think we should want – marriage, family, wealth. But what you lack in gold, you can gain in accomplishments. In the pride of knowing that you can do what others cannot, and that you can teach their children to do the same. I'm quite sure that you will find your place at Miss Castwell's in no time at all."

I gave Miss Morton a tremulous smile, the pity I'd reserved for myself leeching out for her. While Miss Morton seemed at ease with her place at the school, I had to wonder what life was like for her? What was it like to live her whole life alone, within these walls? Mrs. Winter clearly had some plans for my future, but who knew whether she would choose a path I could live with? What if I ended up a spinster teacher, hidden away at this school, teaching the ungrateful daughters of Guardian families?

I felt a rush of guilt for pitying Miss Morton. Who was I to judge her life? Just a scant few weeks before, I'd been up to my elbows in dishwater, unsure of why I was so miserable.

Another knock at the door revealed a Snipe maid in a slate grey uniform dress, carrying a domed tray. She placed it on my desk and walked out without saying a word or making eye contact. More guilt crept into that empty space in my chest, filling me with shame. How could I stand here feeling sorry for myself when I'd been given such an opportunity? If I couldn't make my best effort on my own behalf or Mrs. Winter's, I could do it for Snipe girls like that nameless maid, who didn't think she had the right to look at us directly. I would find a way to make this work.

"Now, eat your dinner, change your clothes and hop into bed and you'll be right as rain," Miss Morton told me. She pointed to a small cordial glass brimming with blue liquid. "The medicine on that tray is important, but a good night's rest is better magic than anything the faculty can teach you."

"How lovely." I nodded, sitting on my bed with a thump as Miss Morton glided from the room. The rolling of my stomach wouldn't allow me to even glance at the tray. And I had a feeling I was going to be suspicious of medicines from well-meaning middle-aged ladies for a while. From the hallway, I could hear the faint patter of slippered feet and hushed conversation as the girls moved down the stairs to the dining hall. And the little bird tapped his beak against my window pane as if he was late for dinner, too.

Tap tap taptaptap.

I was alone here, so very alone, without even the comfort of Mrs. Winter. And that was very scant comfort indeed. No one here knew me. No one cared to help me cover my origins. I barely knew how to fix my own hair. And somehow, I was supposed to know enough magic to get through my classes without posing a danger to myself and others.

I sat there, feeling frozen, as I stared out the window. The cloudy sky faded into night. Ignoring the long-cold tray, I shed my dress, washed my face and slid under the covers. I didn't know what Mrs. Winter had Martha pack in my trunks, and I didn't have the energy to go searching around for a nightgown. I could only hope there was not a fire, because I would end up running out into the hallway in my chemise and bloomers.

Though the bed was even more comfortable than the Lavender Room back at Raven's Rest, I had difficulty settling in. My hair was still pinned up, so I couldn't find a comfortable pillow angle. My hands were achy and raw from the magical abuse they'd taken.

I could do this, I told myself sternly. I could get a full night's sleep, wake up refreshed and start my career as a respectable, ordinary student at Miss Castwell's. I could get through school unnoticed and scene-less. I *would* do this.

Tap tap taptaptaptap.

Outside, that insistent little bird pecked at the window. The rapid beat against the glass seemed to echo throughout my large chamber.

Tap tap taptaptap.

I rolled onto my back, breathing slowly through my nose and staring at the ceiling. I tried to think restful, calming thoughts about kittens, rainbows, and the laughter of babies. But mostly, I thought, "If that bird doesn't stop pecking at the window, I'm going to make it into a feather duster."

Tap tap taptaptap.

I pressed one of the many fluffy pillows to my face, though I wasn't sure whether I was trying to block the sound or smother myself. But I could still hear it, *tap tap taptaptap.*

I bolted up in bed, shouting, "You stop that right now!"

The bird recoiled, as if I'd reached through the glass pane and slapped it. It hopped up and down and then bolted away, flexing its little aquamarine wings in a flounce. I giggled, pressing my lips together to prevent my neighbors from hearing hysterical laughter from a girl in an otherwise empty room. The impression I'd made this afternoon was dramatic enough.

I snorted one last time, punching my pillow into shape. I rolled onto my back and waited for my eyelids to flutter closed. But my eyes were drawn to a strange silver light reflecting on the ceiling. It wavered and danced like moonlight on water... and it seemed to be coming from my bed. I glanced down at my hands. The new metal in my skin was glowing, lighting the room like a cray-fire candle, making it that much harder for me to drift off.

"Oh, come on now."

FALLING into the dream was like tripping over my own feet, descending so suddenly that I didn't even realize it had happened until it was over. The feeling was so familiar, being back in my family's tiny, smoke-stained kitchen, barely lit by the hurricane lamp. I sat on the bench near my father's chair, cracking walnuts into a dented enamel bowl, my fingers scraped and raw at the tips as I pried open the tough shells. Mum stood at the stove, stirring watery cabbage soup. Mary had her head bent over a dress she was remaking into something suitable for the upcoming Harvest Celebration dance on the Rabbit's Warren square.

"It wasn't always like this, you know," Papa said quietly, sipping from a cracked porcelain tea cup. I didn't know why he bothered trying to hide the fact that he was drinking whiskey. While sorting through the dirty clothes, I pulled his hip flask out of his work pants more often than not.

"Before the Restoration, when we non-magicals had real jobs, real lives," Papa slurred slightly, slumping in his chair. "We were the teachers, the builders, the healers. My people were engineers."

The firelight cast an orange glow over Papa's craggy features, the deep, unhappy lines around his mouth. His thinning, grey hair was sticking out in all directions, as if he'd licked a crayfire lamp. His dirty, scarred hands trembled slightly as he lifted the cup to his lips.

"Engineers of what?" I asked, continuing with my work. I'd learned that giving my father my full attention during his nostalgic musings tended to spur them into full rants. Mary ignored him completely, tuning him out by humming some random melody. But I was intrigued. Papa had never revealed this little tidbit before. And I wondered how much he'd had to drink in order to loosen his lips this much.

"Your great-grandfather, Elias. He was a mechanical engineer. He helped develop steam engines for trains. Back before crayfire. Before we used magic to drive trains down tracks, non-magicals used their brains to find solutions – steam, coal fire, machinery."

"Really?"

"They're afraid of us, you know," Papa whispered, leaning over the arm of his chair. "The Coven Guild, they're afraid of what we can do. And we don't need magic to do it. That's why they rose up. They were afraid that we would become more powerful than they are. That's why they keep us pinned down in these slums, telling us to be happy with what they give us. We could have been so much more. I could have been more. And you, Sarah, *you're the one who can change it all. You're not like us. You never have been, not since the day you were born. You can —"*

"That's enough, John," Mum snapped, turning from the stove.

Mary's golden head rose, a pout quirking her lips. "What do you mean, Sarah can change things?" she sniffed. "Sarah can't even change the sheets on the bed without help. I had to do all of the beds on the second floor myself today."

Mum laughed, just a little too loud for it to be genuine. "Yes, yes, Sarah's lucky to have a sister who will help look after her, Mary. What are you working on?"

I frowned at the pair of them as Mary held up the lace trim she was adding to her neckline. Yes, she may have done more physical labor, but if anything, I kept her from getting into trouble. I was the one who snuck Owen's handkerchiefs back into his room when Mary stole them. I was the one who kept Mrs. Winter from seeing that Mary had doodled her name in Owen's school tablets. If anything, Mary needed me to protect her from herself.

Papa ignored their over-bright chatter, adding under his breath. "Your choices in this life won't be easy, child."

My head felt fuzzy and disconnected from my body. Was this really a dream or a memory? I remembered this particular evening at home with my family. My father hadn't spoken after my mother changed the subject at my expense and insisted we all sit down to enjoy our cabbage soup. He slumped dejectedly into his chair and refused dinner in favor of finishing his bottle.

Why did it seem so different, remembering it now? Why hadn't I noticed before, the way Mary complained about me, or the way Mum cowed my father into silence? I'd always assumed that the house was quiet because we didn't want to provoke Papa's "headaches." But how much of that repression had to do with Mum and her attempts to keep my secret?

"What sort of choices?" I asked him quietly.

Papa simply stared at me. "Choose wisely."

MY EYES FLUTTERED OPEN. I sat up in bed, confused by yet another darkened and unfamiliar bedroom. In terms of fatherly advice, "choose wisely" was not exactly helpful. Then again, while Papa was generally the parent I went to when I was in need of a hug or understanding, he wasn't exactly brimming with life lessons. And there was no pressure at all in knowing that every decision I made would affect all mankind. I hoped that the dream version of my father was just being grandiose.

Something he said niggled at the corner of my mind, a relatively harmless turn of phrase. He said that I'd never been like anyone in my family, not since the day I was born. And I was born with magic. Was my subconscious trying to tell me something? Was there something wrong with me from the day I was born? Or was it possible that whatever it was that was happening to me started even before then? Was it was possible that I possessed magic because I was never a Snipe in the first place? What if my parents weren't really my parents?

I remembered ancient Irish folk tales about changelings, about fairies stealing plump human babies from their cradles and replacing them with their own spindly-limbed fairy children to be nursed by human mothers. Most of the tales focused on the human mother's attempts to regain their children. I wondered now, what happened to the fairy children, caught between two worlds, belonging to neither? As I recalled, things didn't work out so well for changelings in fairy tales, uncaring mystical parents, mistreatment and the constant threat of being eaten.

Could I be a changeling? While I loved my family, I never really felt like I belonged with them. I knew I was different, but I always thought it was because they always seemed so strong and hardy, while I was slowly being poisoned into non-magical frailty.

I sobbed, realizing that tears were coursing down my cheeks. Was I really my parents' child or had they simply found me on a doorstep somewhere? Or worse… had my mother betrayed my father with a member of the Coven Guild? It didn't seem likely. Mum was so worn and grey. It was hard to imagine her flirting with a member of the upper crust. Then again, Mr. Winter had always been relatively kind to me, though aloof. Could he be my father? Was this why Mrs. Winter rarely spoke to me before the incident in the parlor? Because she didn't want to be faced with evidence of her husband's betrayal?

Was it possible that in some time where Mum was a younger, less careworn lady, she had caught some Guardian's eye? I just couldn't see it. I'd seen them in the same room many times over the years. There was no spark between them. I knew that any love Mum had for my father had been strained over the years, but I still didn't want to consider the possibility that she'd wandered on him.

No.

This was madness. This was a dream born of exhaustion and the emotional toll of being in a strange new place, not to mention being appointed the keeper of a magical book that I couldn't read. I swiped at my cheeks with the delicate handkerchief with the Brandywine flowers embroidered in the corners. I just needed a good dream-free night's sleep, and I would be fine.

Except for the magical book I didn't understand.

And a new mark on my hands that set me apart from the rest of the students.

And the fact that I didn't really know any magic.

"I have to learn to stop comforting myself," I muttered into my pillow.

7

A FAUX PAS BEFORE BREAKFAST

*A*t the dawn bell, I struggled into consciousness, sitting up and rubbing my hands together. The dragonfly seemed to hum in response. I glanced over to my vanity. Apparently, a maid had come into my room while I was sleeping, unpacked my luggage and laid out my Castwell green dress for the day. Even though I'd entered plenty of chambers with sleeping occupants over the years, delivering breakfast trays and towels and whatever else they required in the pre-dawn hours, I found I didn't like the idea of someone wandering into I room while I was asleep.

I did, however, appreciate the maid's choice of dress. It was one of my favorites, comfortable muslin with a closed collar and pointed sleeves. I also donned the matching gloves. Mrs. Winter may have wanted me to flaunt my dragonfly, but I didn't want to separate myself from the other students any more than necessary on my first day. It frightened me, how much I liked wearing the DuPont gowns. I was used to simple clothes, rough fabrics, but in the gowns, I felt like Cassandra Reed. I was almost a lady.

And while the prospect of growing up, and all the strange new body parts involved, was still somewhat terrifying, I didn't look like the skinny, undersized girl who hid behind her family. I was my own person.

I was sure the thrill of new gowns would wear off if I ever needed a corset, too.

A Snipe girl named Leah arrived as I struggled my way into my gown. She helped me style my hair into a lovely, complicated chignon.

Walking down the shadowed, black-and-white tiled halls didn't help my nerves. The other girls seemed to have divided themselves into pods, four girls emerged from each suite and joined arms, strolling in pairs down the steps in their matching green dresses. Their shoulders were straight, their heads high. Their skirts practically swished in unison. It was unnerving.

Breakfast was less opulent than my morning trays at Raven's Rest, but the kitchens certainly provided the students with a hearty start to the day. Snipe girls in plain grey dresses carried in heaping platters of pastries, bacon, and eggs to each of the tables, where the students placidly took their fill and ignored their servants entirely. I forced myself to take toast and fruit and offer a smile in return to the sweet-faced blond girl who served me. She practically recoiled in shock and bobbled her tray. The other girls stared at me as if I'd just made a considerable faux pas.

I'd faux pas'd before breakfast. This was not going to be a good day.

"Do you mind if I sit here?" a husky voice asked. I looked up to see a tall girl with beautiful teak-colored skin and large doe eyes. Her tightly curled black hair was wound into a high, loose bun that accentuated her high cheekbones. But her clothes did nothing to highlight what looked to be a lovely figure. Her dress, while the usual Castwell green, was cut loose at the bust and hips, making her look a bit like a deflated soufflé. It was trimmed at the wrists and neck with lace in a combination of tan and burnt prune. I recognized the combination of colors as a trademark of the Cowell family, a division of House Drummond that prided itself on the construction of security wards. The Cowells were rolling in money, from what Mrs. Winter told me, why would they insist on dressing their daughter like this?

"Of course," I said, waving toward the opposite seat. "Please."

"Normally, no one sits here, so it's safe," the girl murmured as she dropped into her seat. She sounded resentful somehow, without being so rude as to tell me that she didn't want to break her fast with me.

"Did I steal your table?" I asked, cringing slightly. "Did I take your friends' seats?"

"No, anyone is welcome to sit here," she told me. "But no one else ever does."

"I'm happy to be the first. I'm Cassandra Reed," I said, wrapping my lips around the strange new name.

"Oh, I know. Everybody knows who you are. The Translator. It's all the other girls can talk about. Not that they talk to me about you, of course, but after you, er, departed the library, I overheard – well, never mind what I overheard. Many of them tried their hands at Translating the book, and it didn't even open for them. A new girl coming in and Translating before she was even enrolled, that was bound to bruise their pride. I wouldn't pay them any attention." She blanched, realizing, I supposed, that she had said too much. "Let me start over. I'm Ivy. I'm Ivy Cowell."

"It's nice to meet you, Ivy. And I'm not so sure about the Translating business. I didn't have any idea what I was doing. I just touched the book." I glanced down at my hands.

"I think that's what's making them so angry," Ivy said, suppressing a throaty chuckle. "You weren't even trying."

"No, clearly, I am trying to make enemies on my first day," I said, taking a rather aggressive bite of toast. "I am succeeding. Beautifully."

Ivy snickered. "You're being sponsored by the Winter family. You had enemies before you even got here."

"You might have laughed less as you said that," I told her. "It would communicate less enjoyment at my expense."

Ivy blushed and ducked her head over her oatmeal, but she was still laughing, so I didn't think I'd offended her.

An older slim girl with thick, cornsilk-colored hair and wide, blue eyes approached our table, looking down her nose at me. Her dress was exquisitely tailored with an elaborate brass hammer collar brooch denoting her as a Cavill. The Cavills concentrated their interests on metallurgy and alchemy. They were heavily regulated by the Guild as the government fretted over the House flooding the market with fool's gold, causing the economy to collapse. From what I'd read, the Cavills were bitter rivals of the Brandywines *and* the Mountforts, the Mother House to the Winters.

Flanked by two girls who had clearly tried to imitate her elaborately coiled hairstyle, the blond didn't bother sparing a glance toward Ivy. She dropped an envelope on my plate and did an imitation of a curtsy.

"Miss Reed, I am Callista Cavill. I'm the student body representative, president of the Athena Scholars. Headmistress Lockwood asked us to show you around the school grounds," she said, giving me a smile so sweet it couldn't possibly be genuine. I didn't like her eyes. They were over-bright and reflected nothing, like dolls' eyes. "She wanted to make sure that you were given the *right* sort of introduction to Miss Castwell's."

She sneered down at Ivy, who hadn't looked up from her plate. "Cow."

My brows rose. Had I heard Callista correctly?

Choose wisely.

Mrs. Winter probably would have advised me to welcome any attentions from a Cavill. She would want me to stay on Callista's good side, to curry favor with her, if for no other reason than to protect myself and my secrets from an enemy house.

My mother would have wanted me to travel the path of least resistance. Mary would have wanted me to befriend Callista, if only to try to talk her out of the elaborately worked golden combs tucked in her hair.

But still, Ivy had been friendly towards me first and seemed to have no reason for doing so beyond kindness. I glanced at Ivy, who was staring at me with wide eyes. "Oh, well, thank you, but I believe Ivy was willing to escort me to my first class."

Ivy blanched and flicked her eyes toward Callista, who was glowering down at her.

"Oh, no," Ivy said, shaking her head and standing so quickly, she knocked over her chair. Titters of laughter echoed through the dining hall as she struggled to right it. "I'm suddenly feeling unwell. I'm afraid I will not be able to make it to the first class after all. Cassandra, you should go to class with Callista."

"Oh, al-alright," I stammered, more than a little ashamed at the relief I felt, not having to awkwardly excuse myself from a connection to Ivy.

Ivy was just a few steps away when Callista cleared her throat and called, "Excuse me?"

Ivy stopped in her tracks and turned slowly.

"I don't believe I gave you leave to call me by my given name, did I?" Callista asked sweetly. "Calling me by my first name is a privilege I only grant to my closest, most intimate friends. And trust me, Miss COW-ell, you are not even close to being considered my friend."

I squirmed in my seat, watching in quiet horror as humiliation rippled across Ivy's face. Why was Callista being so blatantly awful to a girl who seemed very sweet and unassuming? Was it because Ivy had African heritage? There were several girls of similar descent sitting in the dining hall, as well as girls whose families originally hailed from other continents.

The Restoration had done much to overcome tensions between these cultures as magic users across the globe decided that they distrusted non-magicals much more than they valued keeping to their own ways. No major House was strictly Anglo-Saxon these days.

Was Callista equally rude to all girls whose backgrounds were different than her own, or was Ivy her favorite target?

To my shame, I looked down to my hands twisting in my lap. To Ivy's credit, she didn't cry or shrink back. She simply nodded and said, "My mistake," and walked out of the dining room.

"Now that's out of the way," Callista sighed, dropping into Ivy's abandoned seat. "Welcome to Miss Castwell's, Cassandra. Given your near-disastrous choices this morning, I am going to take you on as my special friend. And my friends understand the rules here at Castwell's. Rule the first, we do not attach ourselves to pariahs before we manage to finish breakfast. The Cow is social poison, darling. Keep making this sort of mistake, and you'll end up friendless and alone, no prospects, no husband. And you'll have to *work* for a living, just like —"

At that very moment, Miss Morton appeared at my left and laid a hand on my shoulder. "How are you this morning, Miss Reed? Did you sleep well?"

The smug expression that overtook Callista's face was downright sickening.

"Yes, Miss Morton," I said, giving her a tight, uncomfortable smile.

"Well, do let me know if you need anything at all."

"Yes, ma'am."

"Girls, I know I can count on you to make sure that Miss Reed has a pleasant first day," Miss Morton said, her dark eyes staring over the tops of her spectacles.

"Of course, Miss Morton," the trio chorused in an eerily uniform tone while Callista positively simpered at the woman.

Miss Morton gave my shoulder one last pat and departed. Callista's scornful expression returned.

"The unfortunate Miss Morton only proves my point," Callista told me. "Follow my advice, darling, or end up stuck here at Castwell's, teaching the daughters of better families how to go out into the world and have more fabulous lives than you. Now, shall we walk to our first class?"

Choose wisely.

I was standing at a precipice, the sort of choice that could determine how I would fare at Miss Castwell's, and I could feel my toes going over the edge. I wanted to get as far away from Callista as humanly possible, but I didn't want to end up starring in her next dining room spectacle, or worse yet, get treated to my very own bovine nickname.

I wasn't in any sort of position to make someone like Callista angry. A few badly chosen words on my part and she could make my life here at school very difficult. Or worse, she could end up ferreting out the fraud I was perpetrating on the school and Coven Guild society at large. I remembered a snippet of wisdom I'd overheard Mr. Winter giving his son over dinner one evening, when he was having trouble at school. He'd told him, "Keep your friends close, and your enemies closer."

As distasteful as I found her, I would have to keep Callista very close.

I inclined my head in a regal fashion that would have made Mrs. Winter proud. "Thank you for your gracious welcome."

"Good choice," she said, rising from the table. "Shall we?"

I slowly pushed to my feet, resisting the urge to clear the dishes from the table. Callista linked her arm with mine and sashayed out of the room. Her two handmaidens followed as we marched down the hall, and into the solarium. I opened the envelope containing my schedule. I scanned my course list, which included crystallography, remedial symbology, medicinal botany, table etiquette and "independent study." I supposed the independent study was the time I was supposed to devote to the

Mother Book. And then there were electives available to me each day: ritual dance, belomancy, and magical embroidery. I would be so tired from my class schedule that I wouldn't need to worry about insomnia.

"By the by, I know that you're new here, but we typically take our gloves *off* while we eat our meals." Callista glanced down at the green silk gloves I'd chosen to cover my dragonfly

"Thank you for the reminder," I said in as pleasant a tone as I could muster. While we weren't late, walking into the spacious glass-walled room, a dozen or so girls were already seated two to a table, their hands cupping fist-sized blue crystals. Each of them had their heads bent over the crystals, as if meditating.

Morning light poured through the glass panel walls, lending a golden corona to the dark hair of the corpulent woman standing at the front of the room. She stood perfectly still, with her eyes closed, holding a large, cloudy blue crystal aloft. According to my class schedule, this was Miss Selsye, my crystallography teacher.

Anxiety spread, heavy and cold, in my chest. What if I couldn't do any magic when the teachers asked me to? What if they called on me and I didn't know the answers? I'd always been a good student, but these girls had more time to study, private tutors, families who could teach them House specialties. What if they realized I didn't belong?

Ivy was sitting in the back of the class, alone at a table, staring into her crystal with red-rimmed eyes. Callista forged ahead to a desirable table shaded by a potted palm, even though it cut us off from the beautiful view of the manicured lawns. Two younger girls were already seated there, deep in meditation. But when Callista seethed, "Move, now" at them, they hopped to their feet and scrambled out of the way. Callista offered me a sweet smile and dropped gracefully into her seat. I followed suit, watching as the younger girls ducked around the classroom to find empty chairs, now that Callista's lackeys had dethroned two other students sitting behind us.

Now that I was seated, I could make out the little oil lamps embroidered at the rounded collar of Miss Selsye's gown. That would connect her to House McCray, a family that mined and charged rare gems for the crayfire lamps that kept the city well-lit, amongst their many energy-based efforts. Perhaps she was a distant cousin?

Miss Selsye opened her wide blue eyes. If she noticed that she now had an extra student in her classroom, she didn't say anything. Callista sat high and straight in her chair, her face the very picture of an eager, interested pupil. I ran my fingers around the edge of the rounded blue crystal, smiling slightly at the low hum it gave in response.

"Today, we will review the process of charging the crayfire lamps, one of the basic student maintenance duties at the school. As you know, crayfire lamps are made from azurite crystals, due to the valuable copper deposits found within. The copper vibrates at just the right frequency to conduct the necessary energy, providing hours of illumination, safe from the fire hazards or smoke pollution of the lesser Snipe-created methods," Miss Selsye intoned.

I tried to keep my expression neutral, but I couldn't help but wonder if the "lesser Snipe" comments were called-for when discussing *lamps*? Was it really necessary to drop reminders of the Snipes' so-called inferiority into conversation quite so many times per day?

"Aside from being useful in healing spells, azurite also happens to provide an additional 'spark' to nearby magical practitioners, fortifying the strength of their casting work. Now, different crystals require different charging rituals. Depending on their use, you might use sea salt or sunlight or even exposure to turbulent weather. But for today's discussion, we will focus on azurite crystals. Azurite requires a personal sacrifice, if you will, of your own energy. You can't expect something for nothing, even if it's just light to read by. Now, hold your crystals between your palms and close your eyes, imagine the copper deposits deep under the surface, imagine the life force that keeps your heart beating from one moment to the next and then picture that same energy pulsing within the crystal. Picture the cold, still rock giving way to life in its depths."

Clearing my throat, I cupped my hands around the cloudy rock form and mimicked the other girls. I imagined my brain, my heartbeat, connecting with the minerals inside the crystal. Nothing. I opened my right eye and peeked at Callista, whose crystal was glowing bright and clear. A handful of other girls had a subtle azure radiance growing between their palms, but couldn't seem to manage the brightness needed to illuminate the school halls.

Miss Selsye's eyes were now open, and she was giving me a very stern look.

I blew out a frustrated breath and closed my eyes. Clearly, I needed a different picture to motivate myself. I'd floated the vase at Raven's Rest when I was afraid. I was near panic when the Mother Book's symbols were crawling over my skin. Maybe I needed fear to produce effective magic? I imagined myself trapped in a dark room, with only the crayfire lamp for light, and it was cold and useless. I pictured the shadows closing in on me. I imagined how frightened I would be, in that strange room, not knowing what was lurking in the corners. The crystal grew warm in my hands. I peeked through my lashes and saw that it was glowing brighter. I took a deep steadying breath and added more detail to my frightening imaginary room. A cold draft coming from under the door. Eerie taxidermized animal heads snarling at me from the walls. A strange shadow winding its way along the floor, barely visible in the light provided by my lamp.

I was there, in that room, my breath turning to cold fog. Over my shoulder, I heard a tapping noise at the window. Thinking it was that annoying bird from the night before, I turned and saw a gaunt, grey-faced man standing on the other side of the glass, his eyes glazed over and his jaw slack as he pawed at the window. The metal dragonfly on my palms pulsed hot and angry, lashing out at the dead thing watching me. The man became shadow and the shadow became a pair of wings beating against the window.

In my head, I screamed and the light from my crayfire lamp flashed so bright that it overpowered my vision. I blinked back into awareness, surprised to find myself in the solarium, surrounded by my fellow students. And while the other girls' chunks of azurite were glowing and alive with light, my stone was shattered on the table in front of me. And the girls were staring at me. Right, because I needed one more thing to set me apart for the rest of them.

Callista, to my surprise, stepped in on my behalf. More or less. "I told you to take off those silly gloves, darling. The satin is scrumptious, but you're turning into quite the butterfingers. Fashion is important, but it's second to academics, isn't that right, Miss Selsye?"

"Quite right," Miss Selsye said, though she was eying me with marked interest. "Miss Reed, you are excused until you are sensible enough to dress appropriately for my class."

I nodded shakily. "Yes, ma'am."

I stood, careful not to knock my chair over. Callista simpered, "Bad luck, darling. We'll see you after class, yes?"

I nodded, my cheeks flaming with embarrassment, as I fled the solarium as quickly as I could. And the rest of my day didn't go much better. My ritual dance steps were called "heavy and horse-like" by the dancing mistress, Madame Rousseau. My runes were barely legible to the remedial symbology teacher, Miss Chambers. And I hoped to forever block out my disastrous attempts at belomancy, which turned out to be predicting the future by flinging arrows at a coded target. If your arrow landed near a certain symbol, it predicted outcomes like wealth or marriage.

I wasn't sure what was foretold when you missed the target. Several times. It probably wasn't a *good* omen, though.

Miss Morton was the only teacher who seemed remotely happy to see me.

"Difficult first day?" she asked.

"Would mis-throwing an arrow and pinning the hem of Blanche Ironwood's skirt to the ground, so deeply that it takes four students to free her while she glares at you, qualify as 'difficult?'" I asked.

"I think the word would apply, yes."

I groaned and buried my face in my hands.

"It was the same way when I was a student here, Miss Reed. A new girl is introduced to the student body, and it takes a few days for the equilibrium to be restored. They'll accept you eventually. I would suggest that you stop flinging arrows at them. It's low on my list of recommended methods of making friends. Especially with attention from girls like Miss Cavill, whom I've noticed you seem reluctant to befriend."

I bit back any potential response. I didn't want to hurt Miss Morton's feelings. "Did you have a lot of friends when you attended Castwell's?"

She jiggled her head back and forth. "I wasn't *un*popular. But my family… we lost any fortune we had long ago, and have even less in terms of connections. So I didn't have much support here to start, no groups of girls that would take me in on the weight of my name. I chose to spend most of my time in the library with Miss Chance. She was the librarian then, a very kind woman, very supportive of my pursuits. And I hope to do the same that she did, helping young ladies find the books they need to be the best witches possible."

"Even when the young lady in question doesn't even know where to start looking?"

She smiled fondly at me, the frizzled curls forming a sort of grey halo around her face. "Especially those young witches. Look at it this way, dear, when journeys have a difficult beginning, it's generally an easy downhill coast from there." She patted my shoulder awkwardly and then retracted her hand immediately.

"I wouldn't know, I haven't traveled extensively."

"Neither have I. This school, it's been my life for almost twenty years. I worked in the Guild Archive for a bit, right after I graduated... but it didn't work out, sadly. No, I'm more comfortable here. Even when I was a student, I knew there would be no place for me out in the world."

"That's... not particularly hopeful, Miss Morton."

"What I'm trying to tell you, Miss Reed, is that this is home. And you have the chance to make connections I could never dream of. Take advantage. Don't make waves. If some of the more influential girls want to take you under their wings, let them. Girls like that could open doors for you, help you make the connections you'll need to make your way in the world. If you can last a few more days, I think you'll find that you'll survive."

"Yes, but will Blanche Ironwood survive?" I muttered.

She laughed. "Go to your room. Get some rest. I'll write you an excuse for independent study."

"Thank you, Miss Morton."

"Any time, my dear.

I managed to find my room without help, slammed the door behind me and flopped onto the bed. I fervently wished that the mattress would swallow me up and keep me from ever having to face those girls again.

Unfortunately, the mattress didn't seem to have much of an appetite. I sat up, grunting in discomfort at the pinch of my bodice on my ribs. I yanked the pins from my hair and let it loose. The Mother Book caught my eye from my desk. I stood, carefully taking the fragile tome in my hands.

"I don't know what to do," I said to the book. "Everything I touch seems to go wrong... I just need to know what to do."

When nothing happened, I thought maybe the book was ignoring me. Or that maybe I wasn't the Translator after all.

Maybe this overlarge insect imprinted on my skin was just a mistake. I hugged the book to my chest, wrapping myself around it, hoping to feel something besides this crushing embarrassment and disappointment.

The dragonfly hummed, spreading a warm sensation from my arms to my heart, like resting in front of the fire at our old house. I let the book fall away, into my hands and the pages fell open to an entry that hadn't been translated yet. I ran my fingertips over the cuneiform, and they seemed to melt in response, changing and wriggling into tiny gold letters.

An elaborately wrought, gilt-edged illustration melted onto the page, depicting the sigils of the great houses of the Coven Guild. The Mountforts' scales, the Brandywines' flowers, the McCrays' silver lamps, and so on, and so forth. From those major lines sprung the minor houses, the blue compass for House Morton and the Winters' plunging black raven. I would never describe the House as "minor" to Mr. or Mrs. Winter, of course, because I was not insane.

Mountfort House Sigil

At the bottom, smaller and more faded than the others, was a black owl surrounded by silver and gold filigree. I frowned. I didn't know of any House, or even one of the related smaller families, that used an owl in their crest. None of the sigils were labeled, so I couldn't even get a name for this mysterious house. I wanted to ignore the page, to move on to Translating some spell that would make a difference for me or the magical world at large. But I just couldn't stop staring at that silly owl. Why did I get the feeling the owl was important? Why would the book show me something like this when I had so many other things to worry about?

I rubbed my fingertip around the edge of the filigreed frame. The gilt pulsed and glittered in response. I would read up on the old families in the library. Maybe I could find some clue as to what the book was trying to tell me.

"I ask for answers, and you give me more work." I closed the book with a decisive snap. "You are not helpful at all."

8

WHAT TANGLED WEBS WE WEAVE

$\mathcal{I}$t helped to think of the school as a giant household, and we students were there to serve the faculty's whims. We woke in the mornings, had breakfast, then moved about the "house" in perfectly synchronized shifts, but instead of washing or cooking, we were embroidering or dancing or drawing runes. After classes, the girls either retired to the library for study or enjoyed a walk on the grounds with their familiars before dinner. Poor Tom, the stocky young Snipe lad who cared for the grounds, spent most of his twilight hours picking up the familiars' "contributions" from his carefully manicured grass.

After dinner the younger girls, like me, were early to bed, the older girls gathered in study gaggles in their rooms. Though it was still autumn, they were preparing for a ritual called the Spring Interview. The most talented graduates of Miss Castwell's would be invited to join ladies' research guilds, like Mrs. Winter's Demeter Society. But the girls had to prove themselves worthy of these coveted positions with rigorous magical tests. Girls who did not qualify for guild memberships had to console themselves with their mother's matchmaking efforts. It was considered cold comfort to have enough free time to plan your wedding to your fabulously arranged match.

Mail call was held every Thursday immediately after afternoon classes. John and David, Snipe footmen who helped with the heavy work around the school grounds, pushed a heavy cart of extravagantly wrapped care packages into the atrium every week. The packages were filled with pocket money, bottles of hair treatment and silk gloves were doled out to the girls whose families wanted to make sure they knew how missed and cherished they were. Ivy's parents sent her boxes of rose jellies and hair ornaments in the Cowell family colors. Callista's mother showered her with new hair ornaments, beauty tonics and box upon box of chocolate bonbons that she distributed like a queen doling out bread to her favorite peasants.

Receiving one of her bonbons was more than status symbol, it was a weekly re-ordering of social currency accounts. If you received a bonbon, you were in good standing. If you did not receive a bonbon, you had done something to upset Callista and you should scramble to correct that situation immediately.

Girls who didn't receive letters or packages from home were to be pitied. Fortunately, Mrs. Winter remembered this from her school days and on my first Thursday, sent me a box laden with my own bonbons, candied violets, and her specially blended herbal tonics to keep my skin glowing. This treasure trove was accompanied by a large carton containing several new dresses. The carton was slate blue with a large curlicued "D" from Madame DuPont's over the enclosure. It took three housemaids to carry it up the stairs under the careful supervision of Headmistress Lockwood and most of the student body.

Anxiety crawled up my spine, because I knew that the box contained my gown for the upcoming school social, among several others. We were to dress more formally for the social than we did for classes, but not in our full ballgowns. If there was an opportunity for me to disgrace myself before all of

Guardian society and reveal my origins, it was the school social. I was practically failing ceremonial dance. My feet seemed to belong to another person. And I would be wearing the biggest, fluffiest dress to date, just to increase the level of difficulty. I would make a fool of myself. And possibly be arrested by Coven Guild enforcement when I accidentally revealed my underprivileged roots. I would be the first student at Miss Castwell's to be arrested for bad dancing.

As added torture, we were expected to participate in four socials each year. I wondered if I should fake some sort of epiphany involving the Mother Book to keep myself to my room. A Translator could have several epiphanies in a year, yes?

Callista appeared at my elbow, sniffing in a bored fashion. "Is that from Madame DuPont's?" she asked.

Behind Callista's blond head, I saw Ivy's own face perk up with interest. Something about the heretofore unknown slyness in those dark brown eyes had me playing up my connection with the luxurious dressmaker, in a completely bored tone. "Yes, I suppose it's my dresses for the socials. Auntie Aneira arranged for me to have my wardrobe made there. Madame DuPont's staff is wonderfully talented, and so very accommodating."

I may have taken more pleasure in saying that than was proper. I saw Ivy's mouth twitch at the sweet poison in my tone and it took all my powers of concentration to keep my own lips still.

Callista tugged at the neckline of her own tailored green muslin day dress, clearing her throat. "Of course, I recognize the style. All of my school gowns were made there as well."

Behind her, Ivy shook her head and mouthed the word, "No."

I managed to smile without irony and said, "Well, of course they were, darling. Anyone can see that."

Ivy smirked at me, and flounced away, her dark curls bouncing. Miss Morton's advice about letting girls like Callista take me "under their wings" made sense, but I felt better offering this small victory to Ivy.

Slowly, but surely, I learned the routines of the school. The bells rang at dawn, but I was already up and dressed, ready to start my day with the help of Hannah, the housemaid assigned to help me with my toilette. My gowns were my armor, helping me contain the enormous secret I carried around with me.

Every moment of every day, I was on guard, trying to avoid saying something that revealed my formative years in the Warren. I was tensed against my instinct to rise after meals and clear the table, against assuming the submissive Snipe posture and walking behind the other students as we walked to class.

Spending time with Callista, and her two lapdogs, Millicent DeCater and Rosemarie Drummond, was a daily torture. Callista had indeed made me her pet project, eager to keep the Translator at her side for reflected glory. She picked me up at my door every morning like she might pick up the little teacup poodle, Phoebe, she carried under her arm as a familiar. And then, at night, she dropped me off, having learned nothing about me or my opinions. Like Phoebe, a little tyrant made of canine fluff and hatred, I was an accessory.

Cavill House Sigil

I had a better chance of developing a friendship with that silly blue-green bird that insisted on pecking at my window every night.

No matter her target, magic allowed Callista to take social manipulation to a level I'd never experienced at the Warren school, where the worst that could happen was a black eye or finding a frog in your lunch pail. Callista would cast a spell that made it sound like two people were whispering just behind a girl's back, no matter where she went, even in the bathing chamber. And while the victim could never quite make out what was being said, she could hear her name in the muddled conversation. Her victims woke up in the middle of the night, sure that they could feel snakes slithering in their sheets. And there was the none-too-insignificant matter of her somehow weakening the waistline seams of Ivy's day dress, so that it disintegrated while she was walking up the stairs to the classroom wing, exposing her bloomers for all the world to see. While Callista didn't take credit for that one directly, she did take to mooing every time she passed Ivy, making the curvier girl flush red and angry.

The fact that she pulled these nasty little tricks while all of her victims carried sharp ceremonial knives on their person was proof of her vice-like grip on the school's social order.

And all the while, I stood by and did nothing. I sat with Callista at meals, picking at my food and saying little. I sat with her in classes and joined her in the library for study hour. I smiled when it was necessary, laughed when her silly jokes were harmless and stayed quiet and ashamed when they weren't.

I wondered if wearing my new dresses right away was a good idea. Because if Callista was intimidated by the *box* from Madame Dupont's, perhaps my wearing what she knew to be DuPont gowns every day would provoke her into a vengeful frenzy. Ultimately, I decided I should discuss it with Mrs. Winter while I was home for a weekend. This sort of Machiavellian social maneuvering was her specialty.

I managed to get through my first week of classes without making a spectacle of myself. The other girls eventually forgave the slight of my claiming the Mother Book on first day, particularly after I failed to produce any world-changing magical revelations over the next few days. I became part of Callista's clique, faceless and feared.

The teachers were not impressed with me, despite my connection to the Mother Book, because even with Mrs. Winter's best efforts to give me a crash course in beginner's magic, I was not a very promising student. My crystals charged for a moment, only to crack and crumble to powder on my desk. The spells I wrote burned through the page and left embarrassing scorch marks on my desk. I had raw power, marked by fluctuations as a lifetime of suppressors worked their way out of my blood. But I had very little control.

As Miss Dancy, my remedial potions instructor put it, I had "all of the finesse of a painter trying to produce a masterpiece with a pitchfork."

The only subject in which I excelled remotely was medicinal botany with Madame Greenway, and that was only due to growing up as a gardener's child. I knew all of the proper Latin names for the plants, the appropriate temperatures and water and shade for their care. And thanks to Mrs. Winter's tutoring, I could parrot that Balm of Eirin could mend broken hearts and a troublesome cough. Leaving bloodroot on a witch's doorstep could reverse her spells. Garlic had many uses, both magical and medicinal. My display had merited a specimen of Blushing Orchid, a white tropical flower that flushed pink when one spoke to it in a soft, sweet voice. But then, Callista dropped a bottle of sticky, red dragon's blood tree sap down the front of my gown, cooing, "So sorry, darling" after I identified ten plant extracts by their smell. Even Hannah's most dedicated scrubbing couldn't help me get the sap stain from the gown. So I learned that if I wanted to stay off Callista's list of targets, I couldn't excel, even if it was the one area where I showed promise.

By the time I fell into bed each night, it felt like every fiber of my body was strained. I smiled through Callista's discourtesy. I barely had enough energy to clean my face and take my hair down for bed, much less study the Mother Book. But at least I didn't have any more nightmare-daydreams about corpses and owls lurking outside my bedroom. I missed my family. I missed my home. I missed the simplicity of my old life. I even missed the Winters.

My sanctuary was the library, a place Callista avoided at all costs because being unable to speak prevented her precious "socializing." So I would plead a headache or some other acceptable symptom of delicate ladyhood and retreat to the bookstacks. I'd never had enough time to study at the Warren school, but I'd always made good grades. I'd hoped that if I applied myself and read everything I could about the Principals of Magic, chemistry and the histories of the magical houses, that it would just come to me, like osmosis.

But it didn't.

And neither did more information about the strange owl sigil that had appeared to me in the Mother Book. There had to be a reason that book was showing me the owl – and only the owl, no matter how many times I asked to be shown something more. Every day for almost a week, I had no luck with the answers, until one night I woke up to the midnight bell clanging in the bell tower and my face pillowed against a page that had been blank when I started that afternoon.

And despite my exhaustive search of the genealogy section, I couldn't find any mother house that used owls in their sigils. Miss Morton even helped me look through books listing the off-shoot branches in Asia, Europe, and the prison colonies in Australia, but nothing.

Miss Morton was glad of the company though, tempting me to stay past the younger grades' usual retirement hours with offers of soothing chamomile tea and ginger biscuits. She gave me a few books on meditation, which I barely understood, but from what I could gather Miss Morton wanted me to stop *thinking* so much when I was studying the book. I was supposed to leave my mind blank, to open my magic up to the possibilities the Mother Book could offer.

MISS MORTON also found wonderful botany books for me, full of specimens I'd never even heard of – snapdragons that posed a real danger to the cultivator's fingers, humming dahlias that could lull bystanders to sleep with their song before strangling them with tentacles they kept hidden underground, and roses with scents so sweet that the gardener would swear they never wanted to smell any other aroma. But Miss Morton said I had to be careful not to focus too much on one area, so she also plied me with volumes of folk stories, history, anatomy of magical creatures. She even found me a book on proper dancing technique when I confessed my (carefully edited) fears about the social.

Though many of the faculty members were friendly, despite my many classroom failings, Miss Morton was becoming my friend. She offered me advice about the Mother Book, recommending that I sit at a table with the book open, surrounded by all of the genealogy books the library had to offer. She left me to concentrate on my work. I took Wit from the exquisitely tooled leather holster that secured it under my sleeve, and held it over the open Mother Book, begging it to either show me more information on the owl sigil or some other bit of information that would drive me less insane.

I closed my eyes and imagined all of my hope and curiosity focusing on the tip of Wit's point.

I held the knife over the books and was startled enough to send it flying across the study area when I heard a small voice whisper, "That won't work."

I yelped and was immediately shushed by Miss Morton, even while Wit embedded itself through a copy of Levesque's *Guide to Ladylike Broom Use*. The intruder was as small as her voice, pale and delicate as a new reed. She had to be one of the youngest students here, nine or ten maybe? She might have been quite a beauty if not for the hollow cheeks and dark circles under her wide green eyes.

Something in those eyes reminded me of myself, before the Spinning Vase Incident, when I was still on the suppressors. Undersized and underestimated. Too quiet for my own good.

"Has anyone ever told you not to sneak up on people holding sharp objects?" I asked her quietly as I retrieved my wayward knife from where it was embedded in the very expensive-looking book. The girl ducked back behind a shelf as Miss Morton approached to take the damaged book from me with a lift of her greying eyebrow. She pulled her own athame from a holster in her sleeve – dark metal with a rounded, grooved handle-end –

and muttered something I couldn't make out while dragging the tip over the hole Wit had punched through the book. The pages knit themselves together without a mark left behind.

"I'm sorry, Miss Morton," I'd murmured through pursed lips.

"Do try to be more careful, dear," Miss Morton sighed, before returning to her spot at the reference desk.

"So, why won't it work?" I asked the smaller girl, who'd popped back up from behind the bookshelf like a little jack-in-the-box. Honestly, this girl was so petite, that she made me look like a lumbering giant.

"It won't work, because the book has shown you what it thinks you need to see for now," she said. "When you're ready to see more, it will reveal more. For now, you should keep learning everything else you can until you're ready to see."

"That is very helpful, but at the same time, exhausting."

"Being the Translator is often a thankless task," she said, her tone wiser than it should have been at such a young age.

"I'm beginning to understand that," I'd said, turning to slide Wit back into my sleeve holster. "What's your name?"

But by the time I turned around, my small advisor had disappeared. Again. I searched the stacks on the study level, but couldn't find her anywhere. Miss Morton claimed not to have seen any other girl in the library at the time I'd been studying. Had I just been instructed by a ghost? Was Miss Castwell's haunted? Surely, ghosts had better things to do than hang about in the library, teasing students with unhelpful hints.

I didn't see the girl in any of my classes, either. Or seated at the younger girls' tables at meals. Those times were particularly difficult, because I did see Ivy sitting at one of the central tables by herself, while I sat there with Callista, pretending to listen to her endless stories of shopping trips with her mother, of her flirtations with the highest-flying scions of Guardian society.

I tried focus on my own safety, afforded by keeping a relatively low profile at the school and being a member of Callista's clique. I tried to think of my family at home, and my need to protect them. I even tried thinking about the Winters and how I didn't want to repay their trust and effort with losing my composure in a public manner (most likely in the dining hall with a large shrimp fork) and exposing us all. While my first week at school had been relatively easy, I was becoming tired of "easy," if it meant feeling this way.

9

THE STRANGE AND THE FAMILIAR

O ne afternoon, Headmistress Lockwood arrived just as
my remedial symbology class was ending to inform me
I was excused from independent study as I had a visitor. She led
me to the entryway, where I found Owen Winter, examining the
portraits of the school's foreboding founder, Emmeline Castwell.
He held his hat in one hand and a prettily wrapped round box
in the other, both behind his back. Fortunately, the lobby was
empty of other students, so this incident would rate very low on
the dinner gossip scale.

I tried not to let my confusion show on my face as he turned
to greet us. I curtsied and held my hands out to accept the gift
box. In doing so, my hands were outstretched, pinkies touching.
Now that he could see my mark, in full light, for the first time,
Owen's eyes went wide with alarm and something akin to
respect.

There, I thought, let the boy who called it a ridiculous and
embarrassing idea to send me to school stew in that for a while.

"Cousin! How are you? Faring well here in your new home?

Mother didn't want you to know that she was worried – you know how she hates to be seen as a hoverer – so I told her I would come and see for myself that you're settling in."

"Your mother?" Headmistress Lockwood said, lifting a dark brow. "Hovering? I can't imagine."

"She is the most doting and loving of mothers," Owen assured her.

"Miss Reed, you may take your guest to the gardens for thirty minutes and then escort him directly to his carriage. There's no reason to cause distraction by bringing him back into the building."

"Yes, ma'am."

Headmistress Lockwood gave Owen one last knowing look before turning on her heel and walking toward her office. Owen turned his gaze back to Miss Castwell's portrait. "So is there some sort of requirement that to be the headmistress of this school, you must have your sense of humor removed?"

I shushed him. "Please don't get me in trouble."

"Oh, dearest *Cassie*, I mean to do no such thing," he assured me as we walked out a side exit to the gardens. "I only meant to bring you my mother's love and this package."

He tossed the purple box at me, which I caught, much to my surprise. I waited for us to be far from the school building, past the flower beds and the gazebo, even the small reflecting pond. I smiled at Tom, the groundskeeper, as he passed by. He was a sturdy sort of boy, who kept his distance while he cheerfully did his work. Like my father, he whistled old Irish tunes while he raked, which endeared him to me. I didn't speak to him. We girls were discouraged from being at all familiar with any male staff members at Miss Castwell's. Headmistress Lockwood said it caused "unpleasant confusion." Owen wasn't confused at all. He barely looked at Tom as we sat on an ivy-wreathed bench near the treeline.

"Do you practice being awful or does this come naturally?" I asked him.

"It's a talent," he said, preening, even as he flopped onto the granite bench. He paused to take his own dagger, *Sapientem*, from the holster he kept at his hip. He drew the rune for "silence" in the air and a shower of blue sparks arced up from the tip, forming a sort of dome around us before fizzling away. "Now, we don't have to worry about being overheard. So, how is mother's little political pawn this afternoon? No trouble tricking every girl from every Guardian family in Lightbourne, I hope?"

"How is my family, Owen?" I asked, ignoring his jibe. "Are they all right? Is there any trouble? Did your mother send you to warn me?"

Seeing the honest panic on my face seemed to shake Owen out of his teasing. He straightened on the bench and the mocking smirk all but disappeared from his face. "No, nothing like that. Mother honestly sent me to check on your progress. She thought it would look good for the whole family to be seen as concerned about your welfare, since you're supposed to be grieving and you're our beloved cousin and all. Father would have come if he wasn't so busy in the Capitol at the moment. Your family is fine. I wouldn't have teased you like that if something was honestly wrong."

Nodding, I smiled and let some of the tension drain from my shoulders. "So I'm a political pawn?" I sighed. "I think I liked it better when I was just your mother's potential social weapon."

"Well, mother does love her little surprises," he said, smiling as he rubbed the back of his neck. "My father's term is coming to an end, and he's about to lose his seat in the Guild. He's failed to vote for measures that would impose stricter sanctions against the Snipes."

I frowned. "What sort of sanctions?"

"Some in my class feel that Snipes are getting a little comfortable with their positions in Guardian households, too confident, so the new laws would impose fines and other punishments on Snipes who show disrespect for their employers or disregard for the laws."

"So they're creating laws to punish Snipes for not appreciating those laws?"

He nodded. "Yes. And from the disdain in your voice, I can tell that your feelings about those laws reflect my father's. He has been quite vocal about his opposition to the proposal. Our friends and neighbors think that he's getting too soft, which brings us to your sudden addition to our 'family.' A young woman in his household making a social sensation in local circles, could only help his public image, change the perception of him as a weak legislator to one of a doting father figure to a fascinating, though tragic, young woman of some power."

I shivered, clutching my shawl even tighter to my shoulders, ignoring the way Owen's voice dropped when he said, "power."

"And how do you feel about stricter sanctions against the Snipes?" I asked.

He frowned. "I can see why some people might think that the Snipes are becoming a bit... confident."

"Because of girls like my sister?" I asked, feeling an odd mix of resentment and resignation. Mary did go too far in her doomed pursuit of Owen, but I couldn't help but want to defend her. She'd always done so much for me, put up with so much from me, the weak little sister who couldn't carry her own weight. As much as it embarrassed me, there were times I wished she did get her happily-ever-after with her handsome prince, because it was the only thing that would make her happy. But that was madness, and as much as I loved her, I didn't put Mary's happiness above our whole family's safety.

He ignored the question about my sister. "I don't think the laws are appropriate. It seems as though my class would rather legislate their way to respect rather than building a solid relationship with your kind. Perhaps the answer is a change in behavior on our part rather than a change in yours."

I couldn't help but note that despite my change in residence, Owen still grouped me in with the Snipe class.

"Have you spoken to your father about possible alternatives to the laws? He could help with education programs, literature, town hall meetings, something."

"My father wouldn't take my suggestions seriously. He doesn't take himself seriously," Owen sighed.

"Still, I don't understand why your mother would go to all this trouble. Even if your father did lose his seat, it isn't as if that would ruin your family financially."

"No, but it would embarrass my mother considerably, losing a family seat. And of course, there is the small matter of her expectation that I run for the seat when my father retires it. And she could lose face with the Demeter Society, which would crush her. My father would be content to be known as the world's foremost ornithologist. But Mother's from Brandywine stock. She knows the value of power. It's fine for him to putter around his lab, after all, she's a pioneer in botany research. She would never begrudge him his hobbies. However, she's a Senator's wife, and she expects to be a Senator's mother. She will accept nothing less." After a long moment, he added, "An ornithologist is a scientist who studies birds."

"I know what an ornithologist is," I shot back, surprised by the acid in my voice. "I've read a good portion of the contents of your father's library. I'm not stupid."

Owen's brows rose. "I never said you were stupid."

"No, but your expression said it all," I told him. "In fact, it would help if you lowered your eyebrows right now, considering that they've been hanging there since I mentioned my extensive reading."

He burst out laughing, but he ran a hand over his brow, very deliberately relaxing his forehead into a less surprised state. He dropped into the wrought iron chair next to mine. "I'm getting lectured on proper facial expressions by the kitchen maid. This is ridiculous."

"Why are you bothering to talk to me, right now?" I asked, studiously ignoring the "kitchen maid" comment. "We haven't had a proper conversation since you were nine years old and you knocked me off your tree swing."

He looked deeply affronted. "I most certainly did not knock you off of a tree swing."

"You snatched my book out of my hands, pulled my pigtails and *shoved* me off of your tree swing. I landed on my rump in the dirt," I exclaimed. When he continued to shake his head in disbelief, I lifted my hair to show him the tiny scar at my temple, near my hairline. "I hit my head on the way down. I had to get three stitches!"

He moved closer, and I tilted my scarred side toward him. Recognition passed over his face, and his mouth dropped open. "I remember that. You were in *my* swing. And it was my book, by the way. A copy of *Bartleman's Digest of Magical Fungi*. I left it on the swing when I went inside for some water!" he protested. "And as I remember it, you sprang up from the dirt, grabbed the book and hit me over the head with it."

"I did not!" I scoffed.

"You did!" he protested. "You busted my nose! It gushed blood, the sight of which made you hyper-ventilate, pass out and whack your head on the swing." My eyes narrowed and he scooted his chair closer to mine.

"Here I'll prove it. You see this break in the bridge of my nose?" He pointed to the tiniest little bump on his long, noble nose. "You and that bloody book did this. My parents could have repaired it without any effort. But Mother thought that it served as a reminder not to start a fight unless I was sure I would win it. And my father was so angry with me for 'bullying a girl half my size' that he charmed it so *I* couldn't repair it later. "

I started to giggle.

"It was humiliating!" he exclaimed, which made me laugh that much harder. "I had to go to school with a mangled nose and tell the other boys that I started a fight with an older boy in the park and he cursed me! You ruined my otherwise perfect profile!"

He turned his head toward the light, as if to demonstrate his "deformity." I wiped at the tears gathering at the corners of my eyes. "I don't remember any of this. I just remember one day, you stopped talking to me and Mum told me it was my fault for fighting with you. You turned and walked away every time I came anywhere near you."

"I was embarrassed," he said. "I didn't want to admit a sickly little girl got the drop on me. And I was mad at you. Ignoring you became a habit. And as I got older, my parents encouraged me to stay away from you girls anyway. I think they saw how Mary looked at me and it made them nervous."

"So you've always known how she feels about you?" I squeaked, feeling irritated on my sister's behalf. It was one thing to recognize that Mary's behavior was forward, it was another to mock her unrequited love.

"Of course, I know. I'm not stupid, either," he said, pointedly. "I've never responded, in any way. I've never given her any cause to think I felt the same about her."

"Well, I don't think it's helping," I told him. "Because every time you so much as thank her for a plate of toast, she takes it as a marriage proposal."

"What does she think of all of this?" he asked, gesturing in the direction of the school building.

"I don't know," I lied. "Your mother has forbidden me to speak to them."

"And you abided by that? You *are* being a good girl."

"Your mother scares me," I told him. "And don't look at me that way, she scares you, too."

"Well, you scare her," he told me. "Mother doesn't like having her entire outlook on the world changed in a few moments." He paused and fidgeted. "It's not that I don't want you here. Or for you to have a better life. I just hate to see you pulled into something you don't fully understand. I hate to see the danger to my family, too."

"I don't have a choice," I told him. "I can't go back to my old life. These things that I can do, they put *me* in danger. They put my family in danger. This *is* the safest situation for me right now."

And just then, the garden bird with its strange blue-green feathers flapped down next to me on the bench and twittered rather indignantly. It was as if it didn't appreciate being left behind at school and being forced to fly all the way across town to peck at my dress, searching for crumbs.

"Why are you following me?" I grumbled. "Either you stop following me, or I will turn you into a tiny feather-duster."

"What are you mumbling about?" Owen asked.

"This bird," I said, pointing to the winged interloper. "He's been tapping at my bedroom window since I moved to the Lavender Room, tapping and trying to get in. I thought maybe he has a nest in the house, but then he followed me to school, and kept tapping at my window here. And now, here he is."

Owen smiled at me, as if I were something precious and foolish all at once. "When did he first approach you?"

"Before my window?" I asked. "That first day after my moving upstairs at Raven's Rest. He came to the garden and stayed on this bench while I read."

"And did you offer it something to eat?"

I nodded. "A piece of a tart."

"Interesting."

"Why does it keep pecking at me?" I hissed, gently nudging it away from my skirts with a flick of my fingers.

"Where do you think witches get their familiars?" Owen asked.

I thought of the animals that roamed freely at Miss Cast-well's, cats, birds, rabbits, snakes. Dorinda Benisse kept her palomino pony named Gilded Lily in the stables, which she claimed gave her additional power in her glamour charms because he was bigger than all of the other familiars.

"A magical pet store?" I suggested, as the bird nudged at my fingertips with its beak. "Or in the case of your horrible cat, the ninth gate of Hades?"

"Horus is just misunderstood, much like his owner."

I snorted derisively, earning a nudge to my ribs from Owen's elbow. Owen produced a sugar cookie from his pocket and broke off a tiny piece, dropping it in my palm. He nodded toward the bird. I gamely dropped the crumbs in front of the bird, who scarfed them up hungrily. "You don't choose a familiar. When the time is right, the familiar finds you. When you offered the bird food, it completed the bond, and the familiar began serving your best interests, which is awfully difficult to do from the other side of a pane of glass. The poor thing must have been going out of its mind."

I opened my palm, allowing the bird to walk up my fingertips. It cheeped, puffing up its feathers. My bird was siding with Owen. This did not bode well.

"I'll talk to Mother about placing a feeder and perch in your room and getting you one here at school."

"No cage?" I asked. "What about the cats at school, not to mention Horrible Horus?"

"Oh, no, the familiar, who needs a name, by the way, must be able to follow you around. And the cats will keep their distance out of respect for another familiar. Magical creatures have enough control over themselves to resist their more vulgar instincts."

I gently rubbed my finger over the soft feathers on the bird's head. I didn't know how I felt about an animal being sentenced to a life of servitude for me. Also, I wasn't sure how much a bird the size of a sparrow would be able to accomplish for me. I broke off a piece of cookie and offered the crumbs to the bird. "I think I will call you, 'Phillip.'"

"A very dignified name," Owen noted.

"He looks and acts like a Phillip, demanding, imperious, constantly gorging himself on sweets." I gave him a speculative look. "On second thought, I should have named him Owen."

Owen gasped in mock insult. "You know, for someone who complains about my poor manners, you're awfully mean to me."

"Oh, did I hurt your delicate feelings?"

"The cruelty! The heartlessness!" he cried clutching at his chest as if mortally wounded, making me cackle. Phillip hopped about on the bench, chirping to add his voice to the chaos.

"This is what I am referring when to I talk of your poor manners," he told me. "Please make sure you leave these charming tendencies at the door during the school social."

My good mood deflated instantly. "Why did you have to bring up the social?"

"It will be fine," he said. "All you have to do is make a good impression on all of the society matrons. Dance beautifully. Avoid any faux pas that might reveal your origins to the very people who could hand you over to the Guild authorities. What part of that frightens you?"

"The dancing," I told him.

He arched his brow. "Really? Of all that, it's the dancing?"

"I've never danced before in my life. I was too sick to do anything at the Warren dances but sit on the sidelines and watch."

"You could practice," he suggested. "Cast a spell on your slippers so they move your feet for you?"

"I have tried. It is hopeless. And I looked up the slipper spells. Apparently, it only works if you don't take the slippers off for the rest of your life. Because if you do, you'll die."

"You could pretend to faint. The room will be warm and crowded. It's not unusual."

I paused. "That... is actually very helpful. Thank you, I will consider that."

Owen grinned, pleased with himself, as usual. I shook my head. I knew it was probably temporary, like everything in my life at the moment, but it was nice to have my friend back. I hoped that Owen could be someone to count on, instead of someone who waited around Raven's Rest to subtly insult me.

"Mother's going to hate having a bird in the house, you know," Owen said gleefully as he held his hand out to help me off the bench. "It's going to be fantastic."

GOLDEN CAGE

*P*hillip had grown accustomed to his new life of luxury far faster than I had, but now that he wasn't flinging himself at my window to catch my attention, he was far less annoying. I'd expected some censure from Headmistress Lockwood for bringing a wild bird fluttering along with me when I returned to school, but she just rolled her eyes ever so slightly and reminded me that students' families were expected to cover additional cleaning costs associated with familiars. Mrs. Winter sent a special perch carved from driftwood to keep on my nightstand, next to a silver box for his birdseed, and a note telling me how pleased she was that I'd bonded with a small, fashionable familiar, instead of something unfortunate. I got the feeling that she was referring to Dorinda Benisse's pony. Gilded Lily tended to leave a lot of presents for Tom on the lawn.

Phillip seemed to sense when I needed quiet, resting sedately on his perch until it was time to hop on my shoulder to remind me of a meal time or peck at the page of the book I was studying to point out an answer. He accepted little crumbs of the almond cookies I snuck out of dining hall, but refused the sesame biscuits, which I thought showed good taste. The sesame biscuits were the one menu item I didn't like. I felt more settled when Phillip was near. While having Phillip perched on my shoulder while I attempted to Translate the Mother Book didn't make more pages appear, I felt a little more hopeful about working on it with him near me.

Unlike most of the familiars, who wandered freely around the school, Phillip kept to my room. He went so far as to flit away from my shoulder as I walked out to classes each morning, preferring to sit on his perch and stand watch over the Mother Book. Hearing his contented little chirps from my bedside table helped me focus on something besides my worry over the social and go to sleep.

The morning of the social dawned bright and clear, the perfect fairy tale beginning. And yet, I considered any flimsy reason not to attend the "practice" party. I could feel a vicious cold coming on. I was too exhausted from my first week of school to be charming and effervescent. My dress didn't fit. But I knew that Mrs. Winter wouldn't accept any of them, particularly the bit about the dress not fitting. So I allowed Hannah to strap me into the traditional Castwell spring green silk party dress with a wide flounced skirt and short, puffed sleeves. Madame DuPont had embroidered tiny white apples in repeating floral patterns along the hem to show Brandywine allegiance. Hannah had taken special care with my hair, piling it on my head in elegant coils.

I was being watched. The parents, all wealthy Coven Guild adults, stared at me as subtly as possible from behind lace fans and spectacles. Further, since so many of the girls were cowed by Callista's aggressive claim of friendship, they didn't dare approach me to make the proper introductions to their parents. So I stood there, silently, keeping my hands folded with the metal dragonfly pressed firmly against my skirts. Mrs. Winter had written specifically to tell me not to wear gloves to the event, as she wanted it to be well-known that I was the Translator. I felt awkward and uncomfortable, as if the other guests could see through the pretty dress and see the real me underneath. Poor, fraudulent Sarah Smith who didn't want to be seen or studied. I wanted to be in the kitchens preparing trays of food, invisible with no special metal tattoos on my hands or expectations on my shoulders.

I was so nervous about being silently inspected by the magical adults, powerful people who could recognize me as a Snipe far more easily than their daughters, I spent that time mentally reviewing Mrs. Winter's etiquette lessons - no eating awkward foods that would stain my dress, no holding my tea cup from the bottom, no refusing dances from prospective partners, just because I found them physically or morally repulsive.

I didn't even talk to the other girls around me. I barely registered Callista lingering at the top of the stairs, waiting for her mother to arrive. Ivy paced beside me, gnawing at her fingernails and staring off into the distance. The fact that both girls, so far separated on the popularity spectrum, were so agitated made me nervous. What exactly happened at these social dances?

Mrs. Winter was fashionably late, of course. She wasn't the last parent to arrive, but she certainly wasn't the first, sweeping into the school's black-and-white tiled atrium in a silk gown of peacock blue. It was fascinating to watch the sea of wide, ruffled skirts part before her, making way. Even the adults who smiled at her with empty, polite expressions still got out of Mrs. Winter's way when she approached me. Mr. Winter had elected to stay home, as he did not enjoy this sort of gathering… or the people who attended them.

I managed a decent curtsy without falling over or knocking over bystanders and considered it an accomplishment, especially with so many people watching. Mrs. Winter looked… pleased by my efforts? It was an unexpected surprise from a woman who'd spent most of my life peering down her nose at me with a less than enthusiastic expression.

"You are looking lovely, dearest," she pronounced, just loud enough for the other parents to hear as they inched closer. "Madame DuPont was right, this sleeve length is perfect for you. Very appropriate."

"Thank you, Auntie Aneira." I leaned forward, barely close enough to brush a casual air kiss near the vicinity of her cheek. I whispered, "My family?"

"Oh, we're all just fine at home, dear," she said, watching my face carefully. "Missing you terribly, of course, but managing as best we can."

I nodded and gave my best impression of a smile.

"How are your classes? Are you making friends?" she asked. The question felt loaded. And all I could do was nod before Callista swooped in and locked her arm around mine.

"Oh, Cassie and I are the best of friends already," she said, loudly, before dropping a deep curtsy to Mrs. Winter.

Mrs. Winter's face tightened into an unpleasant mask I recognized as "most seriously displeased," the sort of expression she made when it rained on the mornings of her garden parties. I wasn't sure if it was Callista's use of a nickname like "Cassie" or Callista's personality that provoked this response. I was just glad it wasn't directed at me.

"I've been introducing her to the most suitable girls, keeping her from the worst of her missteps," Callista continued.

"Well, how lovely," Mrs. Winter intoned while I gave her a subtle shake of my head. "Miss Cavill, is it?"

"Callista, ma'am, daughter of Jameson and Lucinda Cavill," Callista simpered.

"Yes, I know your parents very well," Mrs. Winter said flatly. Either Callista didn't notice the unwelcoming tone of Mrs. Winter's voice or she was just that good at ignoring it, because at the ripe old age of fourteen, she did not seem at all phased by Mrs. Winter's disinterest.

"Oh, and I see my mother now, please excuse me," Callista said, curtsying again before fluttering across the foyer toward a petite woman in head-to-toe pink lace. She looked like an over-frosted cream puff. The woman greeted her with a cool air kiss and commenced a detailed inspection of Callista's hairstyle.

"Let's go inside before that ridiculous girl brings her mother over," Mrs. Winter whispered. "Lucinda Cavill is a ninny of the first order. She seems to think she can force her husband's place on the Guild committee for Snipe enforcement with ham-handed attempts at flattery. If I have to deal with her while managing your debut into polite society and whatever mischief Owen is going to get into today, I may snap and say something that can't be undone by magical law."

"Must we go inside?" I asked softly.

Mrs. Winter pulled me into a tiny alcove behind a massive grandfather clock and spoke so quietly I could barely hear her. "Cassandra, you are the Translator. The selection of a new Translator is a major event in Guild Guardian circles, no matter where she's from. And the fact that Cassandra Reed comes from nowhere has complicated how we might have handled your entry into society. It's taken all of the influence I have to keep the story out of the newspapers until we're ready to make a formal announcement this week, an announcement we have carefully crafted to deflect any doubt that you are anything but a gently born, delicately bred young Guardian lady. By now, girls from Miss Castwell's have already written letters, detailing your rather spectacular first visit to the library to their families. It's known that I will be attending today's social to observe my niece. And now that those families know that you're the Translator, they're going to want to meet you. If you do not fulfill your social obligations on the first time out, it will give a very poor impression. You cannot tell me that a girl with your natural gifts doesn't have the audacity to get through a little school dance. Now, are you willing to fulfill those obligations or have I greatly over-estimated you?"

I took a deep breath and nodded. "I'm ready."

"Excellent. Now, have I ever told you the story of my first

social here at the school? Headmistress Lockwood was still a student then, and just as severe and rigid as she is now, which as you can imagine made her ever so much fun at parties. Some poor Palmer boy asked her to dance and wouldn't take no for an answer, so she spelled his pants to come loose from their suspenders and drop every time he came near her. I laughed so hard that I dribbled punch down my chin and onto the front of my gown."

I wasn't sure if it was the idea of random pants-dropping or Mrs. Winter doing something so gauche as spitting punch down her dress, but thanks to her well-timed story, I entered the room laughing. My tinkling giggle was barely audible over the soft strains of piano and violin. The school's dance hall was a well-appointed ballroom, slightly less grand than Mrs. Winter's, but certainly warmer with its sage walls and floral brocade furniture. Tall potted palms and peace lilies seemed to burst forth from every corner, creating an intimate, if slightly mossy environment, courtesy of Madame Greenwood. The twenty or so people gathered there seemed to stop talking the moment Mrs. Winter and I walked through the door. And since they were none-too-subtly staring right at us, there wasn't much chance that someone else had interrupted the party.

Mrs. Winter, however, was perfectly poised, basking in the attention as if it were her natural right. "Well, I was young and didn't have the control over myself that I did now."

Owen came forward, looking far more polished and un-gangly than any boy of fourteen had the right to be, and bowed to us both.

"Deep breath," Owen whispered as I rose from my curtsy. "I don't think I could haul you off the floor wearing that much dress."

An ever-flowing fountain of comfort, Owen Winter.

Still, his sarcasm broke through the strange paralysis, and I straightened my shoulders. I lifted my chin, putting on my "best smile." Audacity, Mrs. Winter told me. I would need a touch of audacity.

The students of both schools gathered on the dancefloor, some of them already coupled off. Headmistress Lockwood welcomed us all to the first social dance of the fall semester and announced that Mrs. Eugenia Dalrymple, a Miss Castwell's alumna and grandmother to Ivy Cowell, would serve as this afternoon's hostess. Students were to find their appointed partners and prepare to dance a Spring Reel, a complicated English country dance that was meant to encourage a long and prosperous growing season. As I had a "strained ankle," meaning I had never danced a Spring Reel in my life and wasn't going to be able to start now, my "dearest cousin," Owen, would be escorting me around the room, making introductions and preventing other Palmer students from asking me to dance. While I found this plan suited my "not exposing my dance ignorance to the Guardian world at large" needs, it did upset my "not wanting to spend the afternoon being subtly mocked by Owen Winter" preferences.

Mrs. Winter didn't give one floating fig for my preferences.

"Owen, please go introduce your cousin to our hostess. A distant cousin of mine, you'll remember her from the Yule celebrations on my side of the family." Mrs. Winter waved casually to a woman across the ballroom, who seemed to be trying to taking flight, given the way she was flinging her arm about. She turned and leveled us both with her frank blue eyes. "Children. Behave."

I let loose a breath I didn't know I'd been holding. Owen was staring at me.

"She meant you," I told Owen.

"I'm not the one who was raised in a literal barn," he muttered back.

"And yet, you're the one with the bad manners," I told him, ever so subtly stomping on the instep of his foot under the cover of my puffy skirt. To his credit, his face barely registered the pain.

"They've armed you with pointy shoes," he grumbled.

I giggled behind my hand, Owen led me to a green silk settee where a plump, jowly woman with thick white hair was seated, her black satin skirts furled around her.

Owen's voice was impossibly smooth as he bowed slightly and made the most proper speech I'd ever heard come out of his mouth. "Mrs. Dalrymple, may I present my dear cousin, Miss Cassandra Reed. Cassandra, Mrs. Eugenia Dalrymple." Mrs. Dalrymple peered at me through a pair of silver lorgnettes, her lips pressed into a thin line. I could make out white apple blossoms embroidered on the high collar of her dress, marking her as a Brandywine by birth.

I glanced over my shoulder to where Mrs. Winter was holding court. She gave me a frosty smile, though I'm sure it was more of a facial reminder than a bolstering gesture.

Fortunately, Owen stepped in. He cleared his throat. "Mrs. Dalrymple, I was just telling dear Cassandra about your impressive greenhouses. My cousin has an interest in plants. She just completed a school project on *drosera* plants. Headmistress Lockwood was very impressed by her analysis of their feeding habits."

Mrs. Dalrymple's considerable grey eyebrows shot up, as did mine, because I didn't know how Owen was aware of my first-day tangle with Headmistress Lockwood's carnivorous plant. Did his mother tell him? "Really, my dear? Is Headmistress Lockwood still lording her *drosera aureus* specimen over the underclasswomen?"

"Does she really use the younger girls to feed the plant?" I asked, barely containing the quirking of my lips. "I suspected as much, but I was afraid the other girls would laugh if I asked."

Mrs. Dalrymple shook her head, her grey curls bobbing. "Oh, no, she's always fed that dratted plant from the school's flock of chickens. But she lets the younger girls believe they could be selected to 'donate' to the cause. It serves as a behavioral deterrent."

"I will do my best to behave," I told her.

"Or at least give the appearance of behaving," Owen said in mock solemnity.

I frowned at him and tapped his wrist with my fan, making Mrs. Dalrymple chuckle.

"I don't believe any lady should accept censure from you on proper behavior, young man," Mrs. Dalrymple scolded. "Now, go fetch your lovely cousin some punch while we become better acquainted."

"Of course," Owen said, inclining his head. "And would you like some strawberry tarts, cousin?"

I narrowed my eyes at my "cousin." Strawberry tarts were at the top of the list of "forbidden" party foods as they were awkward to eat *and* capable of producing awful stains. And Owen knew that I'd developed a taste for them before leaving for school.

I shook my head, while giving him the slightest glare. From his expression, I could tell he wasn't the least bit sorry. Mrs. Dalrymple made an exaggerated show of moving her skirts aside so I could sit next to her on the settee. I dropped gracefully to the seat, praying I wouldn't whack the hostess's ankles with my underskirts.

"Are you enjoying Miss Castwell's?" she asked. "Is it very different from what you are used to? Where was that again? Cambridgeshire?"

As Mrs. Winter instructed, I considered the question – and any hidden pitfalls therein – before answering. "Yes, it is very different from Cambridgeshire. And my cousins have been very kind to me, indeed. I don't know where I would be without them."

Technically, it was true. Without Mrs. Winter, I had no idea whether I would be locked up at some Coven Guild Enforcement facility.

"And school? Are you enjoying your classes? Making friends?"

"Everyone has been very kind."

"And the book? I understand you made quite the stir on your first day." She glanced at the mark on my palms.

Now, we had arrived at the heart of it. How to respond to what most Guardians would consider incredible good fortune and privilege, when so far, being chosen as Translator has only meant confusion and strange new skin conditions for me. Mrs. Winter had warned me to be quietly and appropriately proud, but not tiresome. So I simply smiled and said, "I hope that I will be able to Translate useful spells as soon as possible."

"I am glad to hear it. You must meet my granddaughter, Ivy. I'm sure she would be happy to introduce you to some of the younger people here. Your cousin seems to have disappeared in his search for punch. Tragic story. It happens more often than you would think."

I didn't know how to tell Mrs. Dalrymple that I'd not only met her granddaughter, but had stood by and done nothing while Callista terrorized her. So I settled for blushing horribly as Mrs. Dalrymple beckoned Ivy from across the room. She clucked her tongue as Ivy approached in a green dress accented with burnt prune lace. "I don't know why my daughter insists on dressing her in the Cowell house colors. They flatter no one."

I did not let my expression change, because I was having enough trouble marinating in my shame over my treatment of Ivy, even while she fed me information about Callista's wardrobe insecurities. My classmate dropped a curtsy to her grandmother. "Yes, Grandmama?"

"Ivy, dear, have you met the lovely Miss Reed?"

"Yes," Ivy said, carefully, nodding toward me. "We are acquainted."

"Wonderful," Mrs. Dalrymple banged her cane on the floor. "Now, do take her around and introduce her to some of the more pleasant young people."

"Oh, Grandmama, I couldn't do that."

"It's really not necessary," I protested.

"Of course, it is," Mrs. Dalrymple assured me. "Now, run along and be charming."

"Yes, ma'am," I said, curtsying even as Ivy sent me a miserable look. And despite the fact that Mrs. Winter and a good portion of magical society was watching

"I'm so sorry," I told Ivy. "You don't have to do this."

"Why, because you're afraid Callista will see you walking with me?" Ivy asked pointedly. "Afraid she won't hand you your bonbon this week?"

"No." I stopped in the middle of the crush of well-dressed people watching the students dance in intricate patterns on the ballroom floor.

"It's not like you're the only one who stands by and does nothing," she said, her voice softening a bit. "And it's not like I'm her only target, merely her favorite." She cleared her throat and offered me a brilliant smile. "Now, let's introduce you to at least three people, so I can claim that I fulfilled my promise to my grandmother. And then I'm going to go hide behind a potted fern and eat profiteroles."

"I may join you," I sighed. "I love profiteroles."

Ivy snickered and dragged me along. It was difficult to accomplish, moving through the crowd as if I had the right to be there, to enjoy myself, instead of carefully maneuvering around wide hoop skirts and oblivious men while hefting a heavy tray of punch cups. How could I be vivacious and bright when, in my head, I was calculating exactly how many minutes I had before I had to collect, wash, and recirculate the silverware?

But Ivy gamely made the rounds with me, tucking her arm through mine and adding thoughtful comments to her stammered introductions to some of the less intimidating students, such as "This is Kipling Cartwright. He collects exotic snake scales." Or "This is Annalise Chun. She once brewed a dream draught so strong it ate through her cauldron, the table and flooring under it."

It was clearly as uncomfortable for her as it was for me, but I admired her for doing something that put her on edge, despite the help I'd never given her. Owen, on the other hand, had abandoned me completely, standing on the far side of the ball-room, laughing with his friends from Palmer. I thought about doing something that would call his absence into Mrs. Winter's attention, when I heard a gasp from behind me.

The undersized girl from the library, who as it turned out, was *not* a ghost, was standing near a bank of potted palms, her pretty, if a little juvenile, green silk dress had been stained with one of the dreaded strawberry tarts. The sticky red filling splat-tered across her waistline like a bloody wound. Given the way Callista's crony, Millicent, was sauntering away with a triumphant little smirk on her face, I doubted very much the jostle that deposited the tart on the younger girl's dress was an accident. And since Millicent had never had an original thought in her life, I guessed that this was somehow Callista's handiwork.

"Oh, no," the stained girl whispered, glancing around the room, though I wasn't sure if she was looking for help or checking to see who had seen the incident.

"Oh, that poor little girl," I sighed. "That's low, picking on a first-year student, even for Callista."

"Alicia McCray isn't a first-year student. She's just small for her... *our* age. She's not well, never has been."

I looked at the ghost-girl, Alicia, again, noting the wary wisdom around her eyes, the sardonic twist to her lips. She was older than she looked. What could this poor sickly girl have done to draw Callista's "notice?"

"Alicia was born with a condition called 'reverberation.' Her magic is strong, but her body isn't capable of repairing itself from the energy drain involved when she uses it. So the echo of her magic turns inward and festers, I suppose, is the best way to put it. Sometimes, it can explode in large, destructive bursts, which only makes the patient suffer more afterwards."

"Is that why she's small and pale?" I asked. The circumstances sounded all too familiar. What was it about magic that could drain a person's health away so completely? It seemed so counter-intuitive that a force that was supposed to give so much to your life was able to make it so miserable. Then again, my magic was coming back into balance and I wasn't exactly overflowing with happiness.

"I'm not sure," Ivy said. "I've never seen another reverb patient before."

With Callista crossing the room from the left, her eyes locked on the girl's struggle to dab at the stain, I made another choice, and I wasn't sure if it was wise or not. I straightened my shoulders and practically keelhauled Ivy across the floor until we cut Callista off from her trajectory and stopped in front of Alicia.

"Until you can get it home to your laundress, there's no help for it," I told her softly, as she tried to rub at the stain with a handkerchief. "Strawberries and silk do not mix."

"I'm usually not so clumsy," she muttered. The Snipe in me, who had seen enough stained party clothes to know one never *rubbed* at stains, winced.

"I don't think so," Ivy told her. "Millicent is a walking accident – for other people."

I pulled the smaller girl behind a bank of enormous potted palms, large enough to hide us from the rest of the room. I reached into my hair, fumbling against the large satin bow tucked under my hair. With Ivy's help, I finally managed to undo the knot, I stretched the ribbon between my hands and wrapped the wide edge around her waist like a sash. The improvisation hid the offending strawberry marks, and the darker green looked quite nice against her light green silk.

"Keep it, maybe you'll be able to wear the dress again," I said, tucking loose ends of hair back into my coiffure.

"Oh, I couldn't possibly let you do that," she insisted, shaking her head.

"I've never been one for poofy hair bows," I promised her. "I think they make my head look like a sailboat." I splayed my hands behind my head like antlers. She giggled, making her shoulders and face relax a bit.

"Really, I think it looks lovely. I don't think we were officially introduced the other day in the library, when you disappeared after giving me some maddeningly unhelpful advice. I'm Cassandra Reed. This is Ivy Cowell. She enjoys laughing at my expense at the breakfast table. And you are?"

"Alicia McCray," she said, extending her hand to touch mine as she curtsied.

McCray House Sigil

"Lovely to officially meet you," I responded as I returned the courtesy, a near impossibility in the tight corner we'd chosen for our encampment.

"And you as well," Ivy said, dropping in a much more

graceful curtsy than I could manage. "Though I'm not sure I *enjoy* laughing at your expense. It just happened."

"I would have believed that if the laughter hadn't been so loud, but it's possible I earned it later."

"Thank you so much for coming to my aid," Alicia whispered. "I am terrible at these parties, really I am. I would much rather be in my room or in the library, doing, well anything, but talking to people I don't know or do know and don't particularly like. But Mother insists that if I'm going to be a proper young lady, I need to learn to ignore my 'fits of pique' and smile through it all."

I smiled at her, not sure whether it would make her feel better or worse to tell Alicia that I was just glad that she wasn't a library ghost. I guessed it would make her feel worse.

"That sounds very familiar," I said, as we pushed carefully through the palms to ease back into the noise of the party. "And the ribbon was no trouble at all. I would hope that if my dress were damaged, someone would do the same for me. But given the attitudes of some of my classmates, I accept that it's unlikely."

"Oh! Poor Alicia!" I heard a nasal voice exclaim behind me. Alicia jumped slightly at my side. And Ivy cowered. Cowered. And that made me angry.

"Oh, my lady's maid has just the thing to get that stain out," Callista said, clucking under her tongue as she made a great fuss of moving Alicia's improvised sash aside and inspecting the damage to her gown. "Of course, I only offer that help to my dearest, closest friends."

My brow lifted and I wondered why Callista was being so very overt about manipulating Alicia into a corner. What did Alicia have that Callista would want? She was young, so little, people barely noticed Alicia was there. She didn't post any sort of threat to Callista's hold on the school. Why would Callista orchestrate the collision that led to the damaged dress in the first place, so she would have a chance to "rescue" Alicia from her

predicament... Wait. McCray. Alicia was a McCray, as in cray-
fire lamps and crayfire engines. Everybody knew that the
McCrays were *rolling* in money thanks to our society's depen-
dence on their most recent inventions. Maybe Callista was
trying to force a connection to that wealth through "friendship?"

"And of course, as my dearest closest friend, you would
introduce me to your family, including your charming brother."
Callista nodded significantly to a tall, dark-haired handsome boy
standing with several of the older Palmer boys near the garden
door.

And there we had it. Callista was trying to strong-arm her
way into a relationship with Alicia's attractive and very rich
brother. I contained my urge to roll my eyes, but it was a very
near thing.

"Sarah has a wonderful hand with laundry."

I started at the mention of my birth name, thinking perhaps
Callista had ferreted my secret out, and that this was some
twisted attempt to discredit me publically, and in high fashion.

"You'd think she was using magic, but of course, she
couldn't." Callista laughed long and loud, as if it was the
funniest thing she'd ever heard. Alicia offered her polite smile,
but Ivy stared at her tormentor as if Callista had finally lost her
mind. "Isn't that right, Cassandra?"

Callista gave me a pointed look, as if I was supposed to use
this opportunity to praise her management of her servant. But
all I could do was stare at her. She always seemed so controlled
and confident in classes. But I'd seen the same sort of mania in
Mary's eyes, when she looked at Owen. Callista would humiliate
Alicia, put her in the way of greater harm, if she thought it
would bring her closer to her brother. We were fortunate that
there hadn't been a convenient carriage close by, otherwise
Callista might have thrown Alicia under it.

"Doesn't my Sarah have the most wonderful talent for stubborn stains?" she asked again, her too-wide smile still pasted on
as she nodded her head ever so subtly toward Alicia.

I didn't want to play this game anymore. I didn't want to be Callista's lackey, and I didn't want there to be any doubt where I stood.

What would Mrs. Winter do in this situation?

I cleared my throat. "Yes, well, if you'll excuse us, Callista, we were just about to go thank Mrs. Dalrymple for throwing such a lovely social. Good luck with your... stains."

Callista's beautiful face flushed purple in anger, but there were far too many adults present for her to lash out or make a scene. She would get even for my show of "defiance," I was sure of it. But instead of the dread I expected, I felt oddly liberated, so much so that I burst out laughing — which only served to make Callista angrier

I linked arms with Alicia and Ivy and let them lead me toward Mrs. Dalrymple's settee. It felt right to be with these two and not just because I expected we would be safe from any more tart-related "accidents." Despite Alicia's apparent invisibility and Ivy's stigma, I wasn't ashamed to walk with them; not like moving as part of Callista's flock. No one avoided eye contact with me. They didn't clear a path. For once, I felt "a part" of the group instead of "apart."

We hovered at the edge of the dancefloor, where Ivy made her little observations about the dancers — who was related to whom and whose families were feuding. Alicia was quiet, studying the pairings and movements as if she could see patterns that we couldn't. It was no wonder that we rarely saw her around the school building. She was so still and quiet that she was practically statuary.

"What are you looking at?" I asked quietly out of the corner of my mouth.

"My brother," she said, blithely.

I followed Alicia's line of sight to a dark-haired teenager who stood a head taller than most of the grown men present. He turned to face us and I gasped.

The boy from the sidewalk, all those weeks ago, the one I'd

run into. He was Alicia McCray's brother. I didn't know whether to smile or run. He was just as handsome as I remembered, even if his face was tensed by the effort of moving through the crowd, avoiding Callista and her cronies. Rosemarie tried to approach him on the right, he turned to start a conversation with someone on his right. Millicent tried to flank on his left, with Callista closing in on his right, he turned his back to both, so he could be introduced to a classmate's younger sister. All the while, he moved closer and closer to the door.

"Poor Gavin," Alicia sighed. "He does hate these socials. He'd much rather be locked away in his library. He only came today to check on me. Mother makes him."

"I don't know why he hates them," I countered, smiling hesitantly. "That was some of the most graceful dancing I've ever seen. Very fancy footwork."

Alicia did something I didn't expect. She burst out laughing, throwing her little head back and guffawing so long and loud that the dancers nearest us stopped mid-turn to stare. Ivy's brown eyes went saucer-wide and she opened her prune-and-tan lace fan over her mouth to cover her own unladylike grin.

Across the dance-floor, a dark head snapped in our direction. Gavin's dark grey eyes narrowed at the unusual sound of his sister cackling like a loon at a fancy society party. I wanted to hide behind the nearest potted plant. Would he recognize me? Had he given me a single thought since that morning? I looked nothing like the half-grown waif who'd bounced off of him. But still, I felt like he could see through mask Mrs. Winter had painted on me, to the drab, weak girl I'd been.

But then, I saw a natural smile bloom over his face, like the clouds of his polite, distant half-smirk parting to make way for real delight. And I couldn't help but feel that I'd been hit by some nerve-shattering spell. Or possibly a horseless carriage.

"Fancy footwork," Alicia giggled as Gavin moved closer. "I'll have to remember to tell him that later. He *loathed* dancing lessons when he was my age. He actually created a potion that made him appear to have monkey pox, just to avoid them."

"So, he faked having monkey pox every week?"

"At the time, he wasn't thinking in the long-term," she said airily.

"Alicia," he sighed, ignoring propriety and bending at the waist to hug his tiny sister. She giggled and beat lightly at his arms as he picked her up. "I'm just going to take you home with me. You've been at school long enough."

"Not funny," she told him sternly as he put her back on her feet.

"But you're so portable, sister."

I laughed, but I tried to cover it with my hand and it came out of as snort. My cheeks flushed hot as Gavin's gaze snapped toward me.

Oh, no. He'd just heard me snort like a barnyard animal.

"And who is this?" Gavin whispered. "Have you made friends?"

Alicia grinned broadly. "I hope so. This is Ivy Cowell, whose grandmother is hosting our gathering today. And this is a new student, Cassandra Reed, who recently rescued me from a wardrobe crisis. Cassandra, this is my brother, Gavin McCray, he rescues me from everything else."

Gavin smiled that sweet smile I remembered, but there was no flash of recognition as he took my hand and bowed over it. It hurt, just a tiny bit, that he didn't know me, but at the same time, I was relieved. A pulse of warmth fluttered through the metal dragonfly's wing. Gavin startled and turned my hand over in his. "That's quite the magical mark you have there."

"Thank you," I said as he took my other hand and put the two halves of the dragonfly together. "It's new."

Ivy frowned at me. I shrugged. *It's new?* Why didn't I pretend to be mute? Why?

But Gavin didn't respond to my socially awkward volley. He studied my hands carefully, turning the mark this way and that to inspect all the angles. It would have been fascinating to watch if he hadn't been treating my hands as if they weren't attached to my body.

Alicia cleared her throat. "Gavin. Please stop treating Miss Reed like a fascinating lab specimen."

Gavin's cheeks went red and he flashed me an embarrassed grin as he released my hand. "I apologize, Miss Reed. And Miss Cowell..."

Just as he was reaching out for Ivy's hand, Gavin whipped his head toward Alicia. "Wait, did you say something about a wardrobe crisis?"

"Story of my life," Ivy muttered, pulling her hand behind her back.

Alicia's shoulders jerked. "Just a little spill. Cassandra was kind enough to lend me her ribbon to cover the stain."

"That was very kind of you," Gavin said, staring at me, considering. He startled at the sight of something over my shoulder, frowning. "Er, Alicia, I'll speak to you soon. Ladies, it was lovely to meet you, but I have to go. Now."

I turned to see Callista bearing down on us with a bright smile that didn't quite match her determined step. Gavin disappeared into the crowd, ducking in the small spaces between people and reaching the door in remarkable time. Callista's face fell into a disappointed snarl. I turned quickly to keep her from seeing me smirk.

"This party was far more entertaining than I expected it to be," Ivy sighed as Callista flounced back to her flunkies. "I could really use something to eat."

"Agreed." I slipped my hand through Alicia's arm and gently dragged her along with us. "Anything but strawberry tarts."

"That's not funny," Alicia told me primly.

"It's a little funny," Ivy retorted.

We'd almost made it to the refreshment table, when a portly man with thinning grey hair and mutton chop sideburns that barely covered his drooping jowls stepped into our path. And his face seemed frozen in disapproval, as if he smelled something rancid.

"Mr. Crenshaw," Ivy chirped uneasily. "How lovely to see you."

"Yes, well, I don't often attend this sort of occasion, but I was informed that I simply couldn't miss it," Mr. Crenshaw rumbled, his voice low, like a barely repressed growl. His gloved hand clutched at his ebony walking stick, topped with an ornately carved silver owl.

Alicia squirmed under his scrutiny, her wide green eyes bouncing back and forth between us, as if she wasn't sure what to do in this situation, despite her no-doubt extensive etiquette training.

I stepped back from Mr. Crenshaw, whose flat, dark gaze had turned on me. I was reminded, uncomfortably so, of the bird specimens in Mr. Winter's study with their blank glass stare. He reached toward me, breaking social protocol, as if he was going to pull me back into his orbit.

Ivy turned on her heel, breaking protocol even further and walking away without so much as a curtsy. Who was this man and what about him made him so intimidating that Ivy was willing to abandon courtesy so completely at her grandmother's party? I glanced towards Mrs. Dalrymple, who was distracted by condescension toward some other young debutante. I took another step back and I felt the hem of my skirt snag on the floor. I looked down to see the tip of his cane pinning my skirt to the hardwood, keeping me from moving away.

When I looked up, Mr. Crenshaw smirked at me. His eyes, so glassy and empty before, seemed to shift, the pupils becoming so wide that there hardly seemed to be any iris. I felt a tickle at the edge of my mind, like a mouse scratching under the door, trying to get in. I felt oddly detached from the sensation, aware but not susceptible to it. I'd read about this.

Ceremancy, the art of creeping into someone's brain and making them a puppet, controlling their moods and actions. Ceremancy was a "trade secret" of House Mountfort, a skill the family had perfected in the healing halls to calm patients and make them more cooperative during exams. Though the spell only lasted a few moments, it was a skill that made other houses nervous. The Mountforts claimed ceremancy was harmless because of their Hippocratic Oath − a rare leftover from the pre-Restoration Days − prevented them from doing any harm. Though he was a descendant of House Mountfort, it was a skill that Mr. Winter never deigned to practice. I got the impression he found it distasteful, somehow, to root around in another person's skull.

Mr. Crenshaw, who I now realized had a pair of scales etched in the golden cufflinks at wrists, did not seem to have the same scruples. He was trying to mesmerize me, right here in a room full of people. And to what purpose? To make me embarrass myself, the Winter family? Or to gain some sort of unseemly control over me?

I was too shocked to form any sort of response. And I was surprised that instead of terror or paralysis, I felt anger. Indignation. Any control he hoped to gain over me was eroded by the all-consuming rage I felt toward Mr. Crenshaw. Who was this man that I barely knew and who did he think he was, to treat me so in a highly public place? I thought proper young Guardian ladies were shielded from this sort of behavior. I thought I was supposed to be some precious commodity, shielded from distress and boorishness. What was it about me that brought out this predatory urge in people? Could they sense the non-magical blood in me? Did I have an invisible sign on my back that read, "convenient target?"

A flash of heat ran from my chest, down my arms to my hands. The dry, acrid smell of burning paper curled up around my face and I realized it was my silk fan, singeing and smoking under the heat of my grip. Mr. Crenshaw's nostrils flared wide. He glanced down at my hands. I found that I didn't give a damn. *Let him see. Let him know what I could do.* I stepped forward, the heat in my hands building as I reached for the owl's head cane.

"Sebastian, I see that you've met my lovely niece," a cool, elegant voice sounded at my shoulder. Mrs. Winter slipped her arm through mine, giving my wrist a comforting pat while moving my hands away from Mr. Crenshaw's cane. Ivy followed close at her heels, an anxious expression on her face.

"Actually, we haven't been introduced," Mr. Crenshaw intoned while ever so subtly releasing the hem of my skirt from the floor.

"Pardon me, Cassandra, dear, this is Mr. Sebastian Crenshaw, a distant... very distant cousin of Mr. Winter's. He is a member of the Coven Guild Inquiry Commission. Mr. Crenshaw, my niece, Cassandra Reed. She just began instruction at Miss Castwell's."

And suddenly, I understood Ivy's discomfort. The Inquiry Commission was the governing body for investigating "inappropriate" acts by Snipes and Guild Guardians alike. It wasn't so much a law enforcement agency as an agency charged with investigating groups that could be considered subversive or potentially damaging to Coven Guild society. They had much more freedom than any branch of law enforcement, or government, for that matter. The Commission could pull people from their beds, in the middle of the night for questioning under "less than ideal" circumstances for an undetermined amount of time. If their targets were lucky, they would be dumped in the streets of the Capitol with no access to their magic for the next month. If they were unlucky, if they were found to be guilty of undermining the government, they would disappear. And their families would speak of them as if they were long-dead and not well-remembered.

With her pat on the arm, Mrs. Winter was telling me to be cautious. One misplaced word in front of Mr. Crenshaw could mean disaster. I pasted on my best false smile and curtsied prettily, keeping my hands folded against my gown. "It's very nice to meet you, Mr. Crenshaw."

Mrs. Winter continued, "Still, even a novice student like herself recognizes an inappropriate introduction like this. I would hate for any of these girls to think a man could simply stomp up to them like a fishmonger and insist on their attention."

"Surely, with my connections to the school, a little leeway is granted," Mr. Crenshaw insisted, glaring at me.

"You'll find that it is not granted," Mrs. Winter said, her voice as cold as her name.

Mr. Crenshaw looked supremely annoyed to be interrupted, and I couldn't help but feel a little frisson of gratitude for Mrs. Winter's timing. "Yes, well, I imagine that we will be spending a lot of time together over the next few years. We will be monitoring your handling of the Mother Book."

"I was under the impression that Cassandra would be under the supervision of the faculty of Miss Castwells, while she is performing her duties as Translator. I believe all previous Translators were granted a considerable measure of autonomy."

"Previous Translators were selected before the Restoration. There is more at stake now," Mr. Crenshaw said, drawing himself to full height. "We must make sure that Miss Reed is taking her role as Translator seriously and acting in the best interests of society. Or certain measures will have to be taken."

From the menace in Mr. Crenshaw's tone, I didn't think those measures would include cookies and pats on my head.

Mrs. Winter smiled, the warmth of it not quite reaching her eyes. "Oh, I'm sure Cassandra will exceed your expectations."

Mr. Crenshaw sniffed. "We'll see about that. Enjoy yourselves, while you can."

Mr. Crenshaw gave a quick nod of the head and departed. Somehow, the world was still turning. The pleasant chatter of the party and *clink* of punch cups and china plates had continued all this time. No one had noticed the hostile exchange with Mr. Crenshaw or my attempts to incinerate my fan.

"Please excuse us, girls," Mrs. Winter said breezily. "Alicia, it's wonderful to see you looking so well. Ivy, dear, that color lace is very interesting."

Both girls curtsied and made themselves scarce. Mrs. Winter kept pleasant smile in place as she led me out to the front entrance. Owen had made himself scarce, by this point, and I envied him, so very much. Mrs. Winter signaled a Snipe footman to bring her carriage around and turned to brush imaginary lint from my sleeves.

"You handled that well," she said, now that the foyer was empty. "Horrible, puffed up little man. He's a low-level toadie for the inquiry commission, at best. He can't even open official lines of questioning. He can only suggest politely that his betters look into matters he finds suspicious. He's only pressing you because Mr. Winter defeated him in a bid for the appropriations committee. He has delusions of grandeur."

"Aren't he and Mr. Winter both descendants of House Mountfort?"

"Crenshaw has always been jealous of Mr. Winter. Ever since they were boys. Don't let him worry you, dear. But don't let him corner you again, either. The less you speak to him, the better."

"He tried to," I made a vague gesture toward my head and wiggled my fingers, as if trying to pantomime "he dangled a squid over my head."

Mrs. Winter might have rolled her eyes if she wasn't above such unladylike gestures. "Ceremancy, at a school social. How gauche."

"It didn't work. I only felt a little tickle in my brain."

My mentor looked vaguely impressed before returning her expression to its neutral norm and tucking a tendril of hair behind my ear. "You're doing very well, dear. Just continue to do what you're doing. I will say 'hello' to everyone at home," she said as the carriage rolled up to the front of the building. "I'm sure they miss you. I'll send the carriage tomorrow for your visit."

I was struck still while Mrs. Winter was handed into her elegant crayfire carriage. I hadn't thought of my parents once since she'd arrived. I hadn't given much thought to the visit home that weekend. I'd only thought of myself, my concerns, protecting my secret, building my new friendships. What did it say about me that I hadn't thought about sending my family my love as Mrs. Winter was leaving? How could I trust Mrs. Winter's kindness so easily when she'd been such an intimidating figure throughout my childhood? Why did my own mother's efforts to protect me seem so clumsy and wrong by comparison? Was I foolish to feel confidence in Mrs. Winter?

GRIM TALES

*a*s predicted, my failure to help cement Callista's new "friendship" with Alicia meant that I'd not only lost Callista's support, but I'd been demoted to the misfit circle with Ivy. Callista did not meet me in the hallway each morning to join her entourage. Tables in the dining hall were suddenly full when I approached. All the girls in dance class had partners. No one wanted to take turns fetching arrows at my target in belomancy. If not for Ivy and Alicia, I wouldn't have seen any friendly faces all day.

Well, Phillip was friendly. He cheeped happily the moment I walked through my bedroom door, flying to my shoulder and nuzzling his little beak against my cheek. But he was a bird, so I didn't think he counted.

By the time Callista was done telling her version of the social, a large portion of the student body had been told that I'd thrown myself at poor, defenseless Alicia McCray demanding her absolute loyalty before over-indulging in fruit puddings and vomiting in a rhododendron. Oh, and I'd faked claiming the

Mother Book with Mrs. Winter's help – I wasn't even all that powerful, just look at my abysmal classroom performance.

She might have had a point there.

Of course, Callista pretended to know nothing about this when I found her in my dormitory room Friday afternoon, as I finished some last-minute tasks before my visit "home." She seemed to be searching for something, pacing back and forth in front of my desk. The Mother Book? It was still locked in its special cabinet. I could see the padlock dangling from the latch. The warded key was in my pocket. But I did notice that the window had been opened and Phillip was missing from his special perch.

Callista whirled as the door opened, all welcoming smiles and sweetness, though her eyes narrowed when she spotted the book in my arms. I crossed to the window and whistled softly. Phillip came zipping back through the window and landed on my hand. I closed the window and turned back to Callista, brow lifted. I would have to read up on wards. I was under the impression that the school's magic wouldn't allow students to enter each other's rooms without permission. Maybe Ivy would have some advice.

"Callista," I began, keeping my tone even and crisp as Mrs. Winter's when she was correcting Mary. Before I could complete my thought, which was "remove yourself through the door before I make use of the window," Callista practically shouted. "Say no more, darling, you don't even have to apologize. I know that the social was your first gathering of cultured, refined people. Not like your simple farm people from Cambridgeshire. It was overwhelming for you. And I'm sure you didn't mean to insinuate yourself into my conversation with dear Alicia, especially when it was going so well."

Callista crossed the room and took my hands into hers, squeezing them tight. Her grip was so tight, the press of metal against her skin had to hurt, but she never even registered the pain. She tsked over me, as if my social ineptitude was something to be pitied. "For future reference, a good friend would *help* me by complimenting me and playing up my attributes while I'm trying to forge an important social connection. She wouldn't stand there like a lump, distracting that potential friend with her awkward, country ways."

I blinked at her owlishly. Had we been attending different parties? Callista thought that her conversation with Alicia had been "going well?" Did she really think she could bully her way into a friendship, just because she thought it would benefit her?

As if my mark could sense my annoyance, the metal dragonfly on my palms seemed to heat up all at once. Callista hissed, dropping my hand.

"I will keep that in mind for future reference," I said, offering her the barest hint of a smile. "Now, if you'll excuse me."

A soft knock sounded at my door. Callista didn't budge from her spot, seeming relieved at the excuse to stay. I frowned, uneasy at having Callista in my room for a moment longer than necessary. I called, "Come in!"

The "important social connection" herself skipped into my room on her tiny slippered feet, carrying a spray of flowers and a book. You could barely see Alicia through the odd floral arrangement, certainly not comprised any variety of roses I knew. Each blossom was a different color, and the tightly bound petals were shiny and slick.

Alicia stopped short at the sight of Callista, and frowned.

"Little Alicia, darling!" Callista exclaimed. "How are you?"

"Just fine, thank you," Alicia said, in a frosty tone that would have impressed my patroness. Because while it seemed acceptable for me to call her "little" in my head, I was certainly socially savvy enough to know that I shouldn't say it aloud. Callista made a welcoming wiggle of her fingers, to lure her into a… hug, maybe?

Alicia ignored her, walking past her to hand me the flowers. "For you."

"Thank you! They're lovely." I touched the center flower, a lovely bright bloom in Castwell green, and it fluttered open. I realized that while the greenery was fresh and fragrant – almond leaves for gratitude – the rose was made of a long silk ribbon rolled tightly into a blossom shape. As it snaked through the air, the ribbon folded itself and looped like a pair of wings, flapping with purpose across the room and landing in a neat roll on the bed. Phillip flitted toward the ribbon to peck at it, as if he didn't appreciate some other thing flying in his space.

Delighted, I laughed and clapped my hands.

"Fantastic!" I exclaimed. This was the reason to study magic, I told myself, the ability to produce such wonder. One by one, I touched each rose and their ribbons followed suit, unfurling into a ribbon-butterfly and flying across the room.

"They're for you, to say thank you for the social," Alicia told me, beaming sweetly. Feeling slightly guilty for not reading the card before I tugged my bouquet apart, I plucked the card from the foliage. I read it aloud, "With sincere thanks, to replace the kind gift that you gave my sister. Your humble servant, Gavin McCray."

My smile was so broad that it nearly hurt my cheeks. I'd never received such a lovely, thoughtful gift, and I certainly never received such a gesture from a boy. And this particular gesture coming from this particular boy had an ecstatic warmth flooding my whole body. He'd noticed me! And even better, he'd noticed a kindness I'd done his sister. Not the cut of my gown or the smoothness of my complexion, but something true and good in me. Somehow that justified the moments I'd devoted to thinking about Gavin over the last few weeks. He was a sweet boy, who loved and protected his sister. Compared to some of the other Guardian boys I'd seen, he was practically mythical.

And I'd completely forgotten that Callista was still in the room. And that she planned to hook Gavin like a plate-bound trout. Callista plucked at one of the ribbons on my bed with a disdainful sneer she could not hide. "What an odd and unseemly gift."

"Really?" Alicia asked, her eyes wide with feigned wonder. "Because he put so much thought into it. He really wanted Cassandra to know the depth of his appreciation. I helped him choose every ribbon at Madame Beamis's millinery shop."

My lips twitched as Callista tried to row backwards, to recant the insult, but she couldn't. "Well, Alicia, I was hoping to catch you before we all left for the weekend. My mother and I would just love it if you came to tea tomorrow. And if you happened to bring your brother with you, well, that would just be lovely for everyone, now wouldn't it."

Alicia and I both shot Callista incredulous looks. Gavin McCray had to be three years older than us. And, as my Papa would say, Callista was about as subtle as five pounds of fertilizer in a three pound bag. Alicia flushed a pale pink and shook her head, clearly searching for some sort of excuse as to why she couldn't oblige, so I jumped in.

"Oh, that's so sweet of you to offer, Callista," I said, looping my arm through Alicia's. "But Alicia has already accepted an invitation for tea at Raven's Rest tomorrow."

There was an awkward moment, when Callista clearly expected me to include her in the never-issued invitation, but I smiled blithely as she stewed like one of my mother's braised apples.

"Some other time then," Callista sniffed. With her nose in the air, Callista swept from the room.

I laughed, shaking my head, re-reading the card, admiring the precise block printing of Gavin's card.

"She's a *delight*," Alicia muttered, making me snort.

Just then Ivy came bustling into my room, out of breath. She collapsed against my vanity seat and gasped out, "Callista is on her way here."

"Yes, she just left," I said, pouring Ivy a glass of water from the ewer on my nightstand.

"I overheard her telling her minions that she was planning on looking around your room while we were on the belomancy range," Ivy said, mopping delicately at her face with a purple lace-trimmed handkerchief and flopping on my bed – no minor feat in her cumbersome day dress. "And I tried to get up here, but Rosemarie pinned my hem to the ground with a quiver full of arrows. Do you know how long it takes to yank a dozen magically-planted arrows out of the ground and then run up the steps? In a *bustle?*"

"You have suffered," Alicia said, patting her hand delicately.

"I appreciate your efforts," I told Ivy as she drained the water.

"Why would Callista want into your room so badly?" Ivy asked, as I poured her another glass.

"I don't know," I said, biting my bottom lip as I gazed around the room. Nothing in my room hinted at my origins. Could Callista be searching for something incriminating? Could there be rumors circulating about my roots already? "Maybe she's just trying to make trouble for me?"

"She did mention the Mother Book a few times," Ivy said. "But she also mentioned your blue silk fan, so she could be out to steal either one of those. It's a habit of hers, you see. You do something that she doesn't like, she steals something of yours that you *do* like."

"What has she taken from you, Ivy?" Alicia asked.

Ivy took a deep breath and forced a smile. "Nothing I'll miss."

"I feel like I owe you an apology," I told her. "For all of the times I should have spoken up when Callista was being, well, herself. I should have said something. I was too worried about saving my own skin and… I made the wrong choice."

Ivy shrugged. "I understand. You were new. You were just trying to survive. I can't say I wouldn't have done the same. And I'll admit I did reject friendship from you at first. I just couldn't stand the idea that I might start to like you and you'd turn out to be another Callista."

"Fair enough. And I'll find a way to get whatever she took from you," I insisted. "Because I'm the Translator and being able to read the Mother Book should rank some sort of special magic, like reclaiming lost objects from hateful wenches."

"I'm certain that's written in the very small print on the very last page," Alicia said. "Speaking of the Mother Book, I brought something else for you, a special request I had to make of my brother and my mother, but both thought it would do more good for you than in our dusty old vaults." She placed the beautifully wrapped rectangle in my hands and with a touch at the center of the bow, the paper fell away to reveal a weathered brown leather journal with thin vellum pages. "This is the journal of my great-great-great-grandmother, Calpernia McCray. She was the last known Translator."

Grimstelle House Sigil

My mouth fell open as I turned the book over in my hands.

Calpernia's name and 1773 stamped were on the cover. "But this is a family heirloom. I can't take this."

"It will do you more good than it will me," Alicia said. "It's just sitting around our house, collecting dust. My family would consider it an honor if it helps the new Translator. My mother insists."

"Thank you." I gently turned the pages. Calpernia had left plenty of diary entries and sketches, but none of them featured owls.

"Actually, I did have a question." I said, opening the Mother Book and showing her the page depicting the House sigils. I'm familiar with all of the House symbols, but I must admit that I've never seen this owl before."

"That's the Grimstelle owl."

When I shook my head, she sighed. "Well, I only know because my brother used to tell me the stories to scare me when I was little. He was allowed to read Calpernia's journal as a future head of our house. The information has been lost to other families and we don't share it with just anyone. He just loved sitting at my bedside, reading me horror stories of the Ancient House of Grimstelle. It was one of the original seven Great Houses, the only one from France, but it grew weaker over time."

"How does an ancient and noble house grow weaker? I thought that was the point of the inter-marrying and political connections, to build power bases and plot against each other."

Alicia cleared her throat and stroked a finger over the owl illustration. "Well, Grimstelle was once *the* house to watch, generations ago, long before the Restoration. Their specialized skill was connecting with the afterlife. They were highly skilled mediums that could bring forth a host of spirits to speak to the living. They grew very rich, lining their pockets with offerings from people who wanted to bid loved ones goodbye or ask long-lost grandmamma where they'd hidden the key to the silver cabinet, that sort of thing.

"And while they used their riches to further their studies, they barely bothered with other aspects of magic. Eventually, the Grimstelles learned to manipulate the dead, calling their spirits back to their bodies and *moving* the flesh. As they grew in power, the more the Grimstelles were able to accomplish more with the dead. They could make them walk the streets, do their bidding. A few of the Grimstelles were powerful enough to use the dead in their homes as servants. Eventually, they began to use them in less than savory ways to rid themselves of certain enemies, mostly members of the Mountfort household. That brought their actions under scrutiny from the Coven Guild."

Ivy mopped the last traces of sweat from her brow. "So they used the dead as their personal assassins? That's awful."

Alicia shrugged. "There's a certain amount of sense to it. As soon as the enemy was disposed of, the Grimstelle ended the spell, and the corpse dropped to the ground like a puppet without strings. The authorities couldn't take a dead man to jail for murder. And there was no way to tell whose spell animated the corpse. It was the perfect crime."

Ivy tilted her head as we stared at Alicia. "You're just a little bit scary, aren't you?"

She grinned. "Well, that may be true. However, the Grimstelles were scarier. The rumor was that before the Guild stepped in, the House was tinkering with spellwork powerful enough to raise an army of the dead."

I didn't change expressions. "I would ask why, but I'm sure there is some disturbing reason that will keep me awake at night."

"Well, just imagine it, an unstoppable, mindless fighting force that doesn't fear being injured or killed? They could overthrow our entire civilization in a matter of days."

I shuddered. "I knew I shouldn't have asked. And where are the Grimstelles now?"

Alicia gave a shrug of her thin shoulders. "Who knows? The Guild put strict sanctions on them, severely limiting the magic they were allowed to do. They weren't allowed to communicate with the Other World at all. They were fined heavily, wiping out the wealth they'd built up. They were out of practice with the other branches of magic and left without a way to support themselves. Some of the Grimstelles became no better than Snipes, an embarrassment to Guardian culture. Mentioning their name in polite society became taboo. The daughters were quietly married off to other Houses and a good number of the sons changed their names or claimed to be related to other Houses. They became a cautionary tale to young Guardian children. *Don't abuse your magic, or you could end up like the Grimstelles.* Over the course of five or six hundred years, they simply faded away."

Ivy huffed, "Well, I will think of you both over the weekend, when I'm home, alone, staring up at the canopy, unable to sleep."

Alicia giggled.

"Thank you, for the gift, Alicia. I'll take it to Raven's Rest with me and lock it up safe with the Mother Book until I have more time to explore it."

I pulled the key from my pocket, the special key Headmistress Lockwood had enchanted so that only I could use it. I twisted the padlock and felt the warm hum of the lock accepting my magic. With the weekend coming, I was allowed to take the Mother Book home with me, but only because Mrs. Winter contacted the school's governing board – including the unpleasant Mr. Crenshaw – and demanded it. And then she wrote me a letter to demand it. She wanted it known that Mother Book was sheltered at Raven's Rest, even if it was just a few days.

The cabinet was empty.

The Mother Book was gone.

My stomach dropped so fast I felt dizzy. I thought back to that last little triumphant smirk Callista had thrown my way as she walked out of my room. She'd taken it. She'd taken my book. Somehow, she'd managed to outwit a magical lock and steal something that had been entrusted to me. I was sick of this. I was sick of this stupid, spoiled girl causing havoc, never suffering any of the consequences. The dragonfly buzzed angrily on my palms, heating up and sending that burning pain up my arms.

To my right, the long, gauzy green curtains burst into flames.

"Oh, dear," Ivy said.

"We're assuming that Callista took it, yes?" Alicia suggested, pursing her lips while I seethed in the direction of the empty cabinet.

"Who else?" I demanded. "Ivy said she steals things from people she dislikes. She was lurking in my room. She's trying to pay me back for not helping her 'acquire' your friendship."

"So what are you going to do?" Alicia asked.

"I'm going to find the most powerful spell I can to drag that book through time and space, no matter where it is, and plant it right back in my hands."

"Asking Callista to return the book wouldn't be considered a reasonable first step?" Ivy asked.

"If I ask Callista for the book, she'll just pretend that she doesn't know what I'm talking about and she doesn't know where it is," I said, shaking my head. "And I can't help but think this whole situation was designed to put me in the position of begging Callista to pretty-please give my book back. She wants me to look weak, because it suits her twisted social agenda. Well, I've had enough of that. I'm going to do what Mrs. – Auntie Aneira would do. I'm going hit her where it hurts."

"Mrs. Winter wouldn't hit her," Ivy insisted. "Hitting would leave marks."

"I mean, socially. I'm going to go get my book back in a very public fashion, so every girl at this school knows that I'm not Callista's little lap dog."

"I think this is a good plan," Alicia said. "I think we should go to the library to look for a spell right now."

"Good." I nodded, stalking toward the door.

Ivy cleared her throat. "Also, the curtains are on fire."

"Right."

AFTER THE CURTAINS WERE EXTINGUISHED, I marched into the library with Alicia and Ivy on my heels. I'd spent too much time "trying" to do magic. It was time for me to simply do magic.

Miss Morton was sitting behind the reference desk, pencils stuck through her frizzled grey hair as she peered over a pair of half-moon glasses and read *A Treatise on Transcendental Mechanics.*

"Miss Morton, I need a location spell. The most powerful spell that students are allowed to use."

Miss Morton's head snapped up and her glasses slipped down her nose.

"Please," I added quickly.

"Oh, we-well, what have you lost, dear?"

"I would really rather not say," I told her.

Miss Morton's brows furrowed. "All right, then. Will the item in question harm you or your fellow students if it's found?"

"She might harm someone if it's not found," Alicia muttered, only to get her ribs nudged by Ivy.

"No, in fact, it's in the best interest of the school if I find it," I promised Miss Morton. "I don't know where to begin looking, and I think it would save time to just draw the item to me."

"I see." Miss Morton slipped her glasses back up on the bridge of her nose as she scurried around the reference desk. Her footsteps echoed, even under the enormous blue glass dome of the library. I glanced up at the ceiling, while she puttered around in stacks to our left. That blobby shape winked out at me from all the House sigils. I was still frowning at it when Miss Morton came bustling out with a large blue leather book.

"I believe you'll find what you're looking for in this volume.

But I must warn you, some things are better left lost. Once you start looking, you may not ever be able to stop."

"Thank you," I said, tucking the book under my arm and heading out into the hall. I flicked my wrist and Wit slid out of my sleeve.

"Miss Reed, you're not going to just run off and perform an unfamiliar spell willy-nilly, are you?"

I changed the "stabbing" grip on my knife and hid it behind my back. "Of course not. I wouldn't assume that I could do a spell I've never even read simply because I'm the Translator. That would be insane."

Miss Morton smiled, nervously. "Wonderful, now, this particular spell is powerful, but it should be stabilized by at least two coven members to prevent… damage."

I glanced over my shoulder at Alicia and Ivy, who had just taken large steps back. "Oh, thanks, very much."

"What sort of damage?" Ivy asked. "To us or the item that's being called?"

"Both," Miss Morton said.

"I don't know if I would be any help to you anyway," Alicia said. "My brother has spent years layering some very complicated wards over me to keep me from using spells. With my Reverb, well, any help from me would be very unpredictable."

I frowned. So Gavin had placed the spellwork equivalent of suppressors on his sister? Could that be what was affecting Alicia's health? Considering how concerned he was for her well-being, I doubted he knew that long-term magical suppression was bad for her. I would have to find a way to bring that up in conversation without the context of my own experience with suppression.

"What would happen?" I asked Alicia. "If you took the wards off and were able to work magic freely?"

Alicia shrugged. "Gavin will not tell me, but given the faces he was making I have to guess that it would be very bad. Dropping a match in a barrel of kerosene and crayfire crystals, bad."

"That does not paint a pretty picture," Ivy agreed.

"The 'support' positions are mostly ceremonial," Miss Morton assured her. "You don't provide any power. You're just there to prop Miss Reed up, like the legs of a tripod. The most stable cauldron sits on a stand with at least three legs, yes?"

Alicia nodded.

"Well, Miss Reed's magic just needs to feel that your magic is propping hers up if she needs it. It's more about confidence than power."

"I would like to go back to your use of the word 'damage,'" Ivy said, holding up one index finger.

"You know, it occurs to me that this sort of magic would come more naturally if I helped you work with the Mother Book," Miss Morton told me. "I've been reading up on some meditative techniques that might help you."

"I will take you up on that," I promised, adding quietly. "As soon as I find the Mother Book."

Miss Morton frowned. "What was that, dear?"

"Nothing."

THE SCHOOL ATRIUM was a bustle of activity as girls prepared to go home for the weekend. Snipe girls scurried around with piles of gowns thrown over their arms, climbing the staircase. Students stood in clusters, directing footmen regarding their trunks or dropping last minute bits of gossip. Cats and birds, the students' familiars, milled about the black-and-white tile in dizzying patterns, chasing after their witches, as if they were afraid they would be left behind.

Flanked by Alicia and Ivy, I strode into the atrium, the light of mid-day streaming through the glass overhead. Phillip zipped out of the dormitory wing in a blue streak, landing on my shoulder with supportive chirp. I flicked my wrist, allowing Wit to sling out of my sleeve. The handle was warm in my palm.

Slowly, but surely, the other girls paused, watching Alicia

hand me a quartz pendant. Alicia and Ivy held the book open in front of me. I held the pendant aloft while reading the incantation from the book, loudly, praying that I was pronouncing the Latin correctly. By the time I finished the first verse, every soul was still as water, even the Snipes, while I chanted. Callista appeared at the top of the stairs, eyebrows lifted.

I chanted louder, holding the pendant absolutely still, even as the muscles in my arms burned. Phillip hummed along, and I could feel a warm energy flowing down my skin from my shoulder, where he perched, as if he was adding some of his own magic to mine. This felt different than floating the vase or some glamour. This felt... grounded, like Phillip's weight on my shoulder, Ivy and Alicia standing behind me would keep me from failing. Ivy was muttering the correct Latin pronunciations under her breath, adjusting my words without my even realizing it. Alicia simply stared at the pendant intently, as if it owed her money.

With the second verse finished, the pendant started to circle ever so slightly, swinging wider and wider until the chain was practically parallel to the floor. I started the third verse and the pendant stopped mid-circle and pointed toward the dormitory wing. Towards the stairs. Right at Callista.

I smiled brightly and felt the dragonfly wings thrum on my palms, sending a wave of warm energy through Wit. I drew my blade through the air like a conductor, leaving a bright swirling symbol that translated to "FIND." I threw up my arm, pointing the blade at Callista – which I enjoyed, a little more than I should have. Callista's blue eyes went wide, and she dropped to the floor with a squawk, just as I yelled, *"LIBRIS."*

For a second, nothing happened. The atrium stood absolutely still and silent. And I wondered if I'd just made an even bigger spectacle of myself in front of the entire student body, dragging poor Alicia and Ivy down with me.

And then I heard the flapping of what sounded like wings.

The book appeared, flying through the doorway, behind

Callista, flapping its covers like wings. It looped around the atrium a few times, buzzing close to a few girls – nearly smacking Rosemarie in the head before fluttering into my free hand and shutting its covers. Phillip cawed triumphantly, landing on the cover.

I grinned broadly, a golden glimmer spreading under Phillip's feet, as if it was telling me it was glad to see me. I glanced up at Callista, who was sprawled on the floor, an expression of shock on her face. I smiled, sweet as arsenic and cream, and swept my eyes over the assembled girls. I clutched the book to my chest and slid Wit up my sleeve.

The girls parted as Alicia, Ivy and myself made our way up the stairs. I paused at the landing, and Callista scrambled back into a distinctly unladylike crouch.

"You should stay out of my room from now on, Callista," I told her. She glowered at me, rising to her feet.

Phillip wrapped both feet around my free index finger, and I lifted him up to eye level. "You are the best bird familiar a girl could ask for."

He chirped and took a little bobbing bow.

Alicia giggled as we sped toward my room. "I'm so glad that worked."

"Yes, otherwise, it would have been terribly awkward," Ivy said.

"How are you feeling, Alicia? That wasn't too taxing for you, was it?"

Alicia shook her head. "Oh, no, Miss Morton was right. I could feel your magic reaching out for mine, but the spell hardly required anything of me."

Then Alicia's eyes rolled up into her head and she dropped to the floor in a heap of fluffy green skirts.

Ivy and I both shouted and dropped to our knees. I propped Alicia's head against my knees as Ivy checked her pulse and waved a lace fan over her face.

"Should we call for Headmistress Lockwood?" Ivy asked.

"Yes!" I frantically searched the hallway, but found no one to call for help. "How is this the *one time* we find ourselves in an empty hallway?"

"Because if I did this in a crowded hallway, your response wouldn't be nearly this funny."

We looked down to find Alicia grinning up at us, her usually pale cheeks flushed pink with glee. "You should have seen the looks on your faces."

"Oh, you!" Ivy stood and flung the fan at Alicia. She ducked and the fan bounced off of the wall behind her.

"You are horrible," I told her as she cackled.

She shrugged her thin shoulders. "One must find ways to entertain herself."

MIRROR, MIRROR

he streets of Lightbourne looked somehow brighter
and more colorful as the carriage rattled down the
cobblestones. I was going home. I might be able to sneak around
the spells somehow to see my family. At the very least, I would
be able to relax within the walls of Raven's Rest, where my
secrets were known.

Now, as my carriage rattled toward Raven's Rest, I read
through Alicia's ancestor's journal for more mentions of the
Grimstelles. I thought of the stained glass in the library and the
strange blobby bird that looked as if it had been removed from
the glass. What if it hadn't been removed? What if it hadn't
been meant to appear at all? The school had been built
centuries after the Grimstelles were weeded out from Guardian
society. What if some girl, some leftover Grimstelle had tried to
add her family crest to the ceiling to recapture some glory for
her house? Maybe she'd done it badly or a teacher caught her
and undid her work. I found myself feeling sorry for that girl,

the last in her line, trying to claim her place in a world that no longer wanted her.

Still, I couldn't blame the Guardians for not wanting the Grimstelles at their tea parties. The very idea of raising the dead, making them dance like puppets on strings, made me shiver. And an army of them marching through the streets of Lightbourne? The stuff of childhood nightmares. And beneath those upsetting images, an undercurrent of thought gnawed at Miss Morton's assurances that the Grimstelles were long-extinct. Necromancy sounded uncomfortably close to Mr. Crenshaw's talent for mental manipulation he'd tried to use on me at the social.

Phillip landed on my hand and pecked lightly. I grinned, stroking a finger along the velvety blue feathers on his head. He chirped and the dragonfly vibrated in response, glowing warm and gold.

"You're going to want to avoid Horus, Phillip," I sighed. "I don't care what Owen says. He's an ankle-clawing menace."

Phillip bobbed his head.

As the grand old house came into view, I felt the weight of Cassandra Reed slide from my shoulders. I was plain Sarah Smith again, and my skin felt like my own. A pleasant warmth vibrated along the dragonfly on my palms, as if my mark was somehow happy to be home, too. I never thought I would be so *pleased* to see the gates of Raven's Rest, which had meant work and tension for most of my childhood.

But while I wasn't exactly a member of either family under the Raven's Rest roof, at least I didn't have to worry about my hands or my speech or my manners giving me away.

A huge smile broke over my face as the footman, Simon, helped me down from the coach. The shadow of the grey stone house didn't seem so intimidating. Simon ran ahead to open the door for me. I thanked him politely, but felt oddly disappointed when the man I'd known since I was a toddler didn't even lift his eyes to respond. Before I could ask him what was wrong, I saw

Mum in the entryway, dusting some of Mr. Winter's larger avian specimen cases. I guessed that she'd had to take over some of my household duties with me away at school. She turned, caught sight of me in my pretty lilac daydress and gasped.

She rushed toward me, smiling broadly. "Oh, Sarah, just look at you! You're so pretty! So different. And you've grown so tall!"

"Mum," I said, starting towards her with my hands outstretched. The metal dragonfly flashed from my palms as I walked through a beam of sunlight from the foyer window. Mum flinched as the light hit her eyes and she backed away.

"I'm not supposed to talk to you, *Miss Cassandra*. Mrs. Winter forbid it." Mum bowed her head and walked toward the kitchen.

"Mum, I have so much I want to tell you. Please don't leave."

"I love you. Don't you ever forget."

But the door to the kitchen was already swinging shut.

I stood in the foyer of Raven's Rest, on marble I'd scrubbed hundreds of times. It had never seemed so unfamiliar. My own mother couldn't talk to me. When I tried to step close to her, she backed away. Admittedly, this wasn't entirely new. She was always backing away from me. Ever since I was little, she pulled away from my hugs. She was too busy to talk, always bustling around, giving the chores her attention. Giving me my pill every morning was the closest she came to doting on me. Was that it? The pills? The magic? Was Mum afraid of getting too attached to me because she feared she'd lose me? Or because she was afraid I would bring the wrath of the Coven Guild on our heads? Was I the reason Papa started drinking so much? Had I broken my own family without even realizing it?

The grandfather clock ticked away the seconds as saw my childhood through grey, joyless lenses. I felt my eyes well up just as footsteps fell at the top of the grand staircase.

"Mum, what was that noise?" Mary came bustling down the stairs, carrying a basket of table linens.

"Mary!" I'd squealed, nearly tripping over my wide ruffled skirts as I gamboled towards her. Mum's reluctance flew out of my head as I threw my arms around her.

I'd missed my sister more than I thought possible. I'd even missed Mary's teasing, her sly smiles as she needled me with one of her little jokes. But now, Mary wasn't smiling. She didn't return my hug. Heck, Ivy had given me a warmer embrace before I left the school. Mary didn't even seem happy to see me. She tore away from me, putting the laundry basket between us like a shield.

"Don't you touch me," she hissed. Her lip curled back as she took me in from head to toe, like the dress I was wearing was sort of personal betrayal. "Not after what you've done."

I recoiled from her, feeling as if I'd been slapped. "What did I do?"

Mary had always been quick to upset, but her flashes of emotion never ran deep. A pretty bribe or a boring afternoon were usually enough to nudge her through being annoyed with me. But now, now, staring into those eyes felt like falling into a well, a dark, deep pit with snakes at the bottom.

"You think I don't know what's going on here?" Mary growled. "You faked this whole thing. You figured out some way to make it look like you have magic so the Winters would take you in and you could get closer to Owen!"

"Wha-What?" I stepped back from her, my mouth hanging open like a beached trout. I hadn't seen Mary in weeks, and that was all she had to say to me? Did she really think I was capable of this sort of deceit, faking magic? And to believe I'd done it to get closer to Owen, who as far as I knew, hadn't looked at me twice since we were children. The revelation that my basic make-up was somehow wrong, had torn our family apart, turned my life upside down and threatened the very fabric of our society, but all Mary could think of was her silly crush on *Owen?* That was all she cared about?

I loved my sister. I knew she was silly and occasionally vain, but I loved her. That love had blinded me to how deep this obsession with Owen Winter twisted inside of her. She didn't say anything about missing me or wanting me to come home. She was angry at me for not including her in my "ruse." For her to think so low of me cut me to my core.

I felt an angry hum sweep along the metal wings on my palms. I winced, rubbing a hand over the aching burn.

"Why didn't you tell me?" she whined. "I could have helped you. I don't know how you did it, but I could have convinced them that I'm magical, too. And I could be living with you in the lap of luxury, no more chores, no more work. I could be wearing a fancy lady's dress and a bonnet that cost more than our whole house. I could be having breakfast, lunch, and dinner with Owen every day!"

"Do you really think that's what happened?" I demanded. "Mary, I didn't fake anything. The thing with the vase just happened. I still don't know what I did to make it float like that, really. Even after weeks at Miss Castwell's, I couldn't tell you how that worked."

Mary stared at me, for a good long while, her eyes lingering on the neckline of the silk dress I was wearing, as if she sensed there was something not quite right lurking under the material. She gave me a little smile, the smile that meant I was forgiven and everything was right again. But frankly, I didn't know if I was interested in her "grace."

"I'm sorry, Sarah, you know I didn't mean it. My temper gets ahead of me sometimes, but you know I'd never really be angry with you, yes?"

I nodded, wincing a bit as her strong hands clasped around my wrists.

"You were always the better-natured of us, anyway. Always the good girl," she teased. "And you can keep being good to us.

You can use your new place in the household to make life a little easier for us, yes?"

"I don't have any power here."

"We both know that's not true, don't we?" she sniffed, the bitterness creeping back into her voice.

"I'm still as much of a servant as you are, Mary."

"Servants who don't work aren't servants. They're pets," Mary retorted.

Darn it, if she didn't have a point there.

"And as their little pet, you will be able to change things in the household. Schedules, my duties, which areas of the house I'm allowed to enter," she said, her voice far too casual as she toyed with the green ribbon that secured my bonnet under my chin. "And you can help me find ways to spend time with Owen."

"Mary," I groaned.

"He wants to see me, too!" she insisted. "I can tell by the way he looked at me the other morning when I snuck out to bring fresh towels to his bathroom. He misses me, Sarah. This new schedule – the one Mrs. Winter set to keep us from seeing *you* – keeps me from seeing Owen. So really, it's your fault that we're apart. Even with you away at that school during the week, she's keeping up the new schedule so we can 'accommodate ourselves to the change.' But you, you can convince Mrs. Winter that you won't try to see us. Then, she'll lift these silly restrictions."

"So, to help you, I should pretend that I don't care to spend time with you?"

"Please, please, please, please!" she wheedled in a sugary-sweet tone.

"I'll try," I sighed. "Now, would you please tell Mum and Papa that I miss them?"

"Of course, of course," Mary said, picking up her basket. "And you'll talk to Mrs. Winter?"

"I said I would try," I told her.

"Always such a good girl," Mary teased, kissing my cheek and scurrying down the hallway.

"Emphasis on the word *try*," I called after her.

I DIDN'T TRY.

I felt like a horrible sister, lying to Mary. It went against everything in my gut to pretend I didn't want to see my family. I also couldn't help but feel that it was better for Mary to have less access to Owen. Her infatuation seemed to be spiraling out of what could be considered normal and into something *desperate* and dangerous.

Overall, it was a lonely weekend. Now that Mary had tugged her promise out of me, there was no point in talking to me. I didn't see my mother, who stayed in the kitchen under Mrs. Winter's orders. And when I looked down from my windows and saw my father in the garden, he waved, and then turned his back on me. I ran onto the balcony and called out to him, but he hobbled away on his unsteady legs, ignoring me.

To add insult to loneliness, Ivy was unable to make it for tea on Saturday. Her regrets appeared in the form of a note, scrawled in bright pink script on my vanity mirror after breakfast. My shriek of surprise brought Mrs. Winter bustling into the Lavender Room, where I babbled an explanation of someone sneaking into my room and writing on my glass with lip rouge. Mrs. Winter gave me a very amused smile, as she pointed to the note,

"Dear Cassandra, I am sorry I will not be able take tea at your house as planned. My mother planned a series of visits with my Cowell cousins while I'm home without talking to me. Trust me when I say I would rather be taking tea with you. I'll see you at school on Monday.

– Sincerely, Ivy Cowell.

Post-script – Alicia took ill just before I left Castwell's and was not able to make the trip home. So I assume she will not be able to attend, either.

I hope that we can make arrangements for a visit to Raven's Rest at some other time."

Just as I read the last of the post-script, it disappeared and another glowing message appeared. *Post-post-script – I just found out that Mother is planning to take me for a torturous dress-fitting while I am home. Send HELP."*

"How does this work?" I asked, touching my fingertips to the glass.

"Have you truly never seen a scrying message before?" she asked.

"I thought scrying mirrors were for divination, seeking answers in meditation, that sort of thing," I said.

"They are, but when we need to send our close acquaintances a quick note, we just think of that person and use the tips of our blades to write a message on our mirrors. It will appear on which ever glass is closest to the recipient. Generally, they're very private messages, so I suppose it makes sense that you've never seen one."

"But why do you spend so much time writing letters and invitations?" I asked.

Mrs. Winter shook her head. "Well, as I said, scry-messaging is just for quick notes. Paper is necessary for formal invitations and correspondence. How else can you intimidate your friends and enemies with the quality of your stationery?"

"You... can't?" I guessed as she penned an elegant reply on my mirror.

"Now, my question for you is, did you honestly think that inviting Miss Cowell here was a sound notion?" she asked, lifting a brow.

I cringed. She was right. I hadn't thought that through. I didn't have the right to ask anyone to Raven's Rest as my guest, particularly without asking Mrs. Winter first. I was not a member of the family. I wasn't even a guest really. How exactly, did I expect to maintain my story, asking my classmates from Castwell's here, where my family was serving as Snipes? Did I really think I could sit quietly and accept tea and cakes made by my mother? What if Mary passed through the parlor while Alicia and Ivy chatted about school? I wouldn't have been able to stand that pressure. I would have blurted out the whole ugly story and ruined myself.

"I should have asked you before I invited my classmates here," I said. "I am sorry."

"Yes, you should have, but that's not the point," she said. "It's expected that a girl from a prominent family would invite her classmates to see her home. We would have sent your family away for the afternoon. No, what I am telling you, is that you should aim higher than Ivy. Yes, she has a desirable connection to Mrs. Dalrymple, but she's hardly top-tier material. The Cowells are a minor house at best. Alicia McCray is quite the coup, though. She's not a very social creature, from what I understand. And from what I hear from Madame Beamis's shop, you caught the brother's eye, as well. So perhaps your strategy is more appropriate to the situation."

"Or it could be that showing kindness is the right thing to do," I pointed out. "And sometimes, good things come out of that."

"Yes, very amusing, dear," she said absently, glancing over my vanity. She picked up a sheaf of scribbled, ink-blotted papers I'd abandoned before bed the night before. "What is this?"

"A formal thank you note, to Gavin McCray. He sent me that beautiful arrangement of flowers, but everything I write comes across too flirtatious or too bland or too self-serving. It just sounds like I'm trying to ingratiate myself to him, and I get the feeling he sees too much of that already."

"That sounds like a noble intention, Cassandra," she told me.

"Thank you."

"But utterly stupid," she added. When I squawked indignantly she said. "You *are* trying to ingratiate yourself with this boy, whether it's for the purpose of personal gain or romantic interests. Just remember the Golden Rule of Flirtation, 'Dignity before flattery.'"

"And what does that mean?"

"You can pay him compliments. Ask him about his interests. Make him believe that you find him to be terribly interesting. But don't ever, *ever* let him think that you are scrambling to catch his notice. Don't lose your dignity, while flattering his. He will lose respect for you. And then the game is lost."

I sighed. "I planned on saying, 'thank you for the flowers. I think you are a lovely person.'"

"And that is why you need my help. Take out a sheet of paper. I will dictate the note for you. Consider it a tutorial."

"Do you really think that's necessary?"

"Lest you forget an important entry on the House charts you were supposed to memorize, Gavin McCray is the scion from a fine old Yorkshire family that has scores of money tied up in potion supplies. Herbs, exotic animal parts, that sort of thing. He is interested in dragonboat racing, collecting rare ritual swords, and of, course, geology."

"And once every six months, he covers himself in marmalade and howls at the full moon," I added in Mrs. Winter's bouncy narrative tone.

"Well, if it happens to come up in conversation, be sure to mention that you happen to know of the most charming shop in town that carries an array of extra-moisturizing marmalades."

I snickered.

"Mr. McCray's uncle is on several important committees. It wouldn't hurt to encourage a connection between the families."

"I understand," I said, nodding as I took out a sheet of paper and prepared my pen. "But I think I can do that without marmalade discussions, for now."

PAINFUL LESSONS

*C*ith my invitations unfulfilled and a polite, but *warm*, note sent to Gavin via messenger, Mrs. Winter had me spend a good portion of my Saturday practicing my scrying penmanship, tracing letters over the mirror with the tip of Wit while concentrating on a mental image of Mrs. Winter's face. Trailing letters of golden light sputtered to life on her hand mirror, uneven and barely legible. By bedtime, I was able to manage, "somewhat more readable than chicken-scratch," which I took as a compliment.

On Sunday afternoon, I wandered out into the garden to spend some time with the Mother Book. For the past two days, I'd procrastinated, reading the journal of Calpernia McCray instead. It was comforting, reading the thoughts of another Translator, knowing that she saw it as a bit a burden along with the excitement of discovering new magic.

"It's a lonely life, seeing what no one else sees, knowing that no one else living experiences what you do," she wrote. *"Without the comfort of my friends, I would go quite mad."*

I smiled, thinking about how Calpernia's own descendant was keeping another Translator from going quite mad. I would have to come up with some sort of thank you gift for sharing this journal with me. Maybe Mrs. Winter would allow me to ask Mum for a batch of raspberry thumbprint cookies.

Calpernia didn't just write about the Mother Book. She shared funny descriptions of parties she attended, of her life at home with her husband, Liam, and her children. And while she had nothing to say about owl sigils or how to get hostile family members to stop hating you, she indirectly recommended the exact same thing Miss Morton had, stop *trying* to Translate the book and just let it happen.

So now, I sat on the bench by the statue of Hecate, closed my eyes and enjoyed the warmth of the sun on my face. The book was open on my lap, my dragonfly's wings barely touching the pages. I was applying Miss Morton's recommended medita-tion techniques, but honestly, it was exhausting, sitting there, thinking of *nothing.* Not worrying about my family at home or who might figure out that I wasn't who I said I was. Not mentally listing all of the things I had to do that day. Not ques-tioning why I had magic in the first place.

Phillip tittered as he perched on my right hand. My drag-onfly warmed immediately, a signal I'd come to recognize as my magic responding to my call. My mind cleared. That same warmth spread to my arm, through my chest and up to my head. Without being told, I knew I was safe. I didn't need to worry. I had purpose. For the first time in months, I felt my whole body relax. My magic *flexed* and filled the empty spaces inside me, the doubts I had about myself, the confusion I still felt about my family, all of the worries I had about school and the book and the Coven Guild.

I opened my eyes, expecting to see an empty page. But it was filled with a detailed, horrifying illustration of a dead man, shambling down a street in tattered clothes. His face was skele-tal, the skin sagging around a drooping jaw. His eyes were hazy and blank, but his hand was raised, as if he was reaching for me. I yelped and dropped the book on the bench.

"Dash it all, book, I thought we were becoming friends," I whispered, pressing my palm to my thundering heart.

I skimmed over the page now labeled "Revenants." Revenants appeared to be the undead creatures Alicia described in her story about the Grimstelles. They were humans, once living, who had been raised by a necromancer to do his or her bidding. Revenants had no will of their own, the book said, only the direction of their master, repeating over and over in their just-barely-active brain. The brain *had* to be intact for the creature to move. If the brain stem were destroyed, the creature would drop to the ground, harmless. Another way to remove the enchantment was to pierce the creature with a birchwood stake. Birchwood purified, removing the ill-intent of the necromancer.

"That is disgusting," I muttered. More than ever, I was glad that the writing in the book was only recognizable to me.

A portion of the page was left untranslated. I supposed this was the spell necessary to raise a Revenant? I was grateful not to know. It seemed like a good idea to limit the number of people who knew how to raise the dead. I did not want to know what Mr. Crenshaw and his committee would do with this information.

There was more text, about the length a Revenant could stay "active," what personality types made the most effective Revenants. I was fairly certain that Guardians knew that Revenants were dangerous and all-around disgusting. Still, it was the largest portion of text I'd translated so far. And it came with an illustration. I considered this progress.

"That can't be my little Sarah."

I turned to see a tall, burly figure silhouetted against the sunset. His hair was more grey than gold now, the thick, blond hair Mary inherited barely recognizable in its windblown state. His broad shoulders were stooped by age and disappointment.

His broad face, with its prominent brow and capillary-webbed nose, was weathered and permanently sunburnt.

"Papa," I sighed, closing the book and standing with relative ease. I stopped myself from throwing myself at him, remembering Mary and Mum's reactions. But he stumbled forward, wrapping his arms around me and crushing me to his barrel chest. His scent, the earthy mix of fresh-cut grass and sour old whiskey, hit me full force, and I buried my face in his rough green jacket.

"Oh, sweet girl," he whispered into my hair. "I've missed you."

"I'm so sorry, Papa. They won't let me see you."

"I know, I know. Can't fight the Guardians. I know." He pulled away from me. "Just look at you, dressed up so fine. I'm so proud of you."

Papa looked down and winced, dabbing at a streak of dirt he'd left on my skirts.

"It's all right," I told him.

He kept dabbing.

"Papa, it's all right. Stop. Don't waste our time together worrying about my dress."

He nodded. He pulled me to a nearby bench and we sat down. He kept his hands clamped in mine. "I'm sorry that we didn't tell you about all those things you can do. I wanted to, but your mother said it would be better for you if we just pretended you were normal."

He stammered, looking up at me with panicked eyes. "Oh, honey, I didn't mean it that way."

I nodded, my brows drawing close together. "I know."

I saw him patting at his pocket, where his flask would usually be. Where was it? Had Mum taken it? I gave a pained smile. "It's all right. I'm not normal. It doesn't hurt my feelings."

He glanced down at the dragonfly mark, glinting in the sun. "Are they treating you nice? Your Mum said you had some sort of tea party? Did you have a good time?"

"Oh, sure. I was a smashing success. Made a big impression. I think I made some friends."

"Well, that's nice. Just look at you. I've never seen you looking so healthy or so fine. Living with the Winters is good for you."

"It has its good points," I conceded. "But I've missed you so much. You and Mum and Mary. I feel so alone, and I never know if I'm doing the right thing. In fact, I'm sure I'm doing the wrong thing most of the time. I just, I miss you so much."

"I told you, you were meant for greater things than serving, Sarah," Papa said. "I just keep wondering, what if we'd let you go sooner? What if we'd given you over to the Winters when you were born? We discussed it, you know. Maybe it would have been better for you. You would have grown up as a little lady, without those poisons in your system. It would have been right."

"What are you talking about? Why would you even think about that?" I demanded as my father clutched my cheeks between his weathered palms. "Please, just explain this to me."

"Cassandra, Mother is asking for you." I turned to find Owen standing behind us, frowning. There was no disapproval in his expression, only conflict. He didn't want to interrupt this moment with my father. However, from the way he kept glancing over his shoulder, toward the house, it was clear that he didn't want to disappoint his parents, either. "Smith, I believe Mother mentioned giving you the rest of the afternoon off. She said you haven't been feeling well."

"What is he talking about?" I asked.

"It's nothing," Papa assured me. "Just a little tired is all, from getting the grounds ready for winter."

"Owen, could you please give us a moment?"

"Mr. Owen," my father reminded me in a tone that was more habit than anything else.

"It's all right, Smith. She's allowed," Owen said blithely. Suddenly, my father's posture straightened. He jumped to his feet and stepped away from me. The distance between the two of us grew to an impassable gulf. Owen's words had served as yet another reminder that I was separate from my father, from my family.

"I don't want you to worry about us," my father told me. "I want you to make the most of this. You've always been meant for more than I could give you."

"Papa, no."

"I'm not saying this because I want you gone. I love you more than anything in the world, which is why I'm telling you to do whatever you can to make Mrs. Winter happy. You go to that school, and you learn as much as you can. You make a life for yourself out in the Guardian world. You forget you ever came from the Warren." He tapped a finger over my heart. "They're never going to change what's in here."

Papa nodded to me, a little bow that seemed unnatural and wrong. "Be a good girl. Make us proud. I'll give your mother and sister your love."

"Papa." I stood and tried to follow as he strode out of the garden, but Owen caught me around the arms and dragged me back.

"Don't. It was hard enough for him to walk away from you. Let the man do it with a little dignity."

I wilted, closing in on myself until Owen gently dropped my weight onto the bench. He sat beside me, keeping his arm around my shoulders. "Are you all right?" he asked.

I shook my head. "I know I call you 'horrible' on a regular basis, but sometimes, you can accidentally be a very good friend."

"Nonsense, I just didn't want you swooning and smacking your head on the bench." He cleared his throat and moved toward the house, but seemed to stop himself. "Well, I heard that you are making great strides as Mother's show pony. She said you were 'an unqualified success' at the social. You even managed to get Gavin 'This Milquetoast is Too Spicy' McCray to take notice. Congratulations."

He held out an envelope addressed to me in the messy loops I recognized from the card with Gavin's "flowers." Grinning, I reached out to snatch it from him, but a smirking Owen held it out of my reach. "Secret love letters exchanged with a man you are not related to by marriage *or* blood? Explain yourself, young lady."

"All I did was show some kindness to his sister and he sent me a 'thank you' present. It's hardly a betrothal. Besides, your mother knows about the correspondence and fully supports it."

"You made a friend of the Ghost?" he exclaimed. "You really did have a busy afternoon."

"Don't call her that." I scowled as I kicked him lightly in the shin. He yelped and bent slightly. I grabbed the envelope out of his hand. "Alicia's very kind, and funny. And smart. I would be lucky to have her as a friend."

Brandywine House Sigil

Owen frowned at me while he rubbed his sore shin. "I'm sure she is, it's just that she's always so shy. And with her pallor, it's like watching a wraith moving through a crowd, sipping tea. It's unnerving."

"Ivy said she'd always been unwell. I thought you Guardians had Healers for sickly dispositions."

He frowned, shaking his head. "She's an unusual case in that she has survived as long as she has. Reverb patients rarely make it past their twelfth birthdays. I imagine it's only the wealth and resources of the McCrays that have sustained her so far."

"That poor girl."

"Indeed. She could use a friend like you."

"A friend like me?"

"Someone who will understand what it's like to be unusual, to be weak."

"But I'm not weak anymore," I reminded him, making him grin at me.

"No, you're not, and with any luck, one day Alicia won't be, either."

I smiled, nudging him with my elbow. "That's very sentimental of you."

"Nonsense. I just want her do-gooder brother to stop moping about the school, being all broody and noble about the sacrifices he makes to care for his sister."

"There's the Owen I know and... I don't like very much to be honest."

The heretofore unknown flinty tone in my voice made Owen smile for some perverse reason. "I don't remember you being this prissy before."

Despite myself, I snickered. "It's the gowns. They've crushed the humor right out of me. No wonder all your Guild women are so cranky."

"Just wait until you have to wear the full ladies' get-up, you'll be positively insane with rage."

"You really are just horrible, aren't you?"

"And proud of it," he said, beaming and yanking on one of

my curls. I growled and kicked him in the shin. He gasped in mock offense and yanked a different curl.

"Children." Mrs. Winter's voice floated, smooth and cool, over the expanse of lawn. "If you are quite finished, dinner will be served in an hour."

The pair of us straightened immediately, hands behind our backs, stifling our chuckles as we tried to appear the image of proper Guardian innocence. "Yes, ma'am."

"We'll be right in, Mother," Owen assured her. Mrs. Winter nodded, though there was a small worrisome line creasing her brows. The moment she disappeared back into the house, we burst out laughing, with Owen knocking my ankle with his boot and me bumping his hip with the cumbersome bustle on my gown. But rather than letting me stumble, he kept his hand at my elbow, keeping me upright as we struggled our way to the door like two squabbling children.

In the jostle, I glanced up at a bedroom window on the second floor. And I saw Mary, staring down at us with contempt so bright and hot, that I was surprised the window glass didn't melt. I stopped in my tracks, my laughter dying on my lips as I tried to find some way to tell Mary that I was sorry, that we were only letting off steam from a stressful day, that Owen didn't think of me that way. Owen was my friend, just a friend, someone who was helping me find my way in this confusing new life I was living.

Owen stopped when he realized I wasn't following him into the house. He turned, a concerned expression crinkling his mouth. "Cassandra?"

"I'm just waiting for Phillip," I said, smiling absently as I held out my hand for my familiar. The little bird chirped brightly, swooping up from the bench to take his rightful place on my finger.

I glanced up. Mary shut the curtains with a snap, shutting out the pointless apologies I couldn't even make from this distance.

14

DEADLY SERIOUS

$\mathcal{B}$ack at school, more and more pages of the Mother Book were translating themselves. It seemed that asking the Mother Book to come out of "hiding" had opened a channel of communication between us. Information on potions to recuperate after a long illness, a spell to clean water that has been fouled, and oddly, the most effective method of banishing a malevolent spirit into the beyond. I wrote letters, charmed only to be read by a member of the Winter household, detailing what I'd learned for Mrs. Winter. It seemed the best way to report my Translations to… whomever was supposed to supervise me, who wasn't Mr. Crenshaw.

Calepernia McCray's journal had no information to offer about Revenants. She did state that were some things that she learned from the book that she never shared with others, that there was some knowledge that was too dangerous to share, or too frightening. I believed it was reasonable to list walking corpses under "too dangerous" *and* "too frightening."

I spent hours in the library looking for any information on

revenants, but the card codex produced nothing on revenants, the walking dead, necromancy, or the Grimstelles. Apparently, gently bred young ladies did not need to learn about animating the living dead.

Miss Morton couldn't have been more pleased, both with my long hours in her library and my throwing myself in Translating. She pushed me to spend every spare moment with the book, even when the late nights left me tired and listless in class. She said it was important, to the magical community that I learned as much as I could from the book. After all, there hadn't been a Translator in more than one hundred forty years.

Drummond House Sigil

As tired as I was, the more time I spent with the book, the better my classroom performance. My spells accomplished what they were supposed to, levitating objects at will, instead of at random. I stopped blowing up geodes in crystallography. I caught on to the ritual dances, though I still wasn't as light on my feet as Alicia, when she was well enough to join in class. Ivy's theory was that because I wasn't trying to force it, my magic was cooperating more. Suddenly, magic was more than a game, a challenge to see what I was capable of. I could help people, children like Alicia who were born with compromised systems. Maybe I could help her find a cure for her reverb if I kept studying.

More and more of my classmates were being friendly to me, despite being on Callista's dreaded "black list" of students that she'd cut socially. After a heartfelt apology to Blanche Ironwood, she helped me with my grip on the arrows, so I hit the target instead of my belomancy classmates. Charlotte Rasmurti, who was president of her class, joined Ivy, Alicia and me at our dining hall table one morning for breakfast. And before we knew it, the table was full for every meal. Jeanette Drummond, a lovely girl with quicksilver eyes and hair so dark it seemed to absorb the light around her, invited me *and Ivy* to an after-curfew gathering in her room, where about a dozen girls ate sweets and talked about their families, classes, the latest newspaper serial causing a scandal – normal girl things. Alicia joined us, but she fell asleep just a few minutes after the first toffee was unwrapped. Ivy and I tended to linger at the outside of the group, hearing much and saying little, but it felt wonderful to be included. Charlotte's group and Jeanette's group were both different than Callista's. There was no agenda, no back-biting. We didn't have to safeguard every word we said, though I did anyway for obvious reasons. We didn't have to worry about the girls' alliances shifting, just because we didn't do every little thing just as we were asked.

I walked down the hall to my classes and I was greeted merrily by familiar faces and some girls I couldn't even name. I was accepted. I was part of a crowd, instead of standing out. I felt at ease.

For the first time since I'd arrived at Miss Castwell's, I truly thought I had a chance of making a home there.

So of course, the moment I dropped my guard, I was almost immediately attacked.

I was sitting in the garden, enjoying what was sure to be the last of the tolerably cool late November days before winter dug its cold claws in. The weak morning sunlight filtered through the bare tree limbs. I shivered into my green wool coat, grateful for the thick blanket that cushioned me from the cold ground. The fresh air and isolation from the other girls was just what I needed to clear my mind. Just being near so many plants made me feel better.

Ivy was busy with a remedial poppet-making class, and Alicia considered sitting outside in the cold to be a patently stupid way to spend an afternoon. Even Phillip had elected to stay inside on his nice warm perch, eating seeds and laughing at his silly mistress in some silent bird manner.

I was sitting on a blanket under an ancient birch tree on the back lawn, that the students called the Weeping Tree, because it was supposedly where generations of girls went to cry out their broken hearts. My heart was intact, but my brain seemed to be a bit wobbly. The long hours of studying and working with the book were catching up to me.

With final exams approaching in a few weeks, I was spending almost as much time with my potions textbook as I did the Mother Book. Calpernia McCray strongly advised against this, warning that too much time with the Mother Book drained her of her magic and weakened her physically. I told myself that it would only last until finals and the holidays were over, and then I would coast on my good grades through spring – unlike those poor seniors who were facing winter finals *and* the Spring Interview.

And potion making was still difficult for me, because potion ingredients did not behave like kitchen ingredients. They had to be mixed in a precise, detailed manner under certain phases of the moon with certain tools. I had always been what Mum had called a "pinch of this, dash of that" cook, which meant my potions mark was average – and that was only because the teacher, Miss Guiry, was very kind.

I closed my eyes and leaned my head back against the rough bark of the tree, running over the various formulas in my head. *Ground scarab shells mixed with the juice of a floating fig, warmed gently over a driftwood fire for a shrinking draught. Chopped smoking dragon roots combined with minced winter garlic and sea salt for a poultice to treat magical burns. Clippings from a chimera's claws... Well, they exploded no matter what you mixed them with.*

I shuddered. I needed a break, something pleasant to focus on. I drew a piece of elegant stationery from my reticule, creased and limp from being opened so many times. Gavin McCray had taken to writing to me every few days. First in response to the thank you note I'd sent, and then I wrote a thank you in response, and then we got pulled into a sort-of endless thank you note cycle that turned into regular correspondence. He was incredibly intelligent, but single-minded when he was focused on a project. He got incredibly annoyed when the board of directors for McCray Energy insisted that he attend meetings to approve that budget or this hiring. He worried for Alicia and her health. He worried about his mother, who felt she needed to keep up the family's social commitments, even as she grieved the husband she'd lost only two years before. He was annoyed with his classmates, Owen in particular, who didn't seem to take schooling as seriously as he did.

"Most of the time, I feel like I control nothing at all. I feel unprepared and old before my time all at once," he wrote in his latest missive. *"I have all of the responsibilities of my father, but am given none of the respect. I'm supposed to be the head of my house. I'm responsible for keeping the family business on track, but am expected to be the respectful student at school. I am father and son and student and employer and I confess the constant rotation of hats leaves me with a headache some days.*

And now, while moving through these roles, I find myself wondering, 'What would Cassandra think of this design for a long-range crayfire engine?' or 'What would Cassandra think of this journal article on athame metallurgy?' I blame Alicia, who brings you up at every possible opportunity. 'Cassandra prefers herbalism to dance.' when she's trying to avoid lessons with her dance master. Or 'Cassandra never eats soft-boiled eggs.' at break-fast. Or 'Cassandra says it's easier to do your homework with a plate of shortbread.' I've learned more about you from my sister than from five letters from you. You are remarkably elusive with anything resembling personal information. Perhaps I will be better at extracting information from you in person. I received the invitation to the Winters' annual masquerade ball. I very much look forward to at least one dance with you, where I will attempt to interrogate you about your favorite plants and preferred breakfast foods.'

I'd been trying to compose a response for two days. But sadly, Gavin was right. Most of my letters consisted of asking him questions, or repeating the scant details of the origin story Mrs. Winter had given me. I deflected. I obfuscated. I was apparently not as good at hiding it as I thought I was.

How could I answer his questions about my family? About my childhood? About the places I'd been? I didn't want to pile lies on top of lies. But I couldn't exactly tell him about my father the gardener or my house in Rabbit's Warren. I couldn't tell him anything real.

I sighed, staring out over the lawn as if I could read answers in the flower beds. I heard a strange shuffling behind me. I turned to see Tom, the Ward groundskeeper, ambling toward me, arms outstretched as if he was reaching for help. His face was pale as cheese and his mouth was sagging, like he was on the verge of being ill. I'd seen my own father stumble about like this, just moments from losing his breakfast after a night out at the Warren pub with his friends.

I tried to tamp down my irritation. I was not about to help an inebriated Tom pull off his boots and fall into bed, as was my assigned task when my family dealt with my father.

"Tom? Are you all right?" I asked, standing and backing away from the tree.

But Tom didn't answer, still shuffling towards me with that slow, determined pace. His eyes were wrong somehow, the usually bright blue irises drawn back to his eyelids, leaving yellowed orbs in their wake.

Could he be ill? I'd heard of fevers that left people with yellowed eyes and delirium. I would feel terrible if I'd mistaken malaria for Tom being hungover. Then again, I didn't think I wanted him touching me, either way. Want did he want from me? Did he want help? Did he want to hurt me? I glanced toward the school dormitory, but I was too far away to call for help and with the afternoon light, most of the shades were drawn.

There was no expression on his face, just blank, hungry intent. I lost my grip on the Mother Book and my potions text, dropping both to the ground. The thick hedges behind me prevented a retreat. I could dash around him, I supposed. I was wearing sensible walking shoes, but there was no way I could run in these skirts without tripping over them. Then again, Tom didn't seem to be moving very quickly. A phlegmy wheeze escaped Tom's slack lips, a death rattle.

I froze.

Tom wasn't sick. Tom was *dead*.

Tom was a Revenant. Someone had raised Tom from the dead and sent him after me. Had they killed poor, sweet Tom or had he simply died conveniently in some accident and the Necromancer took advantage? A Necromancer. We had a Necromancer on the grounds of a girls' school. How did that happen? No one was supposed to know how to *do* this anymore.

Movement now. Questions later. I felt in my sleeve for my blade. On the one occasion where having a nine-inch dagger on my person would be incredibly helpful, I'd left Wit in its purifying salt bed in my room.

"Don't come any closer!" I exclaimed, trying to put as much authority into my voice as possible.

I was alone. No one was going to help me. Eying Tom's movements carefully, I gathered my skirts in my hands and planted my feet in preparation to dodge. I could hear blood pounding in my ears and heat humming under my skin. I would get around Tom. I had to move as fast as my feet would carry me back to the school building and to Headmistress Lockwood's office. Surely, she had some weapons in there.

Tom's mouth dropped open and the dank, sour smell of new mulch hit my nose like a slap. I retched, pressing my hand over my mouth. He reached toward me, his limp fingers barely passing within two feet of my shoulder as I ducked around him and the tree and ran for the building.

Unfortunately, that two-foot radius was just enough to grab a hank of my hair and jerk me back with shocking strength. I stepped on my own hem, sending me sprawling on the grass. Kicking loose from my tangled skirts, I tried to crawl away, but Tom's hands closed around my shoulders, shoving me into the ground.

I was going to die. Killed by my own skirts.

"Get away from me!" I yelled. His pale lips parted over his teeth, and he let loose a rasping grunt. His cold fingers closed around my throat and began to squeeze. I shrieked, clawing at his wrists. Squirming against the grass, I tried to roll away, but Tom's grip was too tight.

I reached up, pushing at his shoulders, anything to get him away from me. I felt heat, strong and thick, spreading from the metalwork on my hands, burning through the material of my dress. The smoke spiraled up around Tom's face, but he ignored it, wholly concentrated on squeezing the breath from me.

I tried to pull the thick rope of heat back into my hands, away from Tom's body, but as my lungs burned for air, I felt a final push from within my heart and against Tom's shoulders.

"Please," I wheezed, letting that wave of energy loose up my arms and through my hands, against his shoulders. The metal dragonfly vibrated with panicked, angry energy, warming my hands through.

A bubble of white heat exploded around us. Tom was thrown

off of me, and I rolled, stumbling to my feet, tripping over my skirts. I crawled on my knees, kicking off the thick material, winding around my ankles. Something pale brushed against my hand. A branch about the thickness of my thumb. I grabbed it, just as I felt Tom's weight drop on my back. Again, his cold hands wrapped around my neck and squeezed. Gasping, I pushed against the ground with all of my might and squirmed onto my back. In the process, the branch snapped into a jagged point.

Birch purified.

I jabbed the branch into Tom's hand and he lost his grip. I rolled onto my back. For the briefest moment, Tom's eyes went clear and focused on my face. The expression on his face was so frightened that it might have broken my heart if not for his continued efforts to strangle me. With all of the strength I had left, I stabbed the branch into Tom's neck.

Suddenly, a burst of blue-black smoke rolled out of his mouth and his body went slack, dropping to the ground beside me. I laid still on the cold ground, trying to count the body parts that didn't hurt. There weren't many.

I closed my eyes. I owed my life to a stick. Ridiculous.

I wasn't sure how long I lay there, cold and exhausted, the clouds rolling overhead. Tom was still and quiet beside me.

"Miss Reed? Are you all right?"

I looked up to see Miss Morton, standing over me, her head tilted to the side. She seemed to be looking around me, perhaps searching for signs of life from Tom? I lifted my head far enough to inspect the ground around me. "I'm not sure."

Miss Morton crouched over me, reaching for my books. I scooped them up quickly, but I let her help me to my feet.

"What's happened here?" she asked. "Is that Tom? What did – Did he attack you?"

I sat up slowly. "Yes, but I don't think he was entirely under his own power, Miss Morton."

"What happened?" Miss Morton asked, tsking as she

inspected the raw spots on my neck. "You must tell me every-thing, so I can help you."

"I'm not sure," I said, hissing as her fingers prodded my bruises. "I was sitting under the tree, and he just stumbled toward me. He tried to choke me. But I think… I think he was dead, Miss Morton."

Miss Morton frowned. "Oh, no, Cassandra, that's not possi-ble. You were just frightened."

"Miss Reed? Miss Morton?" Headmistress Lockwood's voice snapped from across the lawn. I whipped my head towards her voice and immediately regretted it. My neck was tender. Her steely eyes went wide at the sight of Tom's body. Miss Morton dropped her hands and backed away from me immediately.

"What has happened here?" Headmistress Lockwood demanded. "Cassandra? Are you all right?"

Miss Morton put an arm around me. "Tom attacked Miss Reed."

Headmistress Lockwood peered down at the body and immediately began shaking her head, so hair that her hair shook loose from its prim bun. "Impossible. He's been dead for a day or more," the headmistress said, examining his hands. "You see the blue-black tinge along his fingernails? That's a sign of poisoning, mostly likely fungal."

"He was walking around," I insisted. "He tried to strangle me."

The headmistress peered down her nose, peeling the collar of my dress away from my throat.

"That's not what happened," she told me. "You're just frightened out of your wits."

"I am not," I shot back.

"To make a man walk after death is the blackest magic there is, Miss Reed. The texts on it were sealed long ago," protested Miss Morton.

"Well, someone has opened them up, because he was on his feet," I said.

"Could it be... a Revenant?" Miss Morton gasped, scrambling back from Tom's body and clutching at her collar in horror.

"Don't be ridiculous, Morton. Pull yourself together. Now, Miss Reed, you don't look well," Headmistress Lockwood informed me, pulling at my cheeks so she could examine the whites of my eyes. "Pale, dark circles under the eyes."

"I was just attacked by a dead person," I noted.

"And clearly you have sustained some head trauma if you think that is the appropriate tone to use with your headmistress," she said dryly. "Have you been sleeping lately?"

"When I'm not studying," I insisted. "I just came out here for a little fresh air."

Headmistress Lockwood lifted a dark brow. "But you still feel tired?"

I nodded.

"I am sure our dear Miss Reed is just concerned about passing her exams." Miss Morton tsked, her spectacles slipping down her nose. "Being a first-year student herself, she has to be nervous about being prepared."

"Well, your devotion to your studies is admirable, but not at the expense of your health," Miss Lockwood told me. "Report to the infirmary and have Nurse Waxwing tend to your bruises and ask her for a valerian tisane. It's a tonic that will help with a more restful sleep. Tell no one of what happened today. I will not have you frightening the other girls with wild tales."

I opened my mouth to protest, but she cut me off, adding. "And tell your familiar to keep a closer eye on you."

"Yes, ma'am."

"You are dismissed," Headmistress Lockwood said. "Miss Morton and I will attend to the body disposal."

"Why do I get the feeling that's not the first time those words have been uttered on this campus?" I sighed as I trudged toward the school building.

After the shock wore off, my body and my magic seemed just

to give out, leaving me bruised and listless. I limped to my room, grabbed the Mother Book from its cabinet, collapsed on my bed and slept, paying no heed to the dirt and grass still speckling my skirts.

Ivy and Alicia were *not amused* by my non-appearance at luncheon, dinner, or breakfast. Ivy undid the wards on my door with embarrassing ease and stormed through, with Alicia at her side.

I lifted my head from the pillow and squinted up at them.

"Where *have* you *been?*" Ivy demanded, hands on her hips.

"Stomach ailment," I said, before dropping my head back to the soft linens, wincing as the sore muscles in my neck twinged.

"A stomach ailment that left grassy bits and mud on your skirts?" Alicia asked.

"A very rare stomach ailment," I mumbled.

"Have you seen Nurse Waxwing?" Ivy asked, opening the curtains. Phillip twittered and darted over to the wash basin on my dresser, as if directing her to bring me a cold compress, too.

"Yes," I groaned, shielding my eyes from the sunlight. Alicia climbed up on my vanity and used her blade to scry a message for the kitchens, asking for tea and toast for three.

"You look just awful," Ivy said.

"I feel awful," I muttered.

"Well, that works out, then," Alicia chirped.

"Is this an elaborate ruse to shirk your semester exams?" Ivy asked. "Because we agreed that if we were going to use elaborate ruses, they would be complicated enough to get all three of us out of our exams."

"Trust me when I say no," I said, rolling to a sitting position. I gasped at the pain in my ribs. Sleeping in a four layers of day dress was not something I would recommend to anyone with nerve endings. Both girls looked at me, expectantly.

I couldn't keep this inside. I was holding on to too many secrets as it was. I couldn't keep this from them, too. And if more people rose like Tom, I wanted my friends to be able to protect themselves. I would make them little reticule-sized birch stakes if it would help.

"Tom the gardener, he tried to hurt me," I said carefully.

"Are you all right?" Ivy demanded, rushing to me and checking me over for injuries. "I don't see any bruising, but that can take hours to develop. Have you told Headmistress Lockwood? Should we write your family?"

"Ivy, Ivy, it's under control, I promise. Headmistress Lockwood is handling it now."

"This just doesn't sound like Tom," Ivy mused. "It's not that I doubt what you're saying, Cassandra, but Tom's always so gentle and quiet. Was he drunk? Under a spell? Maybe someone like Callista put him up to it?"

"It doesn't matter. Tom deserves to be fired!" Alicia exclaimed, a sparking angry glower showing behind her green eyes for the first time since I'd known her. "And the authorities should be contacted *now*. He belongs in a prison. And if Headmistress Lockwood won't take care of it, I'm sure my family knows someone who would. Gavin—"

"Don't write to Gavin!" I exclaimed. "Look, the both of you, calm down. Especially you." I pointed to Alicia, who pouted. "I'm fine. I wasn't seriously hurt. And Tom will not be going to prison because Tom is dead."

Ivy's mouth dropped open. "You killed him? With your magic?"

"No."

"Did you use your athame?" Alicia asked. "That's very dark, Cassandra. You can't work with it again or you risk a terrible curse—"

"I didn't stab him with my blade," I told her, deciding to omit the detail about stabbing Tom with a tree branch, for everyone's peace of mind. "And I didn't kill Tom because he was already dead."

Alicia and Ivy stared at me.

"Did you hit your head, Cassie?" Ivy asked carefully.

"No, I didn't hit my head," I groaned, covering my face with my hands. The dragonfly scraped gently at my cheeks, humming with warmth. "Tom was dead. Walking around, but dead. Committed to choking the life out of me, but dead. I thought he was drunk at first, or sick, but he was dead. And he just kept coming for me and I don't think I've ever been so scared."

And for reasons I didn't understand, there were tears streaming down my cheeks. Ivy scrambled next to me on the bed and wrapped her arms around me. She hugged me tight as Alicia climbed onto my other side.

"I don't know why I'm crying now." I sniffed into Ivy's shoulder. "I made it through the attack and talking to Headmistress Lockwood without blubbering all over myself. It's silly. I'm fine!"

"You were frightened and now you know you're safe," Alicia told me. "You didn't feel safe before."

"Are you sure that Tom was dead?" Ivy said. "Necromancy is a magical skill that died off centuries ago, rightly so. It would take a considerable amount of power to do something like that and I don't think anyone here would be powerful enough to do it."

"I'm sure," I told her. "I don't know who could have raised him or why or if they sent him after me or if it was just a coincidence."

"It's probably something to do with the Mother Book," Alicia said. "I hear people talking when they don't realize I'm around. The girls repeat what they hear at home. Some of the more prominent families aren't thrilled with an unknown girl from a minor house being named Translator. Maybe someone thinks that if they take you out of the equation, the Book will select another girl from one of their families."

"You arrived at the conclusion rather quickly," Ivy noted.

Alicia shrugged.

"Mr. Crenshaw didn't seem pleased with my being chosen,"

I said. "And he does have an owl on the top of his cane. Is it possible he could have some family connection to the Grimstelles?"

"It's possible," Ivy said. "But so many people do. The Grimstelles married into a lot of different houses and then disavowed their roots. It's possible *I* have a family connection to the Grimstelles."

Alicia's lips lifted into a smirk.

"I *don't*," Ivy said, whacking Alicia with a pillow and knocking her over. "I'm just saying the owl cane doesn't necessarily mean anything. He could just be an awful person who likes owls but not you. I think you would do better to focus on some of your enemies at the school."

"I don't have enemies," I protested. Both girls raised their eyebrows this time. "I have people I *disagree* with on a philosophical level."

Both girls were smirking now.

"Oh, stop it, both of you."

The girls snickered and I flopped back on my bed. "What am I going to do?"

"You're going to write to Mrs. Winter and keep her apprised of the situation. You're going to get some rest here in your room. I'll order a tray from the kitchens and we'll eat a light supper and you will feel better," Alicia said. "And we will think on this problem until we come up with a solution."

"And we can camp out here in your room for the next few days while you recover, and help you study for exams," Ivy said. "Your crystallography marks have improved, but you are still horrid with ward construction – my specialty. I can help you there. And Alicia needs help with her potions, where you seem to have gained some ground. See? We can all help each other."

When Headmistress Lockwood arrived to check on me, she was not pleased about all three girls planning to miss classes for one girl's "illness." Ivy observed that if Headmistress Lockwood wouldn't approve of the scheme, perhaps I would heal more quickly if she wrote a letter to her gossipy mother asking for a faster remedy for my bruising. It was the most underhanded, sneaky thing Ivy had ever done. I couldn't help but feel rather proud of her. The girls slept on cots in my room in between sessions in Ivy's rigorous study schedule. She'd built a careful web of study periods centered on our strong academic suits, so we could each help each other. And while they slept on their cots, I studied the Mother Book. Well, I stared at the Mother Book, a small crayfire lamp at my bedside casting a soft blue haze on the pages.

I read and re-read the page on Revenants, grateful that the spells used to make them were still untranslated, because I was not ready to know that. But, given the list of signs on the page – cold, clammy skin, inability to speak, insane strength, moving dead person – Tom had definitely been turned into a Revenant. Stabbing him with the birch branch had been the least violent treatment to release his body from the enchantment.

"Why did this happen to poor Tom?" I whispered to myself. "Who did that to him? What does it mean?"

The book's pages turned to the now-familiar chart of House sigils. The top of the page glowed and rippled down to the minor houses, lingering on the Grimstelle owl. "All right then."

15

MASQUERADE BAWL

I didn't recognize myself.

This strange, beautiful creature standing in the Lavender Room's full-length mirror could not be the creature so spindly just a few months ago that I couldn't lift a vase without help.

Madame DuPont had outdone herself, making my costume for Mrs. Winter's annual masquerade. The ball was the opening event to the month-long Yule social season, and invitations were fought over like small principalities.

I studied my reflection, trying my best not to preen. Surely, nice girls didn't preen. My dress was tailored, to give me the illusion of a figure, with straps around my shoulders consisting of deep purple silk larkspur. The underskirts were a lovely blue with filmy purple overskirts, sewn to resemble dragonfly wings. Martha left my hair down, with the exception of complicated braids at the crown with larkspur woven into them. Combined with the silver filigree mask fashioned into dragonfly wings, I looked like a fairy queen.

Phillip hopped on his perch, chirping with approval.

"Thank you," I told him. "You always know just what to say."

Headmistress Lockwood had kept her word. No one outside of herself and Miss Morton knew about the attack. After I'd written to her, Mrs. Winter promised that she would discretely look into any possible descendants of Grimstelles at the school. But every time I spoke to her, she focused on party details. If I asked about the Revenant situation directly, she changed the subject. I assumed that meant she hadn't found anything... or that what she found was so upsetting she didn't want to tell me. Once she no longer had the party as a distraction, I planned to interrogate her... as much as she would allow me.

After Tom's attack, traversing the social snake pit of Mrs. Winter's circle seemed like child's play. I could not plead a sprained ankle to get out of dancing at Mrs. Winter's holiday ball. She'd made it very clear I would be leading the opening dance, "or else." I didn't want to know what "else" could be.

I carefully moved my heavy purple skirts through my bedroom door and, pulling Wit from my reticule, drew a strong ward symbol over the door, while whispering a spell. Both Phillip and the Mother Book were inside, and after Tom's attack, I wasn't willing to risk either, with so many people in the house.

The party had started twenty minutes before, but I wasn't due to make my descent down the stairs for another three minutes. Mrs. Winter said it was very important to arrive at just the right moment. I stepped out into the hall and listened to the muted music, floating up from the hall, echoing from the ballroom. I could hear murmurs and laughter from the guests in the foyer.

I heard Owen's footsteps behind me. "Cassie, could you help me with this cufflink?"

Owen strode down the hall in full evening dress, his dark red hair topped with ravenfeather mask. While the ladies would go all out, accessorizing their already elaborate ballgowns into proper costumes, most of the boys would be dressed like Owen, proper black tie suits and masks reflecting their house sigils. I wondered why the boys bothered coming to the ball at all, when the ladies were demonstrating solely for each other.

Owen skidded to a stop on the carpet when he looked up. "Odin's ravens!"

"Is it all right?" I asked, peering down at my skirts. "Is there something out of place?"

A lopsided grin tilted Owen's mouth. "Not a thing. I just can't believe this is the same knobby-kneed girl I used to know. You look rather acceptable, really."

"Try not to sound so surprised," I told him as I secured the silver raven cufflink through his sleeve.

We peered over the bannister, at the handsome couples in their elaborate costumes. I recognized several girls I knew from school, but not Alicia or Ivy. They'd promised they'd attend. They were still worried about me. Even though I'd kept quiet about Tom's attack, they'd both noticed my lackluster energy, the stubborn circles under my eyes. I'd promised, that now that we were through the semester's exams, I would recover at Raven's Rest before the spring term.

Alicia claimed I'd tried to usurp her place as the pale, wan member of our little trio. Enjoying myself at this party was the first step in their carefully constructed winter break relaxation plan, which also included sleeping over at each other's houses and long, indulgent afternoons spent eating bonbons and reading age-inappropriate novels.

The Winters always took on extra Snipes to help serve on the night of the Winter ball, to make up for the massive work load. I didn't see any members of my own family. Mum would be busy organizing the dishes in the kitchen. My father was all thumbs when it came to fancy occasions, and was kept far away. Apparently, Mrs. Winter knew better than to put Mary in the same room as Owen in a fancy dress suit.

"Ready for this?" Owen asked.

"No," I told him, but he dragged me toward the staircase anyway. Nearly every face in the crowd tilted towards us as we carefully walked down the stairs.

"Head up, shoulders back," Owen whispered gently. "Smile like I've said something very stupid. That should be easy enough to imagine."

I snickered.

"I said smile, not laugh," he muttered, which only made me giggle more.

"Ladies and Gentlemen, I give you, the Translator, my dear niece, Cassandra Reed," Mr. Winter announced in a formal tone as we reached the bottom of the stairs. The adults in the room burst into polite applause. I smiled and nodded my head in what I hoped was an obliging, but humble, fashion as Owen helped me descend the last few steps. It was surreal, having so many adults applaud us as we stood before them in our finery. I supposed this was what Guardians raised their children to be, small adults before their time. That was something I had in common with Owen. We were dressed as grown-ups, were expected to fulfill adult social obligations, and yet had few adult rights and couldn't expect any for years.

I curtsied, and as I bobbed up, I caught sight of Mary through the swinging kitchen door. She saw me standing there arm and arm with Owen, wearing a beautiful dress, being applauded. If looks could kill, I would be stuffed and mounted in one of Mr. Winter's display cases.

Mrs. Winter, resplendent in a gown configured to look like the white queen chess piece, swept toward me, both arms outstretched. She gave both of my cheeks air-kisses.

"Beautifully done, my dear," Mrs. Winter told me, adding quietly, "Though, snickering while mid-stair was a bold choice."

"Owen started it," I told her.

Owen gasped. "Slander and lies, Mother."

"Children, do behave," she chastised us as we followed her into the ballroom.

"No promises, Mother."

I swallowed an enormous lump in my throat as Owen led me toward the ballroom. It was the most beautiful room in the house, with its mirrored walls, vaulted white ceiling and shiny maple floor, lit with hundreds of wax tapers floating in chandelier formations. It was also completely terrifying, because in a few minutes, I would be expected to dance at the center of that room, in front of everybody. More than ever, I wished I was back in the kitchen, with my family, putting food on trays, where no one could see me, no one could judge me. I was on the verge of living out a Snipe fairy tale... if the tale ended with the Snipe-born princess wishing she could turn back into a scullery maid.

Maybe if I wished hard enough, the Mother Book could make me invisible?

This was not helpful. I needed to focus on the task at hand, waltzing without hurting bystanders. I waved nervously to the girls from school, who seemed to be led around by their own bossy adults. Behind us, the orchestra's master tapped the time against his stand. Owen cleared his throat and smirked just the tiniest bit as he slipped his hand to my waist. Over Owen's shoulder, I could see Mr. and Mrs. Winter, in a very proper dance frame. As the host family, the four of us were expected to dance the opening set. Under normal circumstances, Owen and I wouldn't perform in such a capacity, but an exception was being made so I could be formally introduced to the public as the Translator.

Everyone was staring at us. I couldn't hide. And I was going to have to dance. How was I going to remember the steps? What if I stomped on Owen's feet? Or tripped over my own feet?

"Breathe," Owen told me, his gloved hands folding over mine. "Again, if you pass out, I can't haul you off the floor when you're wrapped up in that much fabric."

"You are an awful person," I sighed.

"But a talented dancer, graceful enough to compensate for even the clumsiest of partners."

"Keep going. I'm going to have Phillip attack your eyebrows while you sleep," I murmured through my smile as the first notes of the waltz rang out.

"Really?" he chuckled. "What else?"

"I'm going to ask the Mother Book how to curse you so you only speak in limerick form."

"And then?"

"I'll charm all of the mirrors in the world to cloud over when you look into them."

"That's harsh," he agreed. "Also, you are waltzing, I might add."

I looked down. My purple-slippered feet were moving in perfect accord with Owen's as we moved in a neat box-step. I was dancing in front of people. A lot of people. I needed to stop thinking of how many people there were, before I lost my step.

Over Owen's shoulder, I spotted Ivy and Alicia. They bounced on their toes, waving and grinning in a very unladylike manner that made me love them more than a little bit. Alicia's mother had dressed her as a pixie, in a light green dress with leaf details and a shiny green mask. Ivy's mother had stuck with the Cowell house colors of purple and tan, and she was a... pile of leaves? The shapeless brown and purple gown did nothing for her and the mask sewn with dull fall leaves. Ivy was still lovely, because she was Ivy, but honestly, I was going to have ask Mrs. Winter to introduce Ivy's mother to Madame DuPont.

I saw Owen's eyes go wide, when he turned and caught sight of Ivy. "Be nice," I told him. "Ivy's a very sweet girl, and she gets enough abuse at school. Don't give the other Castwell girls something to tease her about."

"I am always nice," he protested.

"Do you forget, sometimes, that I'm the same girl who's known you since we were both small children?"

He smiled down at me. "No. I never do."

Thanks to Owen's needling, I got through the dance without injuring anyone. We bowed politely, making room for the guests as they invaded the dance-floor. Despite several invitations, I declined hands offered by several of Owen's Palmer classmates. Or... Owen declined for me as he ushered me toward my friends. We bowed politely, making room for the guest as they invaded the dance-floor. Despite several invitations, I declined hands offered by several of Owen's Palmer classmates. Or... Owen declined for me as he ushered me toward my friends.

"Much too exhausted by her efforts, you understand," he told them breezily. "Move along to some other unsuspecting fellow's cousin, thank you."

Alicia and Ivy pushed through the crush, laughing as we threw our arms around each other.

"How are you?" Ivy asked, eyeing me closely. "I hope you got some rest today before they strapped you into that gorgeous gown."

"I am so glad you're here," I told my friends, hugging them both carefully so I didn't rumple their costumes. Around us, the party ground to life like a wind-up toy. Couples moved in carefully orchestrated patterns. Warm, savory foods were circulated by servants who weren't seen or heard. Violin music and floral perfume and firelight overwhelmed my senses, and I was grateful for this little island of quiet, three people who – even if they didn't know everything about me – wouldn't judge me for not arching my pinky correctly when I drank the oversweet cider punch.

"Yes, clearly, no one in the room likes you," Alicia said, solemnly, in stark contrast to her bright mask. "You have no support. You are making a terrible impression."

"No one likes a sarcastic sprite," I told her.

"I've found that's not the case," Alicia said, shaking her glittering head.

Owen cleared his throat in an almost delicate gesture. "I am sorry, ladies, you remember my cousin, Owen Winter. He's interested in horrid cats that swipe at unsuspecting ladies' ankles from under furniture." I giggled as he nudged me in my ribs with his elbow. "Owen, this is Ivy Cowell, who can construct or de-construct iron-clad wards at her whim. She is exceedingly forgiving, even when I accidentally fling arrows at her on the belomancy range. And this is Alicia McCray, who has managed to pack the sarcasm of three Guardian matrons in to one tiny body. In the last two minutes of observing you, she has recorded all of your weaknesses and will use them against you."

"It's true," Alicia said. "You should stop biting your nails; when you are nervous, it's a terrible habit."

Owen's eyes went wide, and he tucked his left hand into his jacket pocket, before he burst out laughing. "Well, now I know why my cousin is so eager to return to school." He bent over each of the girls' hands while they offered him a curtsy. "I see she's found kindred spirits."

"Very nice to meet you," Ivy said, gesturing toward his mask. "That's a lovely representation of the Winter raven. Very... feathery."

"Thank you, and your costume is very... leafy. What is it, exactly?" he asked Ivy.

"I am the spirit of autumn," Ivy sighed, giving me the brief squeeze and waving an exasperated hand at her unflattering gown. "Sometimes, I really hate my mother's seamstress."

Alicia asked her, "Have you set accidental fires when you've visited the dress shop?"

"You know, I think I liked you better when you were silent," Ivy told her, pursing her lips.

Alicia giggled, and bounced on her toes. Owen grinned at their banter. It had to be a refreshing change, I supposed, from the prim and perfect manner in which girls normally behaved in front of him.

"It's not that bad," Owen tried to tell her. "The foliage is, er, really quite lovely."

"Thank you for trying," she told him, blowing a stray curl out of her face.

But even with the newfound spirit that had helped Ivy sass us, she seemed to wilt as Callista approached, dressed in a scandalously cut Queen of Hearts costume, and pointed openly as Ivy's costume, whilst snickering to Rosemarie. Callista threw a meaningful wink towards Owen. Simultaneously, Alicia and I circled our arms through Ivy's, but Owen surprised me by doing more to defend her than we ever could.

"Would you care for a dance, Miss Cowell?" he asked suddenly, turning and offering her his hand.

Ivy's mouth fell open, but she recovered quickly. "Ye-yes, thank you. That would be lovely."

Owen smiled and led her out to the dance-floor and led her in a gentle quadrille. Ivy glowed as she moved, showing more grace than she ever had in our dance classes at school. Across the room, I saw her grandmother, Mrs. Dalrymple, watching Ivy with perplexed expression. She nodded to me. I curtsied.

"That was very kind of your cousin," Alicia noted.

"Yes, well, Owen, doesn't do anything with just one motive." I nodded to Callista, who was giving Ivy and Owen a sour look from the sidelines. "Asking Ivy to dance means that he doesn't have to dodge Callista. Or any of the more dangerous females present. And it earns his mother some cache with Mrs. Dalrymple, who is watching from the settee, very pleased. Overall, it's a coup for Ivy and Owen. Very clever of him."

"Underhanded sneakiness? In a Winter? Surely, you jest," she gasped.

I laughed, but it was covered by the tinkling silver of Alicia's giggles.

"Well, isn't that the loveliest sound in the world?"

I turned to find a tall boy I recognized as Gavin, even wearing a golden mask with plaster flames threading into his dark hair. He grinned at his sister. "The elusive Miss Reed."

I couldn't help but grimace, the tiniest bit, and I forgot to curtsy. It was not my best moment, re-introduction-wise. He reached for my hand anyway and bowed over it without actually kissing my skin, which I appreciated. "The effusive Mr. McCray."

"I believe I've been promised a dance," he said.

"Did I promise?" I asked, even as I took his offered hand. I couldn't help but notice that the dragonfly on my palms seemed to flutter its wings, sending a thrill of warmth that ran up my arm to my heart. Gavin stopped, staring down at our joined hands with an expression of surprise. The dance was a Schottis-che, a slower polka-type dance meant to help encourage harmony between warring families. I couldn't help but appreciate the hint Mrs. Winter was giving to her guests, "behave in my home or be thrown out of it." Unlike the waltz, which had put me in constant eye contact with Owen, the Schottische was danced side-by-side, with Gavin's arm around my waist. And while I'd been reasonably comfortable, standing so close to my "cousin," dancing with Gavin had heat prickling under my arms. I worried that he would be able to feel how sweaty my palms were against his.

"You seem tense," he noted.

"Well, I was warned you were planning to interrogate me about breakfast condiments," I told him.

"Alicia informs me that letter was rude, that a lady likes to keep a little mystery about her. And I should be more subtle in my pursuit of information about you."

"Someone should tell Alicia it's rude to read letters I've hidden in my reticule," I told him.

He laughed, a magical sound that send shivers down my arms. "She's attended school for years and never came home with a story about friends or pranks or anything you would hope your sister would experience. Now, however, it's Cassandra this, and Ivy that. She has a spark now that I've never seen in her, and with her health… Alicia's happiness is a priority for me."

I blushed and ducked my head. I couldn't help it. It just happened

"She's done more for me than I've ever done for her," I said. "And I would like to thank you for the journal you lent me. It's been a comfort, knowing what another Translator thought of the book."

"Anything you ever need, Miss Reed, I would be happy to provide."

"Calling me 'Cassandra,' would be a nice start."

He grinned at me. On the other end of the ballroom, I could see Callista dancing with a boy from House Drummond. Even through her mask, I could see her scowling at me. Though I wasn't sure if she was unhappy that Gavin was dancing with someone else or dancing with me, specifically.

"Alicia said you've improved her botany grade by leaps and bounds."

"I've found a carefully balanced system of bribery and shaming works best while tutoring her," I said. I tried to remember Gavin's interests we'd discussed in his letters, but my mind was blank. All I could remember was "extra moisturizing marmalades," and I was *sure* that wasn't it. Why was this so difficult? I talked to Owen all of the time. I *sassed* Owen. Why did I feel like my tongue was tied in knots? How did Mary do this? No, wait, that was the wrong instinct. I didn't like the way Mary talked to boys. A weird silence hung between us as we moved across the floor with the other dancers.

Gavin grinned. "Well, it's fortunate that you live with the head of the Demeter Society. It should make your Spring Interview a bit easier, when your time comes. Or are you planning to apply to some other research guild?"

I looked up and he was looking at me, as if he was trying to read me. Was this question a test?

"I believe Auntie Aneira would be harder on me than any other candidate," I muttered.

An expression of relief made Gavin's face relax and he laughed. "You're probably right."

The dance wound to a close and Gavin bowed before me. "Thank you for a delightful dance, Miss Reed. I can see my sister, standing behind you, bouncing on her toes and waving for me to bring you back to her."

Laughing, I turned to see Alicia's performance, but Mr. Winter stepped in front of me.

"Cassandra, dear, I am sorry, but Mrs. Winter needs you. Party business, you understand. Mr. McCray, I am afraid you must excuse us."

"Of course, Miss Reed, I hope to secure another dance, later this evening." Gavin inclined his head. I remembered to curtsy, but my cheeks had flushed so hot that I had to stare at the polished ballroom floor. "Until then, I'll have to content myself with letting the pixie stand on my feet while we circle."

I might have laughed, but the tight tense lines around Mr. Winter's mouth were making me nervous. I watched Gavin spin his sister out on the floor and then followed Mr. Winter's sedate but determined pace out of the ballroom to his office.

"Is there a problem, sir?" I asked quietly.

"Not sure yet," he whispered. "Just stay calm and remember the backstory Mrs. Winter created for you. Don't cower and don't panic. Use every ounce of that winsome charm you've cultivated. You'll be fine. We're all depending on you."

"That doesn't help with the panicking, sir," I said, removing my mask.

Frowning, Mr. Winter led me into his office. Despite the fire crackling in the grate, the room seemed filled with shadows and men I didn't recognize. At least they'd removed their masks for this little tête-à-tête. They were standing at attention, arms crossed over their chests, not quite scowling as I entered, but they were definitely lacking the pleasant social expressions I was used to seeing.

Mrs. Winter was standing by the fireplace, her hands folded

at her waist. Mr. Crenshaw was sitting at the center of the table, glaring at me. His gloved hand stroked over the silver owl's head topping his cane.

I had a hard time dragging my eyes away from the owl, the symbol of the Grimstelles, as Mr. Crenshaw spoke. "Miss Reed, we represent the Guild committee on antiquities and artifacts. We have assembled here to discuss your progress with the Mother Book."

Could Mr. Crenshaw be the necromancer that sent Tom after me? He'd been unhappy about the way the Mother Book was being handled. Had he decided to take me out of the equation so another more suitable, non-Winter-related Translator could be found?

The room was quiet.

Because I was supposed to be talking.

I glanced at Mrs. Winter, who was seething though a perfectly poised smile. I cleared my throat and tried to pull on a pleasant expression. "Well, that seems like a lovely party game, what are the rules?"

Mr. Winter snorted, covering it with a cough. His humor, and the pride that lit Mrs. Winter's eyes from across the room gave me courage enough to relax my shoulders ever so slightly. Mr. Crenshaw didn't seem to share Mr. Winter's amusement.

"As the Translator, your lack of contact with this committee is unacceptable, Miss Reed," he growled.

"I sent letters to my uncle, reporting what I've learned from the book so far," I said. "Did he not share them with you?"

Mr. Crenshaw bristled. "Yes, of course, but it was hardly the sort of information we expected from the Mother Book, a good deal of it is information we already have. We expect results, Miss Reed. We expect revelations."

I tilted my head, my stare drifting back and forth between Mr. Crenshaw's bloated face and the owl-head cane topper. What sort of revelations was he expecting?

While I pondered this, Mr. Crenshaw continued, "You

should have appeared before us after the book chose you. You do not have the right to keep that information to yourself. Mrs. Winter has failed in presenting you to us. That is a failure we're addressing now."

I took a deep breath. "Am I to understand you chose to interrupt the social event of the season to chastise me for not answering an invitation you never issued?"

Mrs. Winter smiled at me. This was a good sign.

"You should have known to contact us," Mr. Crenshaw said.

"And how would I have known that?" I asked. "There hasn't been a Translator in almost one hundred fifty years. I wasn't familiar with the protocol. I wasn't even aware that such a commission existed until you mentioned it at the school social, which, now that I think about it, was a perfectly polite opportunity to discuss scheduling a meeting – which you failed to do. But I do apologize. The next time an ancient artifact of immense magical power chooses me as its conduit to magical society, I'll be sure to send you a note."

While my back was straight and my tone firm, my stomach was practically twisting inside out. I was sassy-mouthing the very authorities I'd spent so much time fearing. These men could take me away. They could lock me in some Guild Enforcement facility where the Mother Book would be my only company.

But I was so tired of being afraid. All of my life I'd been afraid of people like Mr. Crenshaw. I wasn't that scared little girl anymore. I was powerful. I was the Translator. Magic had chosen me, when it had every reason to pass me by. I wasn't going to be pushed around by a man with a silly cane-topper.

"Young lady, do you understand your position here?" Mr. Crenshaw thundered. "You are a child. A mere slip of a girl, barely schooled. You are not qualified to Translate the text on your own. You need our supervision."

"I understand my position perfectly well, Mr. Crenshaw. I don't understand yours." I told him.

"My position – my position?" Mr. Crenshaw thundered.

"You should know that your selection as Translator is under review. If necessary, we will take the book back from you until we believe you are fit to serve."

"The book chose me, not you. I do not need your supervision. I will provide you with a complete list of spells and information the book has presented to me since I began Translating. Not because I am afraid of your disapproval, but because they could be of help to other people. Now, if you'll excuse me, I am missing a rather lovely party that my aunt and uncle spent quite a lot of time organizing."

Mrs. Winter inclined her head at me and mouthed the words, "Well done."

I spun on my heel and walked out of the room – without a curtsy – while Mr. Crenshaw fumed. But once I got into the hallway, all of my righteous indignation drained out of me. I needed to hide. I wanted to run into the kitchen and cry to my mother. I wanted to eat about a dozen petit fours.

I heard footsteps beside me and I was relieved when Gavin's voice asked, "Are you all right. You're very pale."

"Just a little light-headed," I told him. "This dress is so heavy and the room is rather warm."

"Should I got get you something?" Gavin asked, his hands closing around my arms, much like that morning when he'd hauled me up from the sidewalk. Did he remember that, I wondered dizzily. Why didn't he remember that? "A glass of water? Tea? Alicia always liked peppermint tea when she's ill. I'm at a loss, here, Cassandra."

"No, I'll be fine," I insisted weakly.

"McCray?" Owen's voice sounded behind us. "What are you doing? Cassandra, are you all right?"

Gavin glared at Owen as I gave a small shake of my head. Owen looked around and looped his arm through mine. He said, loudly, just in case some of the guests could hear, "This is what happens when you over-indulge in lemon tarts, cousin. You know you're allergic. Let that be a lesson to you."

I gave him a weak slap on the arm.

"I'll take it from here, McCray. Try the punch." Owen said as he led me into one of the lesser parlors, the room where Mrs. Winter had couriers wait while she wrote correspondence. This was good. Quiet and cool air were just what I needed.

"Why do you antagonize him? He's a nice boy."

"Because he's a nice boy and I can," Owen told me. "Now what's wrong with you?"

Owen closed the door behind us and I bent over the parlor chair as much as I could in my cumbersome gown.

The Mother Book," I whispered. "They say they don't trust me with the Mother Book because they don't know anything about me. They expect *results*. And then I sassed them. I sassed them severely. What if they look into my background? They're going to find out about me."

"Stop," Owen said, giving my shoulders a light shake. "You can't talk like that, not now when there are ears everywhere. Mother will fix it. You'll see. Mother will find some information or some weakness in the men on the commission and she'll exploit it. You are going to be fine. I need you to listen to me. You are going to be safe. I promise. I just need you to take some deep breaths and go back out to the party before the guests start to suspect something is wrong."

I nodded. I just needed a moment of quiet and calm. "Could I have a few minutes to myself?"

"Of course," he said, stepping away from me. "Just a few minutes. I am going to go get you some water. I'll be right back."

I nodded and closed my eyes. I had to keep calm. I had to keep that courage that had me firing back at Mr. Crenshaw as if he had no right to question me. I had to look every inch the confident Coven Guild member. I took deep breaths, commanding my heartbeat to slow. I wished Phillip was here to chirp and coo in my ear. That always seemed to help.

Within moments, someone threw the door open. I turned

toward the noise to find Mary standing there in her black and white maid's uniform, her face purple with rage. I stepped back, hindered by my giant skirts. My fingers fanned out, and I felt a hot energy running down my arms, gathering in the metal on my palms.

"This is your fault," Mary growled at me in a way that had me reaching for my reticule and the blade hidden inside.

I gasped. "What's my fault? Are Mum and Papa all right?"

"If you'd just been a decent sister to me! If you'd just done what I asked! But no, you had to be selfish and steal the life I wanted, the life *I* deserve. I'm the one who should be out there, in a fancy dress, laughing with Owen. I shouldn't be stuck back in the kitchen working my fingers to the bone."

I tipped my head back and rolled my eyes so hard that they ached. After all this, that was Mary's main concern. Owen. My life hung in the balance. Magical society could be at stake. The dead were walking. And Mary was still obsessed with Owen.

"I'm so sick of hearing about your stupid crush on Owen Winter, Mary," I sighed. "There's more happening in the world beyond your doomed, pointless feelings for a boy who doesn't want anything to do with you. But you can't see past yourself. You've never been able to see past what you want, the shiny thing just out of your reach. Well, I'm done protecting you from yourself, Mary. You're just going to have to grow up!"

"Owen loves me."

"Owen's first instinct is to turn around and run away whenever he sees you."

"You're lying."

"Tell me one thing you love about Owen," I asked her. "Tell me one thing about him, that doesn't have anything to do with his money or his looks, that makes you think he's the love of your life."

"He's so… he… well, you can just tell by the way he looks at me that he's thoughtful and kind and courtly," Mary stammered.

"Owen Winter is a lot of things, but courtly is not one of them," I told her. "Owen is kind, sometimes, and he can be thoughtful. But you have to work through a lot of layers of self-interest and sarcasm before he lets you see that. He has no patience for people who only want to be near him because he's a Winter. I know this because I've taken the time to be his friend. Mary, the person you think you're in love with doesn't exist. You've risked us all, you've embarrassed me, made me cover for you when you misbehaved, all because of some fairy tale in your head."

"Well, I'm not the one pretending to be someone I'm not!" Mary practically shrieked. "I'm not a Snipe in Guild Guardian clothing! You think you're one of them, but you're not! You're just like me, Sarah! You're nothing special!"

A sly, new voice asked, "Is that so?"

Over Mary's shoulder, I saw Callista framed in the doorway, a triumphant smile curling her carefully painted red mouth.

"Callista, don't," I said.

"Are you saying Cassandra is a Snipe?" Callista asked Mary, her tone ingratiating as she stepped closer, removing her Queen of Hearts mask.

"Yes, *Sarah* is my sister. We're both Snipes," Mary insisted, shoving her mussed hair back from her face. "We've served Raven's Rest all of our lives, until *Sarah* was sent to your fancy school."

"Mary, be quiet," I said, shoving her back behind me. "Callista, she doesn't know what she's saying. I think she's ill or enchanted. Something is obviously wrong with her."

"I'm not ill!" Mary shouted. "I'm telling the truth."

And for the first time in my life, I struck out at Mary, not with my fists, but with magic. Wit slid out of my reticule, and I drew a symbol for "quiet" with its point.

Mary was thrown against the wall with the force of it, her lips pressed tight together.

While Mary tried to scream through her sealed mouth, I

turned to the door. "Callista, surely, I can count on your discretion. Embarrass me all you want at school, but I don't think you want to cross Mrs. Winter over an incident with a servant. Not when she's put so much work into this ball."

"Well, you and I never have seen eye to eye on social issues." Callista smirked at me. "I believe I need to go talk to some people. Have a lovely evening, *Sarah.*" And with one last triumphant waggle of her fingers, she flounced away.

I whirled on Mary, who was still struggling against the bond I'd put on her mouth.

"What have you done?" I demanded. "All of our lives, Mary, I've made excuses for you. I've tried to cover up your silliness, your recklessness. No more. I can't help you anymore."

I walked out of the parlor and shut the door behind me, sealing it with magic. I walked into the ballroom, but it seemed like I carried some sort of bubble of silence around me. Conversation died as I moved through the room. People stopped talking the moment I approached them. Mrs. Winter was standing with Mr. Winter at the bottom of the staircase, a stricken expression on her face.

"What. Happened?" she spat quietly through her pleasant mask. "You did so well in the office with that dreadful Crenshaw. You were on the verge of redeeming the evening admirably. What happened?"

"Mary," I whispered. "Mary happened."

16

REMORSE AND RETREAT

*D*espite the usual policy of not leaving the Winter ball before midnight, guests started departing the moment I entered the ballroom. It wasn't exactly a stampede, but the elegant party atmosphere fizzled as guests slowly ebbed out the front door. I retired to my room, pleading a headache. I saw Ivy's stricken face as I passed, but I didn't have time to explain.

I laid on my bed, not giving one care for the gown I was wrinkling to oblivion. I would lose Ivy's friendship. Now that she and Alicia knew I was a liar and a fraud, the only two friends who had ever liked me for me would never speak to me again. I found that to be more devastating than the idea that at any moment, the Guild agents could break into my room and haul me away to a secret lab somewhere.

As Martha helped dislodge me from my gown, Mrs. Winter paced and drilled me on the specifics of the incident with Mary, who had already been sacked and told never to return to Raven's Rest. I had no idea what would happen to her. By firing her, Mrs. Winter had guaranteed Mary would never find employment in any Guardian house in the Capitol. Mary would have to leave home to earn a living. She would have no references, which would mean taking a job in one of the lesser circles. At the moment, I couldn't find it in me to give one floating fig.

"Damage control is key," Mrs. Winter said, still pacing. "We must carry on as if nothing occurred, be seen socializing, shopping, attending meetings of the Demeter Society. You should spend time with your friends, before going back to school in January. Everything as planned."

"Yes, I would think that the students at school will welcome me back with open arms, now that they've heard I've been lying to them from the moment we met."

"Are you trying to be funny?" Mrs. Winter demanded as I slipped into a nightgown and sat on the foot of my bed. "Are you trying to provoke me now by being sarcastic and disrespectful?"

I pursed my lips. "No, that would be ungrateful, and I wouldn't dream of that."

"I understand that you are frustrated and upset right now, Cassandra, but we have to present a united front. I have just as much to lose now as you do. We're in this together. I will not let anything happen to you. I know I haven't always shown it, but I have become very fond of you."

I closed my eyes and willed the gathering tears away. I had not expected that. I had come to respect Mrs. Winter as a mentor, but feelings of fondness? I'd never hoped to be anything more than a servant or tool to her.

"And I am certainly not going to let you drag me down with you."

Ah, there was the Mrs. Winter I knew.

Mrs. Winter stood in front of me. "If someone so much as suggests that you are socially inferior, we will not even entertain the ideas as anything but ridiculous."

"How? People surely heard Mary yelling, they had to hear

what she was yelling. You know better than anyone how quickly the rumors will spread. How do you expect to get away with this?"

"The same way I have 'gotten away with this' for the past decade. With determination, stiff spine and with minimal whining. How many times have I told you, Cassandra, if you believe something badly enough, it becomes real."

"Maybe that doesn't work for everybody."

She laid her hand on my shoulder. "It has to work for you."

Martha peeled the blankets back on my bed and I crawled in. Mrs. Winter pulled the blankets up to my chin. "Goodnight, dear."

Martha moved silently out of the room while Mrs. Winter touched the crayfire lamp and turned the light low. She traced the rune for "sleep" in the air, without her blade, but the symbol's purple outline still glowed against the dim light of my room. The outline wafted toward me, losing shape as it became a warm, calming fog that seeped over my bed.

"Thank you, Mrs. Winter."

She nodded and shut the door.

I turned over, punching my pillow into shape and burying my face in it. How would we all survive this? What would happen to me? Or my parents, what must my parents think? One daughter getting the other banned from the only place she'd ever wanted to call home. Would they be angry with me on Mary's behalf? Would Mrs. Winter decide that I was more trouble than I was worth?

I hated Mary.

I didn't think it would be possible, but at this moment, I honestly, truly, hated my sister. As much as she claimed not to resent me for my weakness, for having to watch out for me all of these years, I'd spent just as much time captive to her jealousy, her "sensitivity," her constant need to be assured that she was the prettiest girl in the room, that one day, if she was just patient enough, Owen Winter would be hers.

She's destroyed both of our lives over a boy.

My eyes drifted shut as the calming warmth of Mrs. Winter's spell seeped into my body. I tried to concentrate on the bright spots of the evening, Alicia's excitement, Ivy's face when Owen asked her to dance, Gavin… Gavin McCray was definitely a bright spot.

I shoved the image of Gavin's smile away from my mind's eye. I didn't need to think about Gavin right now. Obsessing over a boy was what got Mary into this state in the first place. I had more important things to worry about than Gavin McCray, like being dissected by Guardian Enforcement. Surely, the possibility of being dissected was more important than some boy's perfect smile.

MY MIRROR REMAINED clean and clear of any messages from Ivy or Alicia.

Mrs. Winter's attempts to brazen her way through the wake left by my disastrous debut were not appreciated by society at large. She sent summons to her usual minions for afternoon tea. They were ignored. Expected invitations to the Benisse's New Year's Eve Ball were not forthcoming. The parlor was silent, empty of callers and messengers. Gavin's regular letter did not arrive, no matter how many times I willed the ringing doorbell to mean a forthcoming note to me.

It was as if Raven's Rest was holding its breath, waiting to find out just how badly Mary's tantrum had impacted us all. Mrs. Winter was so distracted, she'd forgotten to renew the wards on the kitchen after the party, so I was able to walk right through the door and see my mother. I sat at the scarred worktable, struggling to fight the skirts of my lilac day gown under the tabletop. Mum didn't say one word about not being allowed to see me or talk to me. She simply poured me a cup of tea, set some of her blueberry scones on a plate and brought them to the table for me.

While she doctored her own tea with milk and honey, I stared around the kitchen. I couldn't believe how small the room seemed now that I'd spent time in bigger accommodations. How had all three of us managed to work in such a cramped space? But it was nice to see something was still the same. The same old smoke-stained stove. The same copper pots with the ruthlessly scoured bottoms. Mum's special blue-glazed mug that Papa had given her for her birthday.

I did notice that Mum was digging into the scones without one care for them being special "family" teatime treats. That was different.

"How are you?" I asked.

"Frightened," Mum said. "Mary was sent home, the moment she was dismissed. I had to stay to take care of things for the party. When we came home, she was gone. She ran away and no one's seen her since. I didn't want to come to work today, just in case she came home, but your father insisted."

Mum's lip trembled. "We could have found her another position, maybe moved her to another city. South, where my cousins live. Maybe even Wales. But it wasn't the position she was angry about, it was that boy. She couldn't stand the idea of not seeing him every day, while you…"

She paused and took a sip of her tea, cheeks flushing.

Frowning, I tried to find it in my heart to worry about Mary, to wonder where she was, but I was still so angry with her. I could only shake my head.

"Mum, I'm sorry this happened. But Mary made this mess herself, and I can't fix it."

"I know," Mum said quickly. "I know we let Mary get away with too much. We were always so worried about you, and Mary was such a pretty, easy child. I thought if I gave her enough time, she would grow out of her feelings about Mr. Owen. I thought it was just a phase. I never thought it would go this far. What's happened isn't your fault, sweetheart, none of it. I'm sorry I reacted the way I did in the parlor that day. I was just so scared."

"I know," I said. "And I can't say I would have handled it differently, if I were you. I just wish you had told me."

"Well, it wasn't as if there was a handbook for what to do when your child is born with magical powers she shouldn't have."

"Mum, I don't know what's going to happen to me now. There are rumors circulating about me and I could lose this new life I've tried to build before it even gets started. I might be able to come home-"

"No," Mum said firmly, reaching across the table and squeezing my hand. "You were meant for greater things than working in this kitchen until you die, letting some rich family decide what you do with your life. You do your best to stay at that school, finish your education. And if that's not possible, find some other way to make your place in their world."

"But what about my place in your world? With Mary gone, you and Papa are all alone and you've never... You don't... Mum was it my fault? The way we are? You and Papa not talking to each other. Papa's drinking. The distance between us. Is that because I was born the way I am?"

"Oh, sweetheart." Mum's mouth flopped open, but I noticed that she didn't deny it. "Who's to say? Our life isn't easy, knowing that you're never your own person, that there are so many limits. And maybe you being born with magic did push us all apart, but the cracks were already there. I didn't treat you the way I should have, and I'm sorry for that. But no, this isn't your fault. You did nothing wrong. You didn't ask for this."

She stood and leaned across the table to kiss my forehead. "I've never been more proud of you. Not because you're magical, but because you're strong and you're kind."

I swiped at my eyes with my hands. "Thank you."

Mum sat back with a sigh. I gave her a watery smile and sipped my tea.

"Now, can we talk about that mark on your hands?"

I snorted tea into my nose. "I knew that was going to come up."

BY THE SECOND week of December, Mrs. Winter decided that we'd spent enough time moping around the house and that we would show Lightbourne at large that everything was absolutely normal by spending an obscene amount of money shopping. Mysteriously, Madame Beamis's millinery shop was so busy that the clerk couldn't see us in the crowd of four customers to wait on us. There was no table available at Mrs. Winter's favorite tea house. And finally, I knew we were in real trouble when we walked into Swansea's Potioneer Shoppe, and every woman in the store stopped talking.

Mrs. Winter attempted to smile and greet several of her friends, but they glanced around the room for anything to look at but us. I had never seen Mrs. Winter so unsure of herself, so unsteady. It was downright unnerving riding home with her in the silent carriage.

We arrived at Raven's Rest to worse news. We could hear Owen yelling in his father's study from the front door.

"You had to have known it would come to this! You have to tell them something. Surely, one of mother's cousins will vouch for her story, if she puts enough pressure on them. That, together, with whatever paperwork you can get from the forger, should be enough to convince the inquiry committee, shouldn't it?"

Sharing a worried glance, Mrs. Winter and I walked into Mr. Winter's office with its stark grey walls and abundance of bird skeletons. Owen was more riled than I had ever heard him, his hair disheveled and dressed only in his shirtsleeves. It didn't get better when Mr. Winter answered, "Yes, if I can grease the right palms, it should be enough, but Owen, you must accept that while we may come out of this situation, Cassandra may not. Our hopes for her may be nothing but that, dashed hopes."

Mr. Winter stopped speaking when he saw us in the doorway. Mrs. Winter cross the room and slid her arm through his. The gesture was more affectionate than anything I'd ever seen between the Winters, and I found that oddly comforting. Owen was staring at me as I approached Mr. Winter's desk.

"I'm so sorry," I told them. "I'm sorry it's turned out this way. Maybe it would be better if I just disappeared. You could send me to work for some Guardian family overseas. I could leave the book with you and disappear. I wouldn't use magic again." I glanced at my hands and the dragonfly that glimmered there. "I could wear gloves."

"No, we're too invested, now." Mrs. Winter shook her head. "It would look like we have something to hide."

"Which is convenient because we do have something to hide," Owen muttered, and didn't wait to be corrected, adding, "Sorry, I know that's not helpful."

"It is at times like these that I wonder whether I went too far in asking your family to fake your death," Mrs. Winter wondered.

"Just now, at times like this?" I asked. But instead of glaring at me, a beaten Mrs. Winter merely shrugged.

"School," I suggested after a few awkward moments of silence. "The institute accepts borders, girls who can't go home over the winter holidays. I would be safe there, I think. It would give you time to do some damage control."

"A solid suggestion," she conceded.

"They can't stand up to you forever," I told her, my lips twitching. "Eventually those newly minted spines will crumple under the weight of your icy glare."

Mrs. Winter's tone was scolding, though there was the slightest pleased expression on her face. "Oh, honestly, I don't know what you are talking about. You are so silly sometimes."

17

SCHOOL FOR SCANDAL

Gy move to the school was handled quickly and quietly. Miss Morton was the only teacher left at Miss Castwell's over the break, having no family to visit for the holidays. Only a handful of girls remained, a few students from America and some sulky senior girls who seemed to think they were punishing their families by staying away for the season. Miss Morton was thrilled to see a friendly face willing to help her catch up on shelving in the library. Even she'd heard about my "difficulties" at the party and assured me she didn't believe a word of it.

"Obviously, you are a very talented witch, Miss Reed. You have the sort of power than can only come from a strong Coven Guild family line," she said, cupping my chin in her hand. "In a few weeks, some other scandal will pop up and this will all be forgotten. In the meantime, you must restore your balance, build up your energy stores. Meditate over the book and find that peace within. No matter what, you *must* push through your fatigue and spend more time with the Mother

Book. And in the meantime, we'll have a very merry Christmas here at school."

I tried to believe her. I tried to look at my time at the school as quiet vacation, a chance to gather my strength. I joined the small group of students left in the mostly empty dining hall for meals, where a single table had been laid out with tempting spread of holiday treats. I was surprised to find Callista sitting there. I knew that Jeanette Drummond's family was traveling to France to visit distant relatives in Provence, a venture complicated by Jeanette's allergy to lavender. And Helena Mountfort preferred school to the tense atmosphere at home, where her stepmother had redecorated away any evidence that Helena's beloved late mother ever existed. Jeanette and Helena gave me perfectly polite smiles, but immediately turned to speak to each other. Not exactly a snub, but a civil way of avoiding conversation.

But Callista was supposed to be the cherished darling of her family. Why was she here at school? I was tempted to sit down and ask her that very question. But when I took my seat at Miss Morton's right and caught sight of Callista's triumphant grin, I found I didn't care all that much. Clearly, she was enjoying the chaos she'd sewn by spreading what she'd heard the night of Mrs. Winter's party. I may or may not have made Callista's water goblet disintegrate in her hand.

"I think I'll take a tray in my room for here on," I told Miss Morton, as Callista squawked about water spots on her precious dress.

"That may be for the best, dear," Miss Morton nodded, dabbing at Callista's dress with a napkin.

For more than a week, it felt like all I did was sleep, read, Translate and attempt to contact Ivy and Alicia over scry message. Over and over, I ran the tip of Wit on the glass of my vanity, writing out carefully worded pleas for contact, but they never responded. Gavin's pen was also silent; no letters, not even a card that said, "I'm sorry we can no longer be seen in public together." Phillip abandoned his perch and made his home on my shoulder, nuzzling my cheek, making comforting little cooing sounds.

Callista avoided me, which was a refreshing change of pace. After a few days, Jeanette and Helena issued invitations to join them for late-night chats, but I was too tired to stir from my room. Maybe it was the silence and stillness of the school, normally so filled with life and chatter. Maybe it was not knowing what was happening at Raven's Rest. But I felt like my very soul had been drained out of me.

I was listless and couldn't seem to find the energy to do more than crawl back and forth between my vanity and the bed. I lost track of the days, sleeping away afternoons and waking up in the library with my face pressed against the pages of the Mother Book. I barely ate, except for what Miss Morton brought to me.

The book revealed nothing new to me, except nightmares. I had strange dreams where I was chased down dark cobblestone streets, chased by armies of Revenants. I dreamt of Miss Morton standing over me, forcing my hands onto the pages of the Mother Book. I dreamt of Ivy and Alicia turning their backs on me.

I skipped breakfast most mornings and buried myself in the library. Miss Morton had too much to do, so most mornings, she would tell me which sections of the library needed re-shelving, and then rush out to handle some matter of vital school importance, like Gilded Lily eating the school's entire supply of shrinking violets or Tom's replacement, William, being unable to build a fire in the dining hall without setting a tapestry ablaze. None of the girls staying at the school would stoop to setting foot in the library when they weren't forced to, I had it all to myself. I dedicated an hour or two to Miss Morton's shelving.

And then, I used the keys she unwisely kept on a hook by her desk chair and to search some of the restricted archives. In my defense, she left it hanging right there where I could see it. And it turned out that asking the card codex for information on revenants in a much louder voice didn't not produce results. So, really, I didn't have a choice.

While the restricted archives did have an extensive selection on curses that could turn someone inside out and soul-stealing candles, there were no revenant-related titles. I did find a huge cache of books on the genealogy of "lesser" families. I didn't make judgments. The shelf was actually labeled "lesser families."

I searched any books about families based in France, where the Grimstelles were supposed to originate. I was hoping to find some evidence of Mr. Crenshaw being related to the Grimstelles. On this particular afternoon, I was comparing the French bloodlines with the family trees in House Mountfort – Mr. Crenshaw's Mother House. But I found that every branch of his family, even the brides, was related to some known major House. Yawning, I wiped my eyes and set aside the Mountfort records. No wonder Mr. Crenshaw was so frustrated with his lack of authority in the Guild. Someone with his pedigree should have been heading a Senate office all to himself. Mr. Crenshaw must have been *terrible* at his job.

Frustrated with my lack of progress, I slowly shelved the restricted books back and locked the door behind me. I hung the key on Miss Morton's hook and flopped into the chair where I'd left the Mother Book.

I was so tired. My eyes were aching and it felt like I had cotton stuffed in my head. I promised myself I would go upstairs to take a nap in just a few minutes. But first, I opened the Mother Book on the table and touched the dragonfly's wings on either edge of the cover. I cleared my mind and took a deep breath.

"Show me something," I whispered. "Please."

The pages flapped open to show the house sigils page. Again.

"Very helpful," I muttered, slapping the book shut.

Something fluttered from the back pages of the book. I

picked up the maroon, papery ovals and sniffed at them. Night-glove petals. I flipped through the last few pages and found a sprig of nightglove pressed between the paper. But how was that possible? The only person I knew at the school who favored nightglove was Miss Morton, and she hadn't handled the book in months. I'd stopped bringing it into the library after Callista took it from my room.

I sniffed the flower's faded, spicy sweet scent.

But what if Callista hadn't taken it? What if Miss Morton had taken it from my room and the flowers had fallen into the book while she was handling it? But why? I would have shown her the book any time she asked. Why would she take it from me? I hoped it wasn't true. Miss Morton was one of the most truly accepting people at the school, one of the few people I considered friends at the moment. She was the one who helped me find the spell to relocate the book. Why wouldn't she just tell me she'd taken it and give it back?

I closed my eyes and then opened them to stare up at the ceiling, where the late afternoon light shone through the House sigil constellation window. I spotted the blobby stain I'd noticed on my very first day at Miss Castwell's. I'd spent so much time in the library and I'd been so involved in reading that I hadn't really looked at it again. Mrs. Winter said that the glass had been vandalized while she was a student at Castwell's. What if I was right when I thought that some misguided Grimstelle descendant had tried to add her sigil to the celestial ceiling?

I moved as quickly as I could, exhausted by the act of walking up one flight of stairs to where Miss Morton kept a display of class photos on a large expanse of wall between the astral projection and astrology sections. Each photo featured that year's senior girls arranged on the grand staircase in the lobby, dating back to before the Great Restoration. Mrs. Winter would never admit her age, but I searched back twenty picture frames or so and found Headmistress Lockwood's rigid form front and center. Even as a student, she'd had a permanently exasperated expression. Mrs. Winter was standing a few spots to the right, looking resplendent, even in black and white. I scanned the other girls' faces. In the back, almost hidden between other smiling girls, was Miss Morton. Even at seventeen, she'd looked older than her years. Her hair was already frizzling around her face, her round glasses giving her eyes a wide, plaintive look.

My head swimming, I squinted at the photo, spotting the now-familiar sprig of nightglove pinned to Miss Morton's dress – the sprig of nightglove secured with a tarnished *owl*-shaped brooch.

Why hadn't I noticed that before? Had I become so used to the dull, dark brooch against Miss Morton's dark clothes that I became blind to it?

My limbs growing even heavier, I stumbled down the stairs and approached the House Drummond archive. I opened the thick volume and found the page listing the Morton family.

I traced the connection from the major line from House Drummond to the Morton's roots. Miss Morton's great-great-grandfather was listed as the son of Gulliver Drummond one of the most powerful men in that era's government and a master of training dogs to assist in hunting potion ingredients in the woods. Mr. Drummond also happened to be an acquaintance of Calpernia McCray, and I happened to remember a journal entry in which Calpernia mentioned Gulliver boring everyone at a dinner party with a lengthy description of his dog's favorite places to nap. She wrote that it was no surprise that Gulliver was unmarried with no children, as he was far more interested in his dogs than raising a family.

Miss Morton couldn't be connected to the Drummond family that way. I searched for other Mortons, but all of them had connections to major houses I could confirm. Miss Morton wasn't related to any of those families. It was if she'd materialized from nothing.

Miss Morton had betrayed me. She'd lied to me, pretending

to be my friend. She'd stolen from me. Cold, sharp dread spread through my chest, making it hard to breathe.

I picked up the Mother Book and stood, determined to get back to my room and send Mrs. Winter a scrying message as soon as possible, but my skirts snagged on the chair leg and tripped me up, sending me sprawling across the library floor. I groaned and tried to push up, but my arms collapsed under me. I couldn't move. I didn't have the energy to stand up. I rolled on my back, my eyes not quite focusing on the sigil constellations overhead. The blurry smear on the ceiling seemed to be mocking me. My eyes fluttered closed.

And then, it struck me, Morton. *Mort*. The latin root word for death. Grimstelles were masters of death. Miss Morton was a Grimstelle, hidden right under my nose.

I was an idiot.

I woke to find Miss Morton hovering over me in the darkened library, holding a small cray-fire lamp close to my face. "Cassandra, wake up."

"Miss Morton?" I mumbled. I was so weak I could barely sit up. My head was all fuzzy and my eyes weren't focusing. There was something important, something I was supposed to do, but if felt like a bad dream, something I couldn't drag into the waking world with me. "Time'sit?"

I pushed up, feeling around the floor beside me, trying to find the book. "Where's the Mother Book?"

"Oh, I'm taking it outside, I thought perhaps studying it outside would do you some good, get a little fresh air."

"No," I groaned. "Too tired. I don't think I should be working with the book so much."

"I am afraid I must insist, dear. It will make you feel better."

"No, please," I murmured before slipping under the surface of sleep. I faded in and out while Miss Morton was practically dragging me down the hallway, to a part of the school I didn't recognize. The walls were spotted with mold and the great swatches of paint were flaking from the ceiling. She carried me round and round a dark passage of creaking steps, tucking me under her arm. The book was clutched in the other. How was Miss Morton this strong? We reached a stone chamber with walls that opened onto the school grounds. The flow of fresh air revived me enough to look around.

We were high off the ground, the school's green expanse of lawn stretching out to all directions. The stone chamber's corners were marked by four intricately carved green columns. The bell tower? A wide ladder led to the next level. I could see candlelight through a hole in the ceiling above, reflecting off of the large bronze bell. Miss Morton dropped me into a half-rotten desk chair, the arm falling off under the impact of my weight.

And then I remembered, Miss Morton. Miss Morton was a Grimstelle. Miss Morton had stolen the Mother Book.

"Just a little bit more," Miss Morton cooed, the tarnished owl glinting dully in the low light as she propped the Mother Book into my hands. "You've given me almost everything I need. You've been so very helpful, Cassandra. I can't control the Mother Book. I will never be given that privilege, but all that power flowing through your veins. It's mine. I've cursed the book, you see, to be a sort of psychic funnel, channeling all that lovely power of yours into my magic. You've been draining yourself of your very life force for weeks. It's almost used up, now. I wrote the spell years ago, just waiting for the day a Translator might come along. And when you finally let the book out of your sight long enough for me to take it from your room, I laid my trap. I've learned over the years, hiding my heritage, living in mediocrity, to prepare for the worst and hope for the best. And look how my investment has profited!"

She smiled sweetly, her eyes glittering madly behind her round-rimmed glasses. "Every time you were such a good little witch, obeying my requests to work with the book, meditating so faithfully, you were feeding me your magic, making me stronger. Without you, I wouldn't have been able to accomplish half so much. I certainly wouldn't have been able to use my family's spells to raise poor Tom. I'd hoped that if he finished you for me, that I could take the book, that without a Translator, its secrets would be open to me. But alas, I am just going to content myself with taking your magic."

"Miss Morton, please don't do this," I slurred, falling against my chair, exhausted by the effort of speaking. I felt Miss Morton's cold fingers, tugging at my wrists, binding me with rough hemp rope. "I trusted you."

"Oh, believe me, dear, I know. Do you have any idea how *irritating* it is to hear someone complain about having such a gift drop in their lap? I would kill to be able to do what you do without even thinking about it... well, I suppose, *I will* kill to be able to do what you do."

"Did you change the ceiling in the library, when you were a girl?"

She rolled her eyes a bit. "An act of youthful rebellion. It burned me, every time I walked into that library and saw the Mother Houses sigils, leaving out House Grimstelle. But no one even knew what the Grimstelle owl meant. They didn't know to be afraid. They thought it was some girlish prank, but the experience taught me that temper tantrums wouldn't get me the power, the respect that I wanted. Long years of calculated work, that was my path. And working under that blemish, day in and day out, for years, helped me remember that."

She brushed my hair away from my face in a movement that was almost tender. And the gesture had me closing my eyes like a sleepy child. "You should feel fortunate, to be a part of this, to be a witness to a change in history's guard. I am going to make the Great Restoration look like a garden party. You will help me turn the whole world on its ear. All of those Guardians who have treated you and Snipes like you like dirt over the years, they will understand what it means to be afraid, helpless, to have their choices taken away. I will bring them to their knees."

I squinted at her. "You know about me?"

"Of course, I do, dear," she sniffed. "Mrs. Winter provided far too many details in your story when she applied for you. Aneira never explains herself to anyone like that. Besides, no child who'd had access to library books her whole life would treat them with the reverence you do. But honestly, Cassandra, I don't care where your magic comes from. As long as I can use it to meet my goals."

Staring past her, I could see Phillip on the ledge of the tower, chirping furiously. I swallowed, barely able to produce enough air to make words. I hadn't felt this weak since my days as Sarah, swallowing those suppressors. "Phillip. Mrs. Winter. Ivy. Alicia. Please."

"What was that, dear?" she asked.

I shook my head, wrapping my arms around my middle. The tower was so cold. Or was it me? I felt the holster for Wit under my sleeve. Miss Morton hadn't thought to take it from me. I could use it to protect myself if I could just lift my arms. My eyelids drifted shut. My head drooped forward and I had to catch myself to keep from toppling over. I would get up in just a minute. Wait, no, Miss Morton was tying me to the chair...

GASPING AS I WOKE, I felt warm hands curl around my arms, dragging me away from the desk, against a wall of the tower. The chair made distressingly loud scraping sounds against the stone floor.

"Whass happening?" I slurred, slumping forward. I glanced around and found Ivy giving me a reassuring smile. "Just give us a minute, and we'll have you free, Cassandra."

"How did you get here?" I whispered.

Alicia said, "You called us here. You're annoying little bird was very insistent."

"And your mirror messages were getting near incoherent, we knew something was wrong," Ivy added.

"You got my messages? Why didn't you write back?"

"Our mothers took our athames so we couldn't respond."

"They actually coordinated the effort," Alicia groused. "I was on the verge of stealing Gavin's blade from his room when Ivy climbed up my trellis. She snuck her athame out of her parents' room."

"That's funny," I giggled loopily. When they paused to stare at me, I added, "Because ivy climbs a trellis – the plant. Never mind."

"We broke into my mother's study and took my blade back. Oh, and these are for you." Alicia reached into her pocket and pulled out six letters with my name on them, written in Gavin's messy scrawl.

"What?" The envelopes slipped through my fingers like wet tissue.

"My mother kept them in the same desk drawer where she hid my athame. I think she told the servants not to post them."

"Because of the rumors?" I guessed.

"No, Mother is just very possessive of Gavin, and I would imagine she didn't like how often he was writing you," she said. "Good luck with that. What's taking so long with the ropes, Ivy?"

"Well, Miss Morton may be absolutely insane, but she's a dab hand at tying very complicated knots."

Alicia scowled. "You know, you could speed the process along by using magic. Or that enormous knife in your sleeve."

Ivy scowled right back, whispering an incantation over the ropes binding my ankles and wrists.

"Where is she?" I asked, slowly coming to some form of awareness.

"She's up in the bell tower, preparing for some sort of ritual. She's got the Mother Book with her," Ivy whispered.

"I've been such a fool," I sighed.

Alicia assured me. "I'm sure it's not so bad."

"She's using the book to suck the magic out of me so she can raise an army of the dead to topple the Coven Guild government."

"All right, that is rather serious," Alicia admitted.

"Is there any other adult on the grounds? Can we scry message for help?" Ivy asked.

"There's no time. What she's planning, she's planning to do right now."

Together, they nodded. "And it will be dangerous."

I received more nods and was pleased that they didn't hesitate. These girls were my true friends, there to support me, to help me, even if I was about to do something completely reckless and stupid. They gave me strength, creeping into my limbs and making it a little easier for me to stay upright. "We could probably be seriously injured. If not killed."

More nods, though just a little slower.

They helped me to my feet and held me steady as my equilibrium fought to right itself. "Before we go rushing in to a very dangerous situation without a semblance of a plan, I have to tell you something. I'm not Cassandra Reed. I'm not a Guardian, like both of you. I'm a Snipe. I was a servant in Mrs. Winter's household until a few months ago. I don't know why I can do what I can do. But I will understand if you decide that you want to run home."

Neither girl's expression changed at all; no anger, no hurt, just the same steady exasperation they usually showed me.

"All right then," Ivy said. "Anything else?"

I frowned. "I lied to you."

"Yes," Alicia said.

"Everything you know about me is a lie," I said.

"Yes, and Ivy's not really a descendant of Morgana," Alicia told me. "My mother's family originally made their money selling magic beans. All of our histories are riddled with little inaccuracies. Yours is just bigger than most."

Ivy said, "And we can sort all of this out later. Right now, there's a magic-wielding maniac trying to end the world as we know it."

"I just wanted you to know before you ran at the maniac headlong," I said.

Ivy patted my hand. "We appreciate that."

"You're the same girl who was our friend when no one else was. You're the same girl who defended me from Callista and risked your social neck for Ivy," Alicia told me. "Everything else can be managed."

"Thank you," I whispered, my head bowed. Both girls squeezed my arms gently.

After a silent moment, a thought occurred to me. "Alicia, what would happen if the wards your brother put on you were removed?"

Alicia pulled a face. "I would have a major burst of power, but as long as the wards were replaced, well, it would put me in the sick wing for a while, but I would be OK."

I smiled. Ivy's mouth dropped open as she picked up on my intentions. "Oh... no."

"It will be fine," Alicia told her. Ivy frowned, so Alicia added, "It will be fine, in general."

It took us surprisingly little time to concoct some semblance of plan. I slowly climbed the ladder to the tower, careful to make very little noise. Ivy was going to use all of her ward-manipulating skills to remove the limitations on Alicia's magic while I distracted Miss Morton. Then they would "prop me up" like they had when we'd reclaimed my lost book while I made use of the "banishing of an evil spirit" spell the Mother Book had shown me weeks ago. I figured there was no spirit more evil than someone who was planning to raise an undead army.

The bell tower glowed an eerie green from the light of hundreds of tiny candles. Callista, Jeanette and Helena were bound and gagged, tied to desk chairs. They were slumped against each other, unconscious. Miss Morton was dressed in a positively glamorous black gown embroidered with white owls while she danced around the tower, maneuvering around candle stands and drawing symbols in the air with her athame. Their shapes were dull and sickly grey, fading into the air like a stain. She skidded to a halt when I emerged into the tower.

"Oh, I wasn't expecting you, yet. Very rude, you know, for a guest to turn up early, before the hostess has time to complete preparations."

"What are you doing to them?" I asked, dread sinking in my belly.

"You are witnessing the birth of history, my dear. Thanks to you, I have the magic I need to begin my army," Miss Morton preened. "Three girls from the most powerful families in Light-bourne, here to witness my triumph, to see their power slipping through their fingers before I send them to the great beyond. They'll be the first to rise in my legion."

"And that's why you needed my magic? To turn Castwell's students into Revenants?"

"Not all of them," Miss Morton insisted. "Just the girls from the more prominent families, and the more annoying girls, on principal. Do you have any idea how devastated their parents will be to have their daughters' Revenants shambling around on their lawn every night? They'll be powerless, too busy mourning to stop me."

I stepped carefully around the podium, toward the girls. Miss Morton hissed like an angry cat and sent three blades flying from her sleeve. I cringed, throwing up my arms, and the blades flew off course, dropping harmlessly over the edge of the stone wall. I dropped to the floor, exhausted by the magical efforts.

Who hid *three* blades in their sleeve? That was cheating.

"Shameful." Miss Morton sighed, tapping each girl on the forehead. I hoped that meant that they were merely unconscious and not already dead. "Always cringing. Always so afraid. From what I've heard, the other Changelings were never so pathetic."

"Wait, there are more?" I asked, pushing to my feet. "More like me?"

"Do you really think you're the only one?" Miss Morton laughed. "Oh, my dear, children just like you are popping up all over. Like weeds. More and more are being born every year. You're really not as special as you think you are, Mother Book aside."

"What? Where are they? Why haven't I ever heard of this?"

"It's Coven Guild's deep dark secret," Miss Morton chuckled. "Only a few elite members of the Senate know. Not even your precious Mrs. Winter is aware, and she thinks she's aware of everything. They don't want to start a panic among the Guardians, so they're keeping it hush-hush."

"And how do you know?" I asked. I had to keep her talking, to give Ivy time to undo the limitations on Alicia's magic and give them time to climb up here with me.

"Before I came here, I worked as a government archive clerk, one of the most boring jobs available to Coven Guild members, but the only position available to someone like me with no connections, no status. I handled the reports, archiving every panicked moment and discussion. I knew I simply had to come to the school. That eventually, they would be drawn to the school, some Guardian family would be so terrified of being caught fostering a Snipe witch under their roof, that they would send her here and try to pass her off as a Guardian. And then, I could cause all sorts of trouble. Undo major houses, destabilize the government. Your waking up the Mother Book was a lovely surprise, though. I'd spent years trying just to open the case and couldn't get close to it. But, oh, you have expedited my plans faster than I could ever hope. It all just fell into my lap, proof that even the Fates have agreed upon my destiny."

"These other children? Are they being kept somewhere?"

"No dear," she told me, a mock note of false sadness in her

voice. "Those children were murdered, taken from the families by the time they showed the hint of magic. I've never met a Changeling any older than eleven." She tilted her head, smiling softly at me. "We're so alike, you know, I felt that right away when I met you. You, a girl out of place in a world you don't understand. My house, the great Grimstelles, reduced to nothing. I'm going to change it all, this sick world order that rewards laziness and mediocrity. No longer. I will send my armies into the Capitol. I will topple the very foundations of Guardian society, restore the balance. I will create a newer, better world. I would think that you, of all people, would understand my point of view."

For just a moment, it sounded like music to my ears. No more manipulations, no more lies, no more "guidance" in how to run our lives. Our society was sick. Snipes were servants for no other reason than being born without magic. I wanted to see that change. I wanted to see Callista and Mr. Crenshaw, all of the high and mighty Guardians knocked down a peg or one hundred. I wanted them to know what it was like to work for their bread.

And then I thought of Alicia and Ivy and all of my classmates who would suffer in Miss Morton's "Utopia." And while the current system was unfair, I couldn't punish my friends for being born with magic and wealth any more than I wanted my family to be punished for being born without it.

"But we won't be free, will we?" I sighed. "The Snipes will be just as terrified and helpless as the Guild Guardians. We'll have the dead at our doors, without magic to keep them out. Things need to change. I do want to change the world, but not like this. Not *your* way."

From below, I felt Ivy and Alicia's magic, nudging at my own, letting me know they were there. Alicia's magic was *strong*, like a slap to the back of my head, reminding me how misguided this plan was. I realized I felt alive, refreshed and whole and ready for a fight. I stood, much to Miss Morton's surprise and walked toward the book stand. She tried to stop me, but I flung my hand up, Wit singing out of my sleeve. The force of a shield rune threw her across the tower room and into a column.

Behind us, I could hear my friends coming up the stairs. I turned in time to see Miss Morton flinging a flaming brazier at them, burning coals and all. I screamed, "No!"

Alicia fanned her hands, blade flashing in a symbol even I didn't recognize. The burning coals transformed into lemon blossoms. I stopped, staring at my tiny friend. I'd never heard of changing matter from one form to another, but Alicia had done it. Even Miss Morton appeared impressed.

"So the little mouse has mastered her magic has she?" Miss Morton chuckled.

"It's easy when you have good friends," Alicia said casually, plucking lemon blossoms from her skirt. She picked one up in the palm of her hand and blew on it. The flower spun into the air, aided by a counter-clockwise conductor's twirl of her athame. The blossom grew into a massive black blob of black, oily liquid as it flew towards Miss Morton. Miss Morton rolled her eyes and flicked her wrist. The black slime splashed over an invisible dome-shaped shield over Miss Morton, streaming down as if against glass, where it puddled at her feet.

"And what about you, Cow?" Miss Morton sneered. "I don't see much of a change in you. So much for the healing powers of friendship."

I felt something flare through Ivy's magic, rage, white-hot rage that seemed to singe the edges of my brain. I whipped my head toward Ivy, who was glaring at Miss Morton in an expression of rage I'd never seen on her sweet face. Her dark eyes glittered with a wrathful light that sent a shiver down *my* spine.

"You will not call me that," Ivy told her.

Miss Morton snickered. "What, *Cow?* Oh, you poor poppet, did you actually believe that being the Translator's little flunky made you anything more than the pathetic creature you are? You're nothing, less than nothing. You're not even brave enough to become nothing, *Cow.* You're just like every sad, talentless girl who has shuffled these halls before you."

With Miss Morton's attention focused on Ivy, I turned back to the book. Alicia shifted her body ever so slightly, placing herself between my back and Miss Morton. I turned to the page showing the spell to banish a malevolent spirit into the next world. Phillip lighted on the bookstand, feathers ruffled and agitated, but not making a sound.

Miss Morton scoffed. "You've never fought back in your life. Just go downstairs, girls, while Miss Reed and I finish our business. I'll come for you, soon enough."

"You will not call me that," Ivy said again, her fingers flexing.

"Salt," I whispered to Phillip, who flitted away into the depths of the tower. "Or what?" Miss Morton laughed at Ivy.

"Or this!" Ivy shouted, dropping to the ground and stabbing her blade between spaces in the stones. Flames leapt from the floor, zipping towards Miss Morton as if following a trail of lamp oil. Ivy's fiery anger had transformed into actual fire, and it seemed to be taking on the shape of a bull, running at Miss Morton at top speed. Miss Morton's eyes went wide at the sight a giant flaming cow aiming its horns at her and held up her blade to ward it off.

The bull's nose met the tip of Miss. Morton's worn silver athame and folded in on itself, becoming a tiny ball of smoke and ember. Miss Morton couldn't quite relax, though, because her skirts were in flames. She shrieked beating at them for a second before summoning a storm of dirt and grit from the unkempt tower floor to suffocate the flames.

I rushed to Ivy and Alicia, standing shoulder to shoulder with our blades pointed at Miss Morton. Behind our insane librarian, Jeanette stirred awake, eyes wide in alarm. Her thrashing against her bonds woke the other two girls, who came to just in time to see Phillip drop a small bag of salt into my hand.

Ivy took the bag and threw the salt into the air. She raised her blade and drew restraining wards. The salt landed in a perfect circle around Miss Morton's feet, a stark white contrast against the ash and dirt. Miss Morton screamed in rage and tried to run at me, but the circle held her. Alicia flicked her fingers and the salt sputtered to life, a circle of green energy that surrounded Miss Morton on all sides. Alicia's magic thrilled through the bond, pleased with her creation.

Miss Morton howled, scrambling to protect her already damaged skirts from the crackling walls of ghostly light. She slashed at the walls with her athame, her blade making quickly reforming scratches on her green prison.

Miss Morton hissed through the crayfire. "All that time with the book, sharing your magic with me, I am bound to you now. I am in your every pore. I will return! I am the mistress of Death! My undead armies will rise! I will bring House Grimstelle to glory once again! And I'll do it with your help!"

Alicia and Ivy's magic swirled and danced with mine, not appreciating the insinuation that Miss Morton's magic was stronger. I didn't need an army. I had one. I had Alicia and Ivy.

I smiled, just as frosty as Mrs. Winter ever dreamed of being. "You don't even know me. You're not even half the witch I am."

Phillip flew over my head, beating the air with his tiny blue wings. Alicia's hand rested on my left arm and Ivy's right shoulder pressed to mine. We raised our blades. I looked Miss Morton in the eye and drew the most dangerous symbol in the Mother Book. "*Unmake.*"

Like the spell promised, Miss Morton became nothing. A dark shadow seemed to slip out of Miss Morton's body, rising like dirty green-grey smoke. Her body dropped to the floor and was consumed by the green fire, burning bright for a moment and then collapsing on itself like a dying star. The smoke hovered over the glowing circle before fading away onto the wind.

The three of us stared at the ashy green smear left on the stone. Callista, Helena and Jeanette remained in their chairs, blinking rapidly. In the distance, birds chirped. The world spun on, just as before.

Ivy broke the tension by blowing her hair out of her face and saying, "Well, that was decidedly odd."

"Really? I do this sort of thing every Tuesday before bed," Alicia said in a bored tone, making Ivy laugh.

But while her tone was bored and haughty, I could see in Alicia's expression that she was alarmed. She was staring down at her arm. I could see a mark similar to mine, smaller, but in the now-familiar dragonfly shape, forming around the inside of her left wrist, the hand that had been holding mine during the spell.

Ivy was already moving the neckline of her dress aside to examine her own dragonfly on her shoulder.

"I'm not sure Mother is going to like this," Ivy whispered. "She's worked her whole life to achieve a mark, and never earned one."

"Nonsense," Alicia told her. "Just think of the hideous dresses she'll have designed to highlight it."

"Where did you two learn those spells?" I asked. "I don't remember anything about flaming bulls or flying slime in the books we studied."

"Well, I will admit we studied more advanced spells while we were mastering some of your remedial skills," Ivy said. "I'm sure you'll catch up in no time, considering you just unmade a human being."

I nodded. "Still. You made a bull, made of *fire*."

Ivy jerked her shoulders.

"Would someone mind telling me why the blue Hades I am tied to a filthy chair?" Callista demanded, fully awake and thrashing against her bonds. "Let me loose, now!"

Ivy frowned as Callista thrashed against her ropes. Jeanette and Helena were a bit more polite in their requests to be released. "Do we have to untie Callista?" Ivy asked.

"Yes," I sighed.

"We could leave her up here. Nobody would mind her going missing," Alicia suggested, slumping against me. Her face was pale behind her smirk.

I snickered. "Alicia."

She sighed. "It's just a suggestion."

18

HOTHOUSE FLOWER

*I*t seemed that preventing the rise of an undead army helped raise one's social standing.

I wandered Mrs. Winter's greenhouse, the detached glass garden where she grew her most delicate and exotic specimens, caring for the specimens her friends from the Demeter Society sent to me. The very moment I'd arrived at Raven's Rest, my dress in tatters and covered in Miss Morton's ash, the tributes began arriving. Exotic potted plants, restorative tonics, books to keep me entertained while I recovered from my "dreadful shock," and each of them with a note asking me to attend tea at the sender's home when I felt well enough.

News of our fight to the death with Miss Morton had, of course, spread like wildfire amongst the students, and then their mothers. No one knew *exactly* what happened. Callista, Helena and Jeanette could only give bits and pieces. In their stupor, they only heard twisted fragments of story about the attempts of House Grimstelle to re-establish itself (the gall!) and whispers of necromancy being involved (how distasteful!) Now that society had been re-assured that I was Guardian enough to save three prominent daughters from certain harm, I was welcomed back into the tea-and-tarot circuit with open arms.

With Mrs. Dalrymple leading the charge, all of the proper ladies of the most prominent houses dismissed "those nasty rumors" about my heritage as vicious gossip from the jealous ladies of the Benisse house. After all, I couldn't have prevented a Grimstelle uprising without being a true Coven Guild Guardian. And with the help of little Alicia McCray and Mrs. Dalrymple's own dear granddaughter!

Clearly Ivy and Alicia had been underestimated by society at large, the matrons whispered. Ivy was receiving tea invitations from several matrons associated with the Athena Society, a research guild dedicated to ward construction. And this was without those matrons knowing that Ivy had restored Alicia's protective limitations before Gavin even knew they'd been removed. Alicia had suffered very little reverb symptoms afterwards, just feeling shaky and a little fatigued after our adventure. Ivy was as she always was, steady and exasperated with us both.

I'd begged Mrs. Winter to send them all back, to burn them. I'd had quite enough of Guild Guardian society, thank you, and didn't particularly want to be welcomed back into the fold. But Mrs. Winter insisted that this was all part of her carefully worked plan, and I would not only open these gifts, but write thank you notes for each of them.

I carefully placed heated stones around the potted demon orchid, a rare red specimen that released an odd sulfurous smoke on nights of the full moon. The snow was piled deep against the outer panes, giving the already quiet room an eerie, isolated feel. Mrs. Winter had re-keyed the wards to accept me. She insisted that the warm, moist air of the hothouse would help restore the vitality that had been drained by my ordeal. I wasn't sure about that, but it was nice to have a bit of peace after the bustle of insanity that had marked the last few days.

Of course, that brief peace was disrupted by the greenhouse doors opening. I didn't bother looking up from my orchid specimen, calling, "Go away, Owen. I'm recuperating. And your mother tells me that *not* being thoroughly annoyed is an important part of the relaxation process."

"Well, I don't plan to annoy you, but I certainly understand why you would give your cousin such a warning."

My head whipped toward the sound of the voice that was certainly not Owen's. Gavin McCray was standing in the doorway, holding a bouquet of purple weeping hyacinth – a flower that meant the giver was so sorry, he or she was crying. Through the glass, I could see Mrs. Winter's retreating back. "Gavin. What are you doing here? I thought.. well, never mind what I thought. I'm very happy to see you."

"I'm sorry my mother's actions gave you the impression that I didn't want to continue our acquaintance," he said. "She's been more dependent on me since my father died and, I don't think she appreciated the thought of someone who would take my time or attention."

I raised my eyebrows and his cheeks flushed. I might not have believed the excuse about his mother diverting his messages, except that his letters, which I read during my recovery, had been a series of increasingly urgent pleas for me to respond. The final letter had asked me to send some word, even through Alicia, to tell him that he could hope for my friendship.

"I've moved to the residence halls at Palmer's for the time being," he said, clearing his throat.

"I hate to think that you've moved from your home because of something to do with me."

"It's not because of you," he assured me, standing and crossing the greenhouse to stand near me. "If I don't make a dramatic gesture now, I can only expect more of the same. And I'm on the verge of taking over the family business. She can't treat me like a child and then expect to have the responsibilities of a patriarch. She can learn to respect my choices or she can live separately from me."

"I feel like I could have cleared this up by reaching out to you, but I was concerned that the things people were saying about me might mean you didn't want to contact me again."

"I've learned a long time ago not to listen to the gossip that circulates through the society set," he said softly. "You're one of Alicia's closest friends. If she had any concerns about you, she would have told me. You're a sweet girl, but funny and biting and smart. If any of the society matrons have a problem with that, it says more about them than you."

"Thank you," I said, my own cheeks heating now. "I think you are very nice... also..."

It was all I could do not to roll my eyes. Clearly, this was the biting wit Gavin mentioned.

Smiling, Gavin leaned forward and kissed me softly on my lips, a quick experimental peck.

"I will write to you again, as soon as possible, if that's agreeable," he said, his lips twitching.

"I look forward to your next letter," I told him. "It should be very long, to make up for the recent lack of them."

He took my hand and bowed over it. "I will do my best."

With that, Gavin left me in the greenhouse, walking into Raven's Rest to pay his respects to Mr. Winter. Alone now and suffering a sudden case of sweaty palms, I carefully approached the juvenile specimen of *drosera aureus* Headmistress Lockwood sent me.

I took a dropper from the vial of chicken blood Mrs. Winter had delivered from the kitchen. Better to use the run-off from my mother's dinner preparations than to sacrifice some poor bird. The closed golden bud stretched upwards at the scent of the opened bottle. The beautiful shimmering gold made way for the scaly brown reality as the bud opened up.

"I am not feeding you my blood," I told the little vampiric

blossom. "With my luck, you would grow ten feet tall and start eating people whole."

LATER IN THE DAY, my parents had been allowed a whopping hour-long visit, in the spirit of the holiday season. I'd like to think that some part of Mrs. Winter felt guilty that Mary had run away, leaving my parents with no child to comfort them. But honestly, it probably had more to do with the fact that my father's work was suffering and mother's cooking had become subpar.

My poor parents. Papa looked like he'd aged ten years. And the unhappy lines around Mum's mouth had furrowed even deeper. Hearing that I'd almost died at the fancy school that was supposed to be my redemption hadn't exactly comforted them.

"I just don't understand how any of this happened," Mum said, turning a cooling cup of peppermint tea in her hands, as we sat around the kitchen worktable.

"Have you heard from Mary?" I asked. "Do you know where she is?"

Papa shook his head. "Not since the night of the party."

I waited for the familiar, sinking weight of guilt, for not protecting Mary from herself. But it didn't come. Mary had made the choices that led her here. And for once, I was going to let her feel the consequences.

Mum sniffed. "How did we lose so much so quickly?"

"You haven't lost me, Mum," I told her. "Things are just different now. They were bound to change someday, right? I was always going to grow up, pull away a little bit. It just happened a little bit earlier than we thought."

"I don't know what we were thinking, trying to hide what you could do," Papa said. "It wasn't right, like trying to pretend away a part of you."

"I just wish I knew why I was born like this," I said. "Miss

Morton said that there are other children like me. Changelings who can do magic. More being born every year."

"Why would that be happening?" Mum asked.

"Maybe magic is a living thing," Papa said. "The Guardians talk about it like it's as fickle as wind or water. But anything that involves that much intention, has to be aware of itself. Maybe that ribbon of magic that runs through all Guardians, that spark that allows them to bend the universe to their will, isn't happy with how the Guardians have been using it. So it's restoring the balance. Like in nature; forest fires, they can be devastating, but they can also lead to new growth. Maybe magic is turning the tide, giving power to people that will make better use of it."

Mum and I both stared at my father, who hadn't strung that many clear, coherent sentences together in years. Papa shrugged. "I could be wrong."

Mum did something I'd never seen her do in all my fourteen years. She threw her head back and cackled. Full bellied, throaty *guffaws*. My mouth fell open. This was a banner day for the Smith family doing the unexpected.

And then she snorted. My mother actually snorted.

I burst out laughing, clapping my hands over my mouth as the dragonfly hummed happily. Laughing, Papa reached across the table and wrapped his enormous, rough hand over Mum's and squeezed. Mum wiped at her eyes with her free hand and sniffed.

"It was the right thing for you, to go to that school," Mum admitted, sipping her tea. "I know that now. I was the one who wanted to hide what you are, because it scared me. I was scared that I would lose you, if we told other people what you could do. I am sorry that I gave you the suppressors, that you were so sick for so long. I didn't feel we had any choice."

I nodded. "I... I understand, Mum. I do. I won't say I'm happy about it, but if I had a child who was born with magical powers... No, I am sure I would handle it differently."

"I know that," Mum sighed.

"I could have been very tall," I told her. "You're practically giants, the both of you."

She snorted again. And I grinned.

"Are they teaching you sassy-mouthing at that fancy school?" she asked.

"My personalized curriculum has an *emphasis* on sassy-mouthing."

Papa snickered. "It's good, that you come into a bit more of that. You'll need that, if you're going to find the other children like you. There have to be more out there."

"Find them?" Mum asked. "How exactly is she going to do that?"

Papa shrugged. "Someone has to find them. Who knows where or how they're living? Besides, Sarah needs to know how other children handle their magic. She can't just leave them out there."

Now, standing in the hothouse, feeding my carnivorous plant, I wondered if I could find the other Changelings or if that was just an insane idea. No one else even seemed to know they existed, except for my megalomaniacal former librarian. Where would I even start looking?

Miss Morton had been right about one thing amongst the many, many insane ideas that she'd gotten horribly wrong, the world had to change. I couldn't sit, pampered and pretty, in the hallowed halls of Miss Castwell's, grateful that I'd made it out of service. I wanted to find the other Changeling children. I wanted to help my fellow Snipes make their own way in the world. And with or without Mrs. Winter's support – most likely without – I was going to have to do that from inside their circles.

I heard the door slide open behind me and a blast of cold air had me pulling the collar of my dress closer to my neck. Mrs. Winter was walking into the hothouse, a tray of tea floating behind her. "Feeling better?"

"Stronger every day," I said, nodding. Mrs. Winter gestured for the tray to settle itself on the table next to me.

"Good, you're going to need it over the next few years."

I chuckled. "Years?"

"Yes, darling, years. We're playing a long game here. You barely got through Mary's rather 'informative' tantrum at the ball, and that solely by nature of your distracting the public with that little tiff with Miss Morton."

"My friends and I disintegrated her with the power of our magic."

"Which was a very tidy way to handle a considerable problem," she said.

"You mean, the considerable problem of Miss Morton's attempts to raise an army of the undead?"

"No, I meant the rumors surrounding your Snipe origins."

"Of course," I sighed. "That is obviously the priority."

Mrs. Winter lifted an eyebrow and I added, "But who am I to tempt fate?"

"Well, honestly, most of my circle were leaping at the chance to restore the status quo," Mrs. Winter sniffed. "Really, it might have been exciting for a few moments to gossip about a possible disturbance in my household, but they know what kind of power I wield. They don't want to tangle with me long-term."

And then she patted me on the head. Either Mrs. Winter was woefully under-estimating the zombie army threat, or she was trying to make me feel better through this show of bravado. I was not sure which option made me more uncomfortable.

"You have served your purpose, Cassandra," she admitted. "You've accomplished more than I ever imagined possible. But you mustn't rest on your laurels. You're going to have to prove yourself, over and over, just to survive."

"There's a cheerful thought."

"And on that note, the school opens for spring term tomorrow. Your trunks are being packed as we speak."

"Saving the magical world doesn't get me out of spring classes?"

"No, sadly, it does not."

"How lovely," I sighed.

Phillip darted away from the nearby lemon tree and landed on my shoulder, tittering happily as we walked back into the house. The doors of Raven's Rest opened to me as if I were born to it.

DISCUSSION QUESTIONS

1. Did Sarah's parents do the right thing in suppressing her magic? How else could they have protected her?

2. Sarah worries about her personal integrity after she arrives at Miss Castwell's. Does she maintain that integrity? Or does she compromise too much?

3. How could Sarah have handled her problems with Callista differently?

4. Did Sarah trust Miss Morton too easily? What about Miss Morton's personality drew Sarah in?

5. If you were going to belong to a Mother House, which would you choose?

ABOUT THE AUTHOR

Molly Harper worked for six years as a reporter and humor columnist for The Paducah Sun. Her reporting duties included covering courts, school board meetings, quilt shows, and once, the arrest of a Florida man who faked his suicide by shark attack and spent the next few months tossing pies at a local pizzeria. Molly lives in western Kentucky with her family.

Be sure to check out https://www.misscastwells.com/ for more information on the Houses, when the next book in the Sorcery and Society series is coming out, and fun fan goodies.

Molly also writes adult paranormal romance, adult contemporary romance, and women's fiction:
　　https://www.mollyharper.com/

　f　facebook.com/Molly-Harper-Author-138734162865557
　🐦　twitter.com/mollyharperauth
　📷　instagram.com/mollyharperauthor

CPSIA information can be obtained
at www.ICGtesting.com
Printed in the USA
LVHW020114230719
624964LV00022B/1725/P